Windy City Blues

by

Marc Krulewitch

Smashwords Edition

(Originally Published by Alibi/Penguin Random House.
All Rights Reverted to the Author on September 12, 2018)

Prologue

It was just before nine a.m. when the toddler's mother saw his little hands and cheeks covered in a sticky substance mixed with crumbly white particles. She shuddered, then walked to where the little boy had been looking for the neighbor's kitty under a juniper bush and saw the nearly headless corpse. The woman picked up her son, ran into their apartment, then frantically washed the debris off him, first with soap and water, then with rubbing alcohol. After repeating the routine with peroxide, she called 911.

About ten minutes later, a CPD police cruiser arrived on the scene; two officers approached the woman holding her child and pointing to the juniper bush. Adams, the younger officer, took out a notepad and stayed with the woman as Sergeant Morales slow-walked toward the hedge, carefully scanning the area. White tennis shoes quickly caught Morales's attention. The body lay just off the grass border, barely concealed by the shrubbery. Morales crouched, then used his flashlight to trace the outline of the body, starting from its feet up to a tangle of blood, hair, tissue, and bone fragments where the head should have been. Although Morales was a veteran officer who had seen his share of big city brutality, the shock caused him to stumble backward and slip on the dewy grass. From his knees, he reported the gruesome discovery to his superior over the radio.

After Morales got back to his feet, he directed Adams to secure the area with crime-scene tape, then began to scan the immediate surroundings, where he found a patch of grass covered with blood and debris that Morales assumed had once been part of the victim's head. From this spot, a trail of fragments led to the body. Soon, another cruiser arrived and then two homicide detectives. Morales called Adams over to make sure he got a good look before the medical examiner did his survey and zipped the corpse up into a body bag. Adams tried not to appear shaken as Morales moved the flashlight over the mutilated remains of the human head.

"So what does the condition of the body tell you?" Morales said.

"He got whacked in the head pretty good with a metal pipe or something."

"It's not easy to kill someone with a single whack to the head."

It took a moment before Adams realized Morales was testing him. "So he got lots of whacks. Somebody was really pissed off or sending a message."

"Yep," Morales agreed before noticing three men walking toward them. "Okay, why don't you go over to the crowd and start asking questions? See who lives here, if anyone saw anything, et cetera. I'll start briefing these guys."

At first, Morales didn't recall anything about the detectives other than their names—Calvo and

Baker—and that they had been on the force long enough to have garnered reputations for having once been good cops and having once been physically fit. Instead, on this morning, one might be known as tall and fat, the other as short and fat. They appeared happy, giggling like kids on a school outing. He also recognized Dr. Irvine, the medical examiner, who appeared appropriately somber for someone about to evaluate a victim of brutal violence.

Morales met the three halfway between the sidewalk and the bush. The two detectives breezed past. Dr. Irvine stopped to talk.

"It's pretty bad," Morales said, "but I guess I don't have to tell you to prepare yourself."

Dr. Irvine offered a knowing smile and was about to respond when the two detectives broadcast their disgust and started retreating back the way they had come.

"Looks like a case of old age," Calvo said to Morales.

"The result of a bad migraine," Baker said.

With Adams in pursuit, a young, dark-haired woman came running toward the group. "Hold on, ma'am," Morales said, grabbing the distraught woman's arm. "This is a crime scene."

"My cousin didn't come home last night!"

Adams and Morales looked at each other. The two detectives stepped away. Dr. Irvine headed over to the stiff.

"Wait here," Morales said, then returned with a wallet in a plastic bag. "What's the name?"

"Oh, my god! His wallet!"

"Please, miss, what's the name?"

"Gelashvili. Bagrat Gelashvili."

Morales looked at the driver's license and then back to the woman. His expression said it all. "I'm sorry—"

She screamed and tried to run to the mangled corpse. Adams grabbed her from behind in a bear hug. "No, no, no. You don't want to see him. Please, trust us." She continued struggling and began screaming in a foreign language. Morales radioed for a victim's advocate, then joined Adams in trying to console the woman. Eventually, she sunk to her knees and sobbed.

"What will I tell *Deida*?" she said several times, then, "How can I tell her? How can I tell her?"

Adams and Morales stayed with the woman until a member of Crime Victim Services arrived, put her arm around her, and led her away. Morales approached the detectives, who stood on the sidewalk with the other onlookers.

"I'm Sergeant Morales. Let me give you the few details I know."

Neither bothered with their own introduction. "What's to know?" Calvo said, and chuckled. "That kind of message only comes from one place."

5

"He pissed off somebody pretty bad," Baker said.

"You wanna try to talk to the woman?" Morales said. "She's his cousin."

The two detectives glanced at each other. "Not now," Calvo said. "We'll find her later, after she's had a chance to calm down." Morales watched as the two men turned from him and shuffled a few steps away. Apparently, the briefing was over.

Adams got on the radio and cleared them from the scene. In silence, the two cops drove away in their cruiser. Then Morales detected a small laugh from Adams.

"What?"

"Those two detectives."

"What about 'em?"

Adams laughed again. "I don't know. They seemed kind of—"

"You know what a stereotype is, right?"

"Yeah, but that neighborhood. You don't expect that kind of crime there. And I doubt two fat-slob dicks acting like they were at a backyard barbecue gave the residents a reason to sleep better at night."

"Yep," Morales said and the two were silent again until Morales said, "Just focus on being a good cop. Everything else—that's out of your control."

1

Sheridan Road was the quickest way to Frownie's condo. Named for a Civil War general whose scorched-earth tactics destroyed the commercial infrastructure of the Shenandoah Valley, Sheridan Road now represented a corridor of economic privilege running through the leafy northern suburbs lining the shores of Lake Michigan. Although I was a son of the North Shore, the domain retained no special feelings in my soul nor aroused nostalgic aching. Having gained entrance via my father's illicit profits, I considered my legacy invalid.

My mentor, Sid "Frownie" Frownstein, was a hard-nosed sleuth from the old days who had skillfully hoofed that muddled line between investigation and collaboration until he withdrew to a lakefront penthouse with spectacular views of the shoreline and a hobby restoring antique cars. Despite his age, Frownie still clearly remembered the days when the cliché hard-boiled detective originated—the "Bogart Bullshit" days, he liked to say. He'd always been out in the lead, taking life where he wanted it to go. But at age ninety, life was catching up fast. Frownie's best advice? Don't trust no one.

It had been too long since my last visit. I was ill prepared for how significantly his body had deteriorated. Sitting upright in bed, leaning against an enormous reading pillow, Frownie wore a T-shirt that hung on his skeletal frame like a towel over a clothesline. A disconnected IV bag dangled from a pole. If I softened my gaze, I could evoke the image of a cadaver. Then he spoke.

"Hey, Julie! C'mon over here, ya little schmuck. How the hell are ya!"

The voice, still deep, clear, dripping with a blue-collar Chicago accent straight out of central casting, covered me like a warm blanket. Had I closed my eyes, I could've been back in my childhood, ensconced under Frownie's desk while he reminisced on the phone with former clients and past "operatives."

When I leaned down to kiss his cheek, Frownie hooked his left arm around my neck and pulled himself up to hug me. He had all the weight of a laptop computer. I carefully lowered him back to the pillow, fearful his bones would snap.

"I look like I was in a concentration camp. But I ain't this body. It's just a skin and bones costume that's wearin' out. Hey, doll, get over here. I want you to meet someone." Frownie's live-in nurse walked into the bedroom. I guessed she was around sixty, fit, attractive, long hair colored blond. "This little putz ain't related to me, but he's taken the role of the grandson I always never wanted."

The three of us laughed and I introduced myself.

"I'm Helen. Nice to meet you, Jules." Helen walked to the other side of Frownie's bed and examined the catheter bag.

"They wanna hook me up if I get too dried out," Frownie said and pointed to the IV. "Right, honey?"

"We want you to be comfortable. Maybe Jules can convince you to stop fighting us." She winked at me and turned to leave the room. "Call if you need anything."

"Not a bad piece of ass to be hangin' around an old fart like me, eh? So what's up?" Frownie closed his eyes and waited. I had the feeling he was toying with me, that he knew exactly why I was there. Just as I was about to answer his question, he said, "It's your old man, ain't it?"

"He acts like I'm sticking a knife in his gut. And just because I want to include homicide—"

"Don't go makin' it all nice usin' words like 'homicide'! You mean *murder*! Killin' human beings! Who do you think you're talkin' to?"

"Okay, okay, murder—"

"For chrissake, Julie, you already did it. You got nothin' to prove. You investigated Snooky's murder and you solved it. And you didn't get killed in the process. Don't you see? You won. Move on. You can make a damn good livin' with all the other investigatin' they do these days."

"Dad wants a guarantee that I'll never take another murder case. I can't do that. And I'm not gonna lie to him. Do I gotta remind you it was Dad who got out of prison two months ago, then knocked on my door and *gave* me my first murder case?"

"Yeah, yeah, but that was *Snooky*. Your old man's no dummy. He knew what Snooky meant to you. And he knew you'd go after his killer no matter what. But he didn't know you would've taken murder investigatin' as somethin' to call your own. So do me a favor. Tell me why the people-killin'-people business is so goddamn important? Then maybe I can understand a little bit."

Frownie was a realist. Depending on my answer, he could accept how things were, even if he didn't like it. "Fine," I said. "You want the truth? I loved it. I loved every goddamn second of it. I don't know why, but I never felt more alive than when I was investigating Snooky's murder."

Frownie looked away, nodded his head, and said, "That's what I was afraid of. That's what your old man didn't count on. By the way, you still seein' that broad? Susie Somethin'? You sounded kinda happy about that."

"No. Didn't work out. No big deal. So what do I do about Dad?"

Frownie turned back to me. "First of all, don't go guilt-trippin' yourself. You're his son. His flesh and blood. When you're a father, you'll understand. But for now, that's his problem. In the meantime, try to ignore his comments. But if he keeps pesterin' you, just tell him you don't got no murder case and to stop worryin' about it. And if you do take another murder—well, you'll figure it out. Why worry about somethin' that ain't happened yet?"

We both laughed. There was something about Frownie's voice that sunk into my bones, reassured me that everything would be all right.

"That's true. Who the hell even knows when I'll get another murder case? Maybe I'll *never* get another one!" I stood to leave.

"Uh, before you go," Frownie said. "You should know. Your dad's kind of losin' it a little bit. Upstairs. You know what I mean?" Frownie's expression reflected the pain he felt telling me this.

2

Contentment and well-being had not been sensations overly familiar in my life. The farther I drove from Frownie's condo, the less I held on to the warmth of his words. By the time I stepped into my office building's lobby, the accustomed pessimism had returned and I realized that the four hundred square feet that made up my new office had become a refuge of sorts—from what, I wasn't sure.

I settled behind my desk with the newspaper. A half hour or so later, a thin, boyish-looking man standing on the landing outside my office caught my attention. The fact that the door was wide open and I was the floor's only occupant added to the strangeness of his presence. Early twenties, I guessed. He leaned against the wall next to the unmarked door of the room across the landing. His dapper suit was comically too large, as if he were a child dressed in his father's clothes. He held his arms tightly against his chest, suggesting I had been the subject of his gaze for some time.

I lowered the paper and said, "Can I help you?"

The stranger's expression changed to a serious grin. He straightened himself up, walked through the doorway, and extended his hand. Tiny ears held back neatly tapered blond hair. Blue eyes carried resignation and anguish, as if he were destined to carry a heavy burden. I shook his hand.

"You're Jules Landau, aren't you?"

"Yes," I said, and became somewhat annoyed when the stranger didn't respond with an introduction but walked slowly past to linger behind me. I swiveled my chair around. "Do you mind telling me who you are?"

The man walked back to the front of my desk. "Isadore Himmel," he said. "Call me Izzy."

An ill-fitting name to match his ill-fitting suit. "So what do you want, Izzy?"

"What do I want? What does anybody want? The truth, of course." Izzy's posture gave him the appearance of leaning backward. His hands resided deep in pockets engulfing half his arms.

"I'm not in the mood for games," I said. "Are you interested in hiring my services? If not, then take off."

"Tell me," Izzy said. "I was ten minutes or more outside your door. Yet it took that much time for you to question my arrival here."

At some mental level, I'm sure I had been aware of someone loitering outside sooner rather than later, but an article about Asian carp invading Lake Michigan had engrossed me. "The door was open. What were you waiting for?"

"I'm supposed to hire a detective who's not even curious? Are you sure you're in the right profession?" His eyes narrowed.

Was this just some nut who had wandered in off the street? "Okay, Izzy. What is it you want to find the truth about?"

The little man strolled around the room, looking my almost bare white walls up and down as if searching for imperfections. He stopped to examine my framed credentials and said, "You heard about that code enforcement officer who was murdered?"

I searched my memory. "I don't remember a cop being killed. When was this?"

"*Parking* officer," Izzy said.

I'd never heard of a parking officer ever being killed. Had it happened in Chicago it would have been big news, if only to satisfy the grouchy multitudes who would revel in the murder of someone who wrote parking tickets. Even the most timid Chicagoan was only too happy to provide a scorching indictment of city parking policies. "You stumped me again, Izzy. When did this happen?"

"A week ago. His name was Jack Gelashvili. Viciously beaten to death near Foster and Western."

"They got meters in that neighborhood?"

"The meters are innocent; he lived there."

"So he wasn't killed on the job?"

"Does that matter?"

"No, but it explains why I didn't hear about it. You knew the victim?"

"No. But I want you to find his killer."

I suppressed seeing providential significance in Izzy's offer of murder investigation number two on the heels of my conversation with Frownie. "Why? There are hundreds of murders each year. What's this guy to you?"

Izzy sighed loudly. "It's sad that I need a reason to care about a fellow human being slaughtered practically in his front yard. But if you must know, *I* also live in the neighborhood, with my three-year-old twins. Noah and Carolin. They saw a crowd and an ambulance and police cars. They sensed something bad had happened and it touched their hearts. They'll never be the same—I can tell. So you see, it's my front yard, too, where an innocent man's blood was spilled."

"How *innocent* was he?"

Izzy shook his head in disgust. "Blaming the victim now? He was asking for it? I was there when

14

they took his body away. You should've seen this young woman, a family member I assume, screaming, crying, beseeching over and over, 'Why?' And you ask only about his innocence?"

"I just wondered if you knew something about the guy. Who were his friends? What was he into? That kind of thing. And how did you find out about me, anyway?"

"*The Partisan.*"

Izzy referred to Ellis Knight's article detailing how I'd solved Snooky's murder while exposing rampant police and city hall corruption. The lengthy, purple-prosed feature received both praise and criticism for the writer's use of omniscient narration to reveal the alleged thoughts and motivations of all major characters. *It's the substance that matters!* Knight kept saying over and over throughout Snooky's investigation, maniacally laughing through his giddy twenty-something demeanor. Despite the article giving me an undeserved reputation as a murder investigator, I saw an increase in finding birth parents and cheating spouses that allowed me to afford a small office on the top floor of a converted vintage four-flat in Old Town. The owner had successfully resisted the forces of change since its 1927 construction, leaving in place the magical qualities of musty air, scratched tiles, poor lighting, and neglected wood finish. The indifference cheered me up for some reason.

"I really don't have a lot of experience—"

"That case gave you *momentum,* Landau. Exploiting momentum is what drives men like you to find answers. Not everybody has this genius."

Genius? I understood neither the logic nor the premise of this statement. "It's been two months. How much momentum could be left?"

"The potential is what matters. And I sense you're a man with nothing to lose."

He implied recklessness? "Ellis Knight's article was more creative writing than facts. Maybe it's Knight who has the momentum—whatever that means. No offense, Izzy, but I really have no idea what the hell you're talking about."

Izzy walked to the room's only window and stared out over North Avenue. "My apologies," he said. "The Boston Marathon bombing affected me deeply—the randomness of its victims in particular. That neighborhood was home to many. But that case was solved. Now there's a murder on the block where I live. I need to know why a life was extinguished so close to where my children, my neighbors, and I lay our heads to sleep."

"Okay, I get it. A corpse shows up on your doorstep. What did the police say?"

"Zilch. Nobody knows nothing. It's as if bodies showing up in this neighborhood should be viewed as the new normal."

"Bodies show up everywhere in every city. Usually, it's only relatives or close friends of the victim who seek out a PI."

Izzy reached into his breast pocket and took out an envelope. "There are fifty one-hundred-dollar bills in this envelope," he said and dropped it on my desk. "There will be fifty more when you've found the killer. Is that enough to care more about this murder than my motivation for hiring you?"

I peeked inside the envelope. The nuance of Ben Franklin's smile had two hundred years of capitalistic influence behind it. What chance did I have against such momentum?

3

"Yeah?"

Police detective Jimmy Kalijero answered his cell phone as if expecting a timeshare solicitation. Many years ago he ran the sting that nabbed my father for illegal gambling. On my dorm wall at college, I had the framed *Chicago Sun-Times* article with the photo of Kalijero smiling proudly as he led a row of cuffed suspects to jail. That Dad was careless enough to get caught pissed me off, but I had to admit I felt a kind of deviant prestige for having a jailbird father.

"Yeah, right, Kalijero, you don't recognize my number or my voice."

No response, then, "Oh, of course, it's Landau calling. How completely logical because he calls me all the time because we're such good pals."

It had been two months since we last worked together, but I was still pretty sure we had spoken a few times since then. "I deserve the guilt trip, Jimmy. I promise to call more often."

"What do you want, Landau? And no, I still can't accept a son of the Chicago Landau family as a legitimate private investigator."

Kalijero referred to my family history, starting with Great-Granddad, who made his fortune among his immigrant brethren of pushcart peddlers working the open-air market of Chicago's Maxwell Street. From this miserable residue, Great-Granddad guaranteed a dependable stream of extorted money and earned the monikers of iron-fisted boss, political dictator, chieftain—and scoundrel. In addition to ward committeeman, he also held offices with fancifully arcane titles such as city collector and city sealer of weights and measures. Some of my relatives called him the smartest man they ever knew and pointed to his chauffeur-driven limousine on a municipal salary as proof. Others pointed to the same thing and damned him as a gangster. Regardless, those who knew of him understood why Great-Granddad's scandals inspired passion sixty or more years after the man died penniless in my father's childhood bed.

"Jack Gelashvili ring a bell?" I asked Kalijero.

"Why should it?"

"Murdered last week near his home in Budlong Woods."

"So why should I know about this murder out of six hundred or more stiffs we find each year?"

"Gelashvili was a parking officer."

"Gee, what do you think the motive was?"

"Cold, Jimmy. He worked for the police department, asshole. How about showing a little respect for those that do the cops' shit work? Would you like to spend your days writing parking tickets? By the way, he was off duty when they bashed his head in."

I thought I detected a conciliatory grunt.

"You got me, Landau. I should've known about this guy. They probably had a special ceremony for him, but I haven't been paying attention like I used to. I'm very nearly burnt out. I figure about fifteen thousand people have been murdered during my career."

"You're still relatively young for a Greek god. You got your pension locked up; why don't you do something else with your life?"

"I wouldn't know what to do—and I don't need advice from you. How's Frownie doing?"

"I've never seen him so carefree," I said. "He stays in bed most of the day, but his spirits are high and his mind is razor sharp. He's fighting to the end like it's a game. 'I'm not my body,' he told me the other day. 'Who needs a goddamn body anyway? I'm just a spark bouncing around my brain.'"

Kalijero chuckled and said, "Sure sounds like he's losing it to me."

His comment angered me for its small-mindedness. I wanted to like Kalijero, but that would require ignoring his unenlightened condition.

"How about finding out for me who's on the Gelashvili case?" I asked. "See if I can chat with them a little bit."

Kalijero sighed. "You think I can just snap my fingers and the whole goddamn department falls at my feet? I'm one of your contacts, is that it? Your man in the CPD . . . ?"

Geez, what nerve had I hit? I let Kalijero rant a while longer until I found a break and jumped in. "You sure are a surly son of a bitch, Jimmy. And it's a damn shame you hate your life so much that you feel the need to shit all over someone who just wants to help find a little justice for some poor bastard who got wasted . . ."

It was my turn to rave, which I did with gusto, reaching deep into that angry bag of frustration we all carry around with us for such occasions. At what point the call dropped, I had no way of knowing.

4

At home the next morning, I ate breakfast and fired up my new laptop to search the *Republic* archives for Gelashvili. The article I discovered was barely long enough to warrant a byline. "Forty-five-year-old Jack Gelashvili of 2415 West Farragut Avenue, found dead from blunt force trauma near his home. Robbery motive inconclusive, although his apartment was ransacked. No one is in custody and Foster area detectives are investigating."

Unmarried, living with his cousin and mother, Gelashvili, according to neighbors quoted in the article, had a pleasant personality and was an all-around terrific guy. No mention of what he did for a living. A glorified obituary, really.

The reporter's name was Peter Ross. I called the *Republic,* then endured ten minutes of being transferred around different offices before someone figured out Ross was a stringer and that the Gelashvili article had been his first with the *Republic.* With great reluctance, I called Ellis Knight, my *Partisan* contact and an affluent white kid who had acquired an annoying fondness for ghetto slang.

Knight answered with, "Another exclusive exposé? You got a one-eight-seven? Already, already, already!"

"Calm the hell down. Why don't you give Ritalin a try?"

"Why else would you call me? We gonna memorize Bible verses together?"

"Do you know a freelance reporter named Peter Ross?"

"Yeah, I know Ross. What do you want with him?"

"I want to ask him a few questions about an article he wrote."

"What article?"

"How can I get in touch with him?"

"What article?"

"Try to stay calm. A guy got murdered and I'm looking into it."

As if a dog could ignore a piece of raw meat. Knight exploded into the freaky uncontrollable behavior that was his trademark, first begging for the story then saying I owed him for helping my career. It might be funny if it wasn't true. On and on he went until I hung up.

As if on cue, the phone rang seconds later.

"Can you keep a goddamn grip on yourself?" I barked at Ellis. "Do you want to give it a try?"

"Don't give me any orders, Landau," Kalijero's gravelly voice said. "I didn't have to call you back. In fact, I don't ever have to talk to you."

"Sorry, Jimmy, I thought you were someone else. You want to yell at me some more?"

"Baker and Calvo."

"Baker and Calvo?"

"The two detectives assigned to the Gelashvili case. They're both a couple months from full pension benefits for a career of half-assed police work. That means they can do shit all day and it don't matter. It says a lot that these two clowns got the case."

"Meaning it's low priority."

"More like it's *no* priority. And there was no special ceremony or acknowledgment for Gelashvili. It's like the guy didn't exist."

"Why'd you call me back?"

"I don't know. It's not as if I want to be your drinking buddy. But that guy, he deserved better. I mean he worked for the cops. Someone should try to find out . . . " Kalijero groped for words.

"What? Just say it."

"The *way* they killed the guy. They turned his head into a pulp—somebody's way of sending out a sick message."

"Whose way?"

"That kind of memo usually comes from organized crime. Gangs, Mafia."

"That's one memo you'll be glad not to get."

Kalijero hung up on me for the second time in two days.

5

Leaning against the butcher block island, I re-counted the money Izzy had given me, fully aware a black and white cat sauntered back and forth from the kitchen to the living room, lashing her tail and meowing every four or five steps. About the time I reached the thirtieth C-note, my ankle erupted in pain. Punim was hungry.

I dropped a pile of livers, kidneys, hearts, and gizzards into her bowl and then prepared a sandwich of raw tofu on rye with sliced tomatoes, fake mayo, and toasted ground sesame seeds. I ate and once again confirmed I had fifty portraits of Ben Franklin in my possession. The phone rang.

"I know how to get in touch with Ross," Knight said.

"So you're gonna help me?"

"Only if you promise me exclusive rights to the story behind the murder."

"There might not be a story behind the murder. What's Ross's number?"

"I want it in writing—that only I get the story. I've got the papers at Mocha Mouse for you to sign."

Had I not already come to terms with this bizarre character—assistance from him would require tolerance, acceptance, and surrender—I might have allowed my anger to ruin what had been a perfectly good morning.

Investigating a murder meant wearing a shoulder harness again. I holstered my .40-caliber and headed to a coffee shop named for a saxophone-playing rodent. Knight himself, in his black horn-rimmed glasses and dark wiry hair piled high, seemed an appropriate caricature for a diner with a Buddy Holly theme. Probably the strangest kid I ever met. A privileged white boy dreaming of the "hood," oblivious to how idiotic his unconvincing ghetto slang sounded. His toothy grin annoyed me the most. I knew he'd be at his usual table, the one in the back surrounded by ten chairs, nine of which were empty. Knight fantasized of one day leading an Algonquin Round Table of tabloid journalists. He had a long way to go.

"Good to see you again, Jules." Knight fidgeted with a sheet of paper.

I took a seat three chairs away. "Let's get this over with."

Knight pushed the paper at me. "I should've told you to bring a lawyer. I'll give you a couple of days if you need advice."

I noticed "Gelashvili" was mentioned in the first paragraph. "You saw Ross's article?"

"I called Peter. A parking officer hunted down; brain scrambled; fifty-eight bucks in his wallet? Credit cards untouched? Apartment ransacked? And you're going to tell me there's not a story there? Even the meth heads, whores, and drunks hate those parking Nazis."

I read through the agreement, three paragraphs stating in no uncertain terms that in exchange for unfettered access to Peter Ross, I would reveal any and all information regarding the murder of Gelashvili to Ellis Knight and only to Ellis Knight. What bullshit.

"Just in case you're getting ideas, Ross won't talk to you until I tell him you've signed."

"Yeah? And if you get the big story, you gonna share a byline with him?"

Knight stared at me a moment. "That's none of your business."

"Okay, Ellis." I scratched my name out on the designated line. "You own me. Now give me his number. And he better be cool, or I'll shove this agreement down your throat and let you void it out your ass."

I slid the document back to Knight, and he dug out a piece of paper from his pocket. "Here's his number," he said and handed it over to me. I grabbed it and walked out.

6

On the phone, he sounded older than I'd expected; when we met up in person, he looked about mid-fifties. "Peter Ross?" I asked. He sat on a bench at the park near Diversey Harbor.

"That's me," he said through whatever he was chewing.

He was skinny and well tanned in a brown, worn-out, leathery kind of way. His face reflected a lifetime of missed deadlines and spiked stories. Every few seconds he turned his head and spit out sunflower seed shells. Gross. I sat at the other end of the bench. "So what do you know about Gelashvili's murder?"

Ross finished the seed he was working on and ejected it. "Well, I know the cops weren't eager to figure it out. Considering Gelashvili was one of their own, I thought that was really crummy."

"I gotta believe your original article was a lot longer than what got published."

"Hell, yes, it was. I had a whole feature on his family. Georgian immigrants. A real powerful, tragic human interest story. The death of the American dream. But the *Republic* hacked it down to an impotent piece of shit."

I waited for Ross to expand on the emasculation of his piece, but he offered only more violent evacuations of black shells.

"What did the city editor say about it?" I asked.

Ross spit in disgust and faced me for the first time. "That useless bastard? He's got his nut sack hiding so far up, he has to spend all his money on a stud service for his wife. At first, he was psyched up, thought we had a real scoop. And then bang! Somebody says 'boo' and he shits himself. I asked him what was going on and all he can say is he got a call from the big boss, Konigson."

"What about the cops? Did they tell you anything?"

"They got a couple of Laurel and Hardys pretending they give a damn. Every time I asked them a question, they'd look at each other and smile. Then one of the morons would give me the 'it's an ongoing investigation' bull crap and laugh."

His defeatist tone intrigued me. "So you're just going to roll over? Don't you want to know why the Gelashvili investigation is being shut down?"

Ross gave me a poisonous look. "You want truth? Is that it? I should be Zola and Gelashvili my Dreyfus? His head reduced to rubble and nobody cares. That's the only truth that matters anymore. Fuck your truth!"

I liked getting people fired up. "Why did you agree to meet me?"

"Knight's paying me a hundred bucks. He's using me to rope you in so you have to give him the inside story. If you showed up, that means you signed his contract."

"Why didn't Knight just ask you himself?" A kid on a skateboard flew past us, failed at executing a kick-flip, but still landed on his feet while the board went off the sidewalk.

"Because I hate that little fuck. But I'll take his money."

"You're a true friend."

"He's a punk with a rich daddy. Truth or no truth, he'll never have to worry about making a living."

"Why does that piss you off?" I knew why, but I couldn't resist.

"Damn it! I just said why. Truth! You have any idea how I've had to compromise myself just to make a buck? You think I want to write meaningless articles about guys no one cares about getting beaten to death? But I gotta make money. I've wasted a lot of time. In fact, I've wasted my life."

His dejection was palpable and entirely uninteresting. I placed my business card on the bench and walked away.

7

As a kid, we always had the *Sun-Times* in the house. The *Republic,* I later learned, was the conservative paper while the *Sun-Times* leaned toward the progressive side. My great-granddad was part of Mayor "Big Bill" Thompson's political machine during Prohibition. Both the *Sun-Times* and the *Republic* existed in one form or another back then. And both accused Great-Granddad of terrorism. He once shared a headline with Al Capone. I wondered which paper Great-Granddad read.

Despite Republic Tower's landmark status as a quintessential example of neo-Gothic architecture, I saw only a skeletal monolith of spikes, spires, pointed arches, and gargoyles. Medieval ignorance and suffering peasants with torches and pitchforks also came to mind. It was into this house of pain I walked, seeking answers from the eighth-largest newspaper in the United States. Famous quotations chiseled into the granite walls recalled the divine duty of a free press and created not just a lobby but a "Hall of Inscriptions." An enormous relief map made of shredded money spoke many column inches about a newspaper baron's true religion.

"I'd like to speak with Mr. Konigson," I said to the receptionist, whose only response was to stare at me as if waiting for the punch line.

"You want to talk to Sam Konigson, the CEO of the Republic Media Group?"

It was my turn to wait for the punch line—but I was the joke. "Okay, how about the city editor?"

"I need to see an ID." I complied, she wrote down some information, then gave me a guest pass to hang around my neck. "Go to the twentieth floor and try your luck. His name is Wilbert Palmer."

Peter Ross had told me Konigson called his editor directly. It seemed odd a CEO would personally call anyone not from upper-level administration just to maim a story. Even I knew a collection of managers, associates, deputies, and assistants dwelled between a CEO and a section editor.

Another receptionist awaited me as I stepped off the elevator. I had had a cult-like love for 1970s television like the *Mary Tyler Moore Show* and *Lou Grant,* and old movies from *Citizen Kane* to *All the President's Men,* and the newsroom appeared exactly as I expected.

The woman behind the counter looked like a college student. An open copy of *Advanced Reporting* confirmed my suspicion.

"I'd like to talk to Mr. Palmer please."

"Is he expecting you?"

I smiled. "I doubt it."

She frowned and picked up the phone. "Someone here to see Wil," she said and returned to *Advanced Reporting*.

Seconds later a gloomy-looking man—just barely as old as the receptionist—rushed up to me. "Yes?"

"Mr. Palmer?"

"I'm Dylan, his assistant."

"Assistant to what?"

"To the city editor."

"I'd like to talk to the city editor."

"Unless he's expecting you, send him an email."

In the back, I saw a glass room with a long conference table. At the head of the table a balding man sat alone, staring out the window.

"I want to talk to him about a murder. I'm a private investigator." I showed him my identification.

"He's too busy to see everyone who stops by. Send an email."

"Busy, my ass. That's him staring out the window in the conference room, right?"

The man glanced behind and then back to me. "Mr. Palmer communicates only by email unless you have an appointment!"

His non-denial told me I guessed correctly. I reached for my wallet.

"Here's twenty bucks," I said and stuffed the bill into his shirt pocket. "And here's twenty for you." I dropped another bill onto *Advanced Reporting* and blew past the assistant to the city editor.

They caught up to me as I opened the glass door of the conference room. The three of us entered together.

"I just want to talk about Gelashvili—" I said but was immediately drowned out by the youngsters begging forgiveness.

Then a woman about my age came in. "What the hell's going on?" she asked.

"And you are?" I asked.

"I'm Mr. Palmer's assignment editor." If Palmer gave a damn, he didn't show it. I think he barely glanced our way. "Brenda, get back to your desk. Dylan, what's going on?"

"He just barged in—"

"Now, just wait a goddamn second. Dylan here took twenty bucks to let me come in." I plucked the bill out of his shirt pocket and dropped it on the floor.

"He's lying!"

While Dylan voiced his outrage, I sat next to Palmer and introduced myself.

"Why was the Gelashvili execution given about as much space as a standard obit?"

Palmer turned and looked at me. His hairline receded uniformly past the top of his head. From above, I supposed he resembled a half moon. His face had a plump, healthy glow despite his sixty or more years. His eyebrows looked professionally groomed. Gold cuff links matched gold tie clip. Gucci, I guessed. Our eyes momentarily met before he turned back to the window. A large hand fell upon my shoulder. I looked up into the face of a security guard who suggested it was time for me to leave. I was able to fling a business card onto the table before the officer escorted me out the door while demonstrating the arm lock restraining position. A real control freak.

8

At two o'clock, it had already been a long day. Back home, I dropped the stomach and intestines of an unidentified animal into Punim's bowl. The gloppy thud brought her running into the kitchen where she attacked the entrails like the sweet little kitty-cat she was. I needed some couch time. To assist her digestion, Punim would soon curl up on my lap, and the two of us would drift off together while the facts of the case swirled around my subconscious and Punim chased and devoured the small animals of her dreams.

The cell phone ended my nap. Punim voiced her irritation and ran off. On the phone a soft male voice. "Uh, yes. You want to know about Mr. Gelashvili?"

I recognized the voice. "Mr. Palmer?"

"May I ask why you should care about Mr. Gelashvili?"

"He was murdered. I'm being paid to find out why."

"Don't you believe the police can figure it out?"

"When my investigation is finished, I'll tell you what I believe."

"And what makes you think I can help your investigation?"

"Why would the CEO of a giant media corporation take the time to personally call a city editor just to kill a story about a guy who writes parking tickets?"

Deep sigh, then, "Where shall we meet?"

Palmer insisted we meet in "your neck of the woods," and I gave him directions to Mocha Mouse. I got the idea Palmer had not ventured much north of downtown. He kept asking how to spell major streets like Halsted and Armitage. When I told him just to tell the cab driver the address, he informed me he was going to travel by "elevated train."

From my table, I watched a tall, plump, white dress shirt with gray slacks walk into a wood-centric, bebop-jazz-themed coffee shop of graying ponytails, pierced noses, and enough tattoos to be measured in square yards.

"Coffee, tea, various fruit-based drinks?" I said.

"Nothing, thank you," Palmer said, sitting down before wiping his head and forehead with a monogrammed handkerchief. He leaned forward on his elbows and looked me straight in the eye. He wore no rings although his fingernails were clean, even, and polished. "I've become so accustomed to communicating by email," he said in an East Coast aristocratic accent I recognized from old movies. "Now, please, what did you want to know?"

I had the feeling he was anxious to talk.

"The stringer who wrote the original article about Jack Gelashvili's murder, Peter Ross, told me you relayed a message from Konigson saying the article should be hacked down to an insignificant nub. Is it true?"

"Mr. Ross was very upset about this. While I had no obligation to explain anything to him, I did tell him Mr. Konigson had personally called me. I had no more information to share with him."

"Got anything to share with me?"

Palmer dabbed his forehead again. "I'm not sure. That is, you are correct to think it unusual for someone in Mr. Konigson's position to personally call an editor. I must say, it piqued my curiosity as well. I had never expected to speak to the man, yet there he was on the phone, wanting to talk to me."

Palmer reminded me of a painfully shy, über-intelligent child desperately trying to break out of his shell.

"What exactly did Konigson say to you?"

Palmer laughed or coughed, I wasn't sure which. "Well, he told me to make sure there's not a human interest story surrounding Mr. Gelashvili. When I told him a good article had been written by Mr. Ross, he spoke quite harshly and used crude language. He threatened me, actually."

Palmer turned his attention to an area of thrift-shop couches arranged in a circle where tie-dyed kids held hands with closed eyes, creating a kind of peace-circle ambience. He looked like he wanted to ask me about it. "Don't ask," I said. "Now, why didn't the all-powerful Oz just tell you to kill the story?"

He laughed or coughed again. "In retrospect, I think fear. He was afraid other media sources might pick up the story and try to investigate. An obit of a poor immigrant would help discourage investigation by sending a signal that the case had been looked into, so why bother?"

"Sounds like you've really thought about this," I said. Palmer didn't respond. "Konigson was afraid of something related to Gelashvili's murder. But when he demanded the story be nothing more than a glorified obit, he didn't even bother making up a reason?"

"I'm afraid that's pretty much what happened. That arrogant—" Palmer suppressed a thought.

"What is it?"

Palmer looked at the meditating kids. "The arrogance of money. One with money need not fear consequences."

Had the corrupting influence of money been lost on Palmer only to have been found with Gelashvili's murder? "You could've told me all of this on the phone."

Palmer took a deep breath. "Yes, it's perfectly normal that you should wonder why I came all the way up here to meet you. And to be absolutely honest, I'm still processing my motivation as well. Perhaps it was just the timing. Mr. Konigson's phone call stirred up emotions inside me. I was never one to question the way things were, and suddenly I'm conflicted. You were the first person to directly ask me about the Gelashvili article. Now that someone else is demonstrating a keen interest, I feel compelled to discuss my internal struggle." Palmer leaned back in his chair and briefly closed his eyes.

"So what are you doing here?" I said.

Palmer straightened up and gave me a quizzical look. "How do you mean? We agreed—"

"No, I mean here in Chicago? I would never have pegged your personality surviving a big-city newspaper."

Palmer smiled and nodded. "I know now that you are correct. The *Republic* chose me, and not the other way around. In fact, my entire life has been chosen for me."

"Before you tell me the story of your life, can you make it remotely relevant to the squelching of the Gelashvili article?"

Palmer thought for a second. "Yes, I think what I have to say will be relevant, if only parenthetically." He looked squint-eyed and then rubbed his forehead. "Actually, it may be more relevant than either of us realizes. I have a feeling that insights previously unrecognized may surface—if you don't mind listening to me."

"By all means, sir. Tell me your story."

"My family comes directly from the New York of the Gilded Age . . ."

Palmer began his story of childhood WASP ostentation complete with exclusive private schooling for children of the super-rich who also possessed remarkable intellectual gifts. That the written word became the source of Palmer's fascination delighted his mother, although his father would have preferred that his son's encyclopedic mind took advantage of the less subjective world of finance. As he spoke, the phrase "proper breeding" repeatedly flashed through my brain.

Palmer had spent his life in a bubble, focusing only on the journalistic and literary tasks put in front of him and excelling at each level. Family contacts ensured that opportunities to work at the most distinguished publications were available to him. As a gesture to his father, he also obtained advanced degrees in finance and law, earning one of the top ten scores in the country on his CPA exam. Palmer's cultivation amidst the elite publishing families of Manhattan guaranteed a symbiotic relationship with the media's gradual corporatization and culminated with his appointment to oversee all of the Dow Jones consumer-oriented publications.

"Over the course of many years in New York financial publishing, I realized I was an oddity," Palmer said and, without any detectable change in his aristocratic inflection, began deriding himself for a life of shallow nearsightedness. Purely out of curiosity, I asked him to elaborate. "Wall Street," Palmer said. "Specifically, the blatant way investment banks controlled the country."

I didn't know if I had ever been so underwhelmed. "Are you kidding? *That* came as a surprise to you?"

Palmer stared at me for a solid five seconds. "Have you ever seen Mr. Konigson?"

"Only newspaper headshots of his shaggy face."

"I've never seen him without three former navy SEAL bodyguards surrounding him. I used to see nothing peculiar about living this way. Gradually, my eyes opened. My revulsion for the controlling gentry stems from having lived among them so long. Someone as far removed as you from the *elect* of finance has the ability to see much more clearly than someone like me, who had known no other reality."

Palmer's deadpanned sincerity filled me with shame.

"Excellent observation. But did you think Chicago would be a bastion of provincial virtue?"

Palmer smiled. "Chicago was not New York. That was enough for me. I had been groomed to one day own or run a media company. Many argued I shouldn't settle for being an editor. I, however, welcomed the reduced role in the journalistic *scheme*."

When Palmer spat out the bitter taste of "scheme," he said more than all his preceding words combined. Perhaps I should investigate how far a disillusioned journalist would go to get the truth.

"So what I know for sure is that we have a media billionaire personally ordering one of his hundreds of mid-level deputies to kill a story of no consequence about a person of even less consequence. I certainly appreciate you coming to meet me, Mr. Palmer, and I sympathize with your career disappointment, but as I said earlier, you could've told me this on the phone."

Palmer stared at the tabletop while drumming his fingers. "So what am I doing here?" he said still looking into the table. After a minute he said, "I'd like to offer my expertise, to see if I can find a financial angle to the murder. My understanding is that money almost always plays a role in such crimes. This information could be my contribution to not allowing a man's death to be callously consigned to the status of a footnote. Nobody should have that much power. Who's to say it won't happen to me or you?"

9

The following morning I pondered the lowering angle of mid-October's sun, along with the gradual decline of relative humidity. In particular, how this overture heralded the best time to be in the Midwest. Chicago's well-deserved reputation for crappy weather sometimes eclipsed our memories of the delightful days that visited each autumn. This morning began as one of those days. Outside my window, the ash trees had just begun their metamorphosis, and something about the way the breeze spoke through their leaves inexplicably evoked nameless but pleasant feelings of peace. Then the phone rang.

"To some, a neighborhood is as significant as an entire world. There is no difference."

It took a few moments, but I recognized the unmistakable inflection as belonging to Izzy. "What do you mean?"

"Something local may be globally momentous. I'm ready for an update on your progress."

"It's been what? Two days? And I don't remember progress reports as part of our agreement."

What I imagined as Izzy's version of shouting came next. "You think I'd give a stranger five thousand bucks and then wait for my phone to ring? You think I give five grand to any Tom, Dick, or Harry who calls himself a private investigator?"

That I could be so effectively humbled by Izzy's tongue-lashing only intensified my curiosity about how such a bizarre personality could have developed in any life form.

Izzy insisted we meet at my office. When I arrived, he was already waiting on the landing in the same cross-armed posture he had presented upon our first meeting. I had a feeling he'd called me from there. Without a word, I unlocked the door and took a seat behind my desk. Izzy sat in the guest chair.

"I apologize for my tone," Izzy said. "It is not my nature to speak in such a manner. But sometimes nature is mutinous." Izzy sighed, stood up, walked to the window, stared out over the madness as he had done on his first visit. "A hundred years ago, who would've imagined an entire universe would exist solely to control where one could park an automobile?"

I waited for more and then said, "All morning I thought only of hearing your contemplations on parking."

"How one with your shallowness could have solved a purse-snatching, much less a murder, I find remarkable. Many billions are spent on and earned from parking. Laws are written stipulating how long an automobile may stay in one place before that law is broken. When the first car was created, did this idea come to mind? You don't know in advance where things will lead, Landau. I walk into your office and you assume a barrier should exist between client and professional. Yet I am the one who gave you the money on which all depends. Either you include me in whatever details I desire or our agreement ends and you will forfeit the funds I have given you—on a prorated basis, of course."

I wondered if my parents ever imagined that their son would complete thirty-five years of life, become a private investigator, but still allow himself to be emasculated by a scrawny apparition of a man.

"Palmer is a disillusioned newspaper editor who also has many years of executive experience in the corporate media." I filled him in. "He's going through a career-life identity crisis. He has offered his expertise in the finance world. That is, if money played a role in Gelashvili's murder, he will seek out the evidence."

Izzy walked back to the guest chair and sat. "Within minutes you again disappoint me. At the very least you should know this investigation implicates corporate media masters and others that their tentacles reach."

"Or it could be simple and straightforward. We don't know anything yet."

"Did you know Dagestan means 'land of mountains'?"

It dawned on me that I should expect all conversations with this guy to be filled with seemingly pointless questions that he would employ as part of a larger riddle. "Why would I know that?"

"A small country with big mountains. Do you not see the symbolism in a perceived contradiction?"

I wanted to say, *What symbolism and perceived by whom?* but then it dawned on me. "The Boston bombers. They were from Dagestan."

For the first time I saw Izzy smile and thought I caught a glimpse of his real self—youthful, unburdened, optimistic. "Maybe I misjudged you," he said, and then his face morphed back to that dour façade of an old man. "What's next?"

I wanted more of an explanation to the Dagestan-mountain thing, but I was learning. "Next is my first interview with the murder victim's family," I told him.

10

I paced the sidewalk in front of Gelashvili's building, trying to prepare myself for the agonies of bereavement. Frownie's voice echoed the importance of staying emotionally disconnected. I would tell him "detached" was a better word, and he would tell me to use any goddamn word I wanted as long as I stayed "fucking disconnected."

A bit of red on a sugar maple diverted my thoughts. Gelashvili lived in one of those lush neighborhoods that never came to mind when one thought of Chicago. Only ten miles from the downtown delirium, parts of Budlong Woods looked classically suburban with tidy frame cottages behind perfect squares of grass. Other areas reeked of urban bungalow paradise surrounded by carefully

44

sculptured hedges and multicolored flower beds. Gelashvili lived between these worlds in a red brick four-storey apartment building.

A female voice responded over the apartment building intercom. "Yes?"

"My name is Jules Landau. I've been hired to investigate Jack Gelashvili's death. May I have a few minutes of your time?"

The extended silence approached the threshold of re-ringing or walking away. Then, "Just a moment."

I held the doorknob anticipating a weak buzzing from the latching mechanism, but instead watched a petite woman with shoulder-length jet black hair descend the hallway stairs in white corduroy slacks and a yellow scoop-neck T-shirt. The word "lovely" came to mind.

She opened the door enough to reveal a beautiful face with a hint of Asiatic influence. Late-twenties at most, I thought. I gave her my investigator's ID, my driver's license, and a business card. The door fell against her toe as she studied them. She looked again at the credentials and then back to me. Then she pushed open the door and handed back all the documents. I returned the business card to her and asked that she keep it. Her brown eyes momentarily held mine, and then she slid the card into a front pocket. I saw, perhaps, the smallest of smiles.

"My name is Tamar Gelashvili," she said as we climbed the stairs. "I live with my aunt who was Bagrat's—I mean, Jack's—mother."

"I'm sorry for your loss."

Tamar didn't respond. When we reached the third-floor landing she said, "My aunt speaks very little English. And her despair is indescribable."

The third-floor apartment reminded me of a basement dwelling that had only a couple of window wells for light. As my eyes adjusted, I noticed heavy curtains covering a large picture window and candles burning throughout the room. Each candle appeared strategically located near a black-and-white photograph or a medieval icon depicting an ancient Christian saint. In the background, several haunting voices chanted quietly in an unrecognizable language. Tamar approached me carrying two folding chairs. She handed me one.

"Come," she whispered.

I followed a few steps and jumped when I realized I had completely missed the living, breathing figure in a rocking chair nearby. An old woman faced a man's portrait on a corner shelf above a candle. Tamar put her chair to the side of her aunt. I sat on the other side with a partial view of the woman's veiled head and her right arm. *Whistler's Mother* came to mind.

Tamar leaned forward, whispered to her aunt, then turned to me and said, "How can we help you?"

46

"Is your aunt comfortable with my presence here?"

"I doubt she's aware of your presence."

"What language were you speaking?"

"Georgian. We're from Georgia, a small country—"

"On the Black Sea near Russia, Turkey, Armenia."

The candlelight reflected off her teeth when she smiled. "I apologize for assuming."

"For assuming all Americans are ignorant morons? That can't be helped. Jack's given name was Bagrat? How long had Bagrat been living in Chicago?"

"When my cousin realized his name in English sounded in translation like a bag of rats, he changed it. That was five years ago, when he arrived with my aunt."

I laughed. "Why did he leave Georgia?"

"It was becoming unsafe for him. He was a Moscow-trained scientist. He had always worked with Russians and had many Russian friends. But he lived in a region that wanted to be independent of Georgia. Russia supports this independence, but the Georgian government does not. Jack was not political. He didn't care one way or another. But there were those who wouldn't accept the idea of being neutral. You had to take a side."

"Five years ago Bagrat arrived with his mother in the U.S. Did they know anyone besides you?"

"Nobody. And he hadn't seen me since I came here as a child—although we always kept in touch. He and my aunt took care of me when my parents were killed by a bomb in the marketplace. I was only two. He was a big brother and a father to me. But there was a civil war raging and they both wanted me safe. When I was seven, they somehow arranged an adoption through a refugee organization. I was raised by a Georgian couple whose parents had fled the Stalinist takeover and settled in Chicago. I still remember saying goodbye at the airport . . . " Tamar's face crumbled as a wave of grief swept over her. She quietly sobbed into her hands. I wanted to believe my desire to comfort her would have been just as strong had she not been beautiful and intelligent.

As quickly as the anguish flooded in, so it also subsided. Tamar wiped her eyes and laughed. "I'm sorry. I thought I had regained my control. At least I didn't start tearing my hair or scratching my face like the west Georgians."

"Please don't apologize. If you don't mind me asking, how was life with your adopted parents?"

"They were wonderful parents, already about sixty when I arrived. No children of their own. They've long since retired to Florida. It was a great comfort for them to know *Deida*, Jack, and I were together again. They are in poor health and I see no reason to tell them the horrible news."

"How did Bagrat the scientist become Jack the parking officer?"

"His specialty had something to do with chemicals and heat and metals and things I couldn't even imagine. And even though he had permanent residence status, finding a job in his field seemed impossible, especially considering the language barrier. And he wasn't a young man anymore. The Georgian community was always helpful to immigrants. The super of this building is Georgian. He helped us get our apartment. But Jack didn't want to work construction or drive a taxi. His attitude alienated a lot of people. They thought he acted superior and arrogant. Over time, he realized he needed to lower his expectations and just focus on making a living."

"How did he end up working for the cops?"

"The super, Ivan, had been a math professor back home. He and Jack became good friends. Ivan was also good friends with the owner of the Kutaisi Georgian Bakery, where I work and where lots of cops hang out."

"I'd like to interview Ivan. Can you introduce me?"

"I would, but he has since immigrated to Canada. Vancouver, I think."

"Too bad. So Ivan had a connection with the police that he used to help Jack?"

"Pretty much. I didn't talk to the police much, but Ivan had gotten to be friends with several of them. When he found out Jack needed a job, he asked his police friends for help. Next thing we knew, Jack was writing parking tickets."

Although I had never been there, the bakery Tamar mentioned was one of those institutions that defined neighborhoods. Devon and California streets meant, *near the Georgian bakery*. "Did he know how unpopular this job was with the public?"

"I believe so. But by then, he didn't see any choice."

"The article in the *Republic* said his apartment had been ransacked. Obviously you were not home, but what about your aunt?"

"When the police arrived, she was lying on her bed just staring at the ceiling. By the time I got here, she knew something bad had happened to Jack. I had to confirm her worst fears."

"What did they take?"

"As far as I can tell, nothing. But they were definitely looking for something."

A shrill cackle from the rocking chair startled me. Tamar whispered something in her ear. I barely perceived a kind of guttural mumbling from the aunt, but Tamar responded with more whispering and the two conferred in this manner until Tamar kissed the old woman on the head and turned back to me.

"My aunt needed to remind me that Jack was a scientist and how proud the whole village was to have him as a son. Then she said Jack was now with

Apostle Andrew." Tamar pointed to one of the icons on the walls. "My aunt asked what I thought Jack and Andrew talked about." Tamar's eyes narrowed just slightly, but enough to darken her appearance. "I hope they talk about cutting out his heart and roasting it on a skewer—whoever did this to Jack. Sorry, what were you saying?"

Wow. She did have a dark side. "Parking officers regularly find themselves in hostile situations. How did Jack handle himself? Do you know if he made real enemies?"

Tamar thought for a moment and then shook her head. "Actually, it seemed like he made a lot of friends. His coworkers teased him for being too lenient, but a lot of people appreciated his approach. I mean, he wrote plenty of tickets, but he didn't mind giving people breaks. He said he was amazed at how grateful people were when he voided someone's ticket."

"Did he have a social life? Girlfriends?"

Tamar hesitated. "He didn't show much interest in dating until he came home one day and told us about meeting Lada. He was writing a ticket to her car when she approached him. They started talking, and he found out she was Russian. They started dating. After a few months, he acted like a boy in love." Tamar started laughing. "We found out later that Jack's coworker Rich actually set it all up. Russian, Georgian, it was all the same to Rich."

"So Rich and Jack were pretty good friends?"

Tamar considered my question. "At first, I thought maybe they would be. But Jack couldn't figure him out. Nice one day, doesn't talk to you the next. I don't think he's very healthy. If you want to talk to Rich, he always works this neighborhood. You can probably find him."

"Do you know Lada's last name?"

Tamar had to think. "Sobor-something," she said. "I'm not sure. Rich should know."

"What did you think of Lada?"

"She was only a few years older than me, which was strange. But she was very sweet and very pretty. Jack was a healthy man, after all, so I would never begrudge him a little happiness. The more I got to know her, the more I liked her. She even helped take care of my aunt. But there was a lot of mystery around her. She drove a fancy Mercedes, wore beautiful clothes. We never knew where her money came from."

"What did Jack say about her money?"

"He dismissed our questions with 'It doesn't matter' or 'What's the difference?' So I let it go. If Jack was happy, I was happy for him."

"And?"

Tamar sighed. "Out of the blue, Lada called him and said she was having immigration problems and needed to go back to Russia for a while. She promised to keep in touch and said she was confident her connections would get everything resolved. Jack never heard from her again. He became very depressed, although he tried to hide it."

"When was this?"

"About a month ago."

"How about enemies in Georgia? Is it possible he was killed to settle an old score? Is there a Georgian mafia in the United States?"

Tamar frowned. "Mr. Landau, I appreciate your interest in finding my cousin's killer, but I'm quite confident his murder has no connection to organized crime, vendettas, ritual sacrifices, or any other conspiracies dominating the current cinema. He was a scientist by training, but he also knew he had to leave that life behind and accept the status of an average working American."

A blush of shame crawled up my back and over my shoulders. I thanked a nameless entity for the dim light.

"I could blame Hollywood for my shallowness, but that would be too easy."

"Blaming is easy. But movie plots often have a basis in reality. Who can take the blame for Georgians being one of many tragic peoples from the Caucasus?"

"How about the public? Could there have been a citizen whose parking ticket was the final insult from a miserable life, and your cousin just happened to be the recipient of this misplaced anger?"

St. Andrew's candle started flickering wildly then blew out. The old lady made a series of throat-clearing sounds. Tamar stood then walked to a small console table against the wall and took a book of matches from the drawer.

"If there were such people," she said as she re-lit the candle, "I wasn't aware of it. He never spoke of threats or anything like that. Except for his sadness after Lada left, he was always quite happy when he came home. Although, in the weeks leading up to his death, he did seem distracted. But he insisted everything was fine." Tamar sat back down.

"He may not have been aware of it. I mean, a guy comes to his car and sees a parking ticket on his windshield written three hours earlier and then takes it out on the first parking officer he sees."

Tamar's response was swift. "So he followed my cousin home and then waited around, or came back another day so he could kill him when he wasn't wearing his uniform?"

Good point. "Unlikely. In Jack's case, it seems someone laid in wait—premeditated murder—as if they had already picked out where they wanted to put his body."

Tamar sighed again. "I know I must prepare myself for Jack's death to be filed under 'random act of violence.' One detective suggested a gang initiation rite. Another implied mistaken identity."

"The police found cash in his wallet, so robbery clearly was not a motive. But they did ransack the apartment, so they were looking for something. Did he wear anything of value such as jewelry or an expensive watch that was missing?"

"Nothing like jewelry. Although he always wore a *chotki*—it's a bracelet of prayer beads that once belonged to his grandfather. Its only value was sentimental. I assume it got torn off and scattered about."

A somewhat awkward silence followed. Then I said, "Perhaps it will help to know there are others who won't be satisfied with some half-assed speculation from a couple of deadbeat cops waiting to retire to the doughnut shop."

Tamar gave me a curious look. "One of those *others* hired you?"

"Yes. One of those others is paying me to find the truth. And for what it's worth, I give you my word that the truth will be found."

In this business, offering promises or guarantees was nothing short of stupid. But men often say stupid things in the company of beautiful women.

11

"I took another murder case."

Frownie's smile vanished. He turned away from me and, if possible, appeared older. The guilt hit me hard. Why hadn't I expected it?

I stared at the profile of a man old enough to remember his uncle Davey pathologically describing hand-to-hand combat at Belleau Wood, until one day Uncle Davey stuck his army-issued Colt revolver into his mouth and pulled the trigger. The bloodshed of Prohibition gangsters, the privation of the Great Depression, the mass slaughter of the Second World War, and every other human tragedy since were deeply embedded into Frownie's consciousness. Yet here he sat in his last year of life, tears brimming forth as if I was destined to relive all of history.

Then a surprise.

"Of course you're goin' to tell me," Frownie said with a laugh. "What—you're gonna come visit and lie to me?" He laughed again. "But you gotta tell your old man, too. Don't keep secrets from your father."

"I'll talk to Dad soon," I said, then told Frownie about Izzy showing up at my office and described his bizarre personality and the cash he carried with him.

"That's the gumshoe biz. At any time some nut shows up and gives you a pile of money. But you can't let the money alone make up your mind. Ya gotta know what you're gettin' into. The money's not always worth it."

He was right, although I would have to think about it later to determine what role the money played. I told Frownie the details of the case while he stared straight ahead as if calculating the various components into an equation. As I waited for him to share my enthusiasm, I realized how much his approval still meant to me.

"Tell me about the stiff," Frownie finally said.

"An immigrant from one of the former Soviet republics just wanting a middle-class American life."

"I don't like it. They say them Russian mafia guys are more cold-blooded than anything we had in the old days. And you got this corporate prick with more money than God. That combination scares the hell outta me. And it should scare the hell outta you, too."

"Hang on a second, Frownie. I'll give you the corporate money angle but not the Russian thing. The guy was from *Georgia,* a separate people and culture with their own tragic history."

Frownie continued staring and then perked up. "Ah, what the hell. What do I know anymore? This editor, Palmer, who got the call. You're sure he's in your corner? He know what he's gettin' into?"

"So far he's acting born-again. A true believer. He wants to find a financial angle to the murder. I expect him to stay pretty much in the background."

Frownie looked at me. "Why's he helpin' you, anyway? What does he give a damn?"

"I'm not sure. Trying to make amends for something in the past, I think."

Frownie clearly did not like the idea of Palmer being involved in the investigation. "Just remember.

If he stumbles upon some money angle—those guys are the first to disappear. And I don't mean they volunteer."

It was still pleasant, although the sun had sunk low enough to remind me of the fool's paradise that autumn induced and how the slightest chill revealed the vulnerability of a cotton T-shirt. I found a parking place three blocks from my apartment. Had a parking deity blotted out the sun and permanently guaranteed for me this space, I would've accepted it without complaint, even at ten below at two *a.m.*

Before going home, I stopped at Tasty Harmony, a take-out utopia only a few storefronts from my apartment. It was run by some kids I met when I stopped at their Fort Collins, Colorado, eatery and begged them to open a restaurant in the 2700 block of North Halsted Street, Chicago. Six months later, I discovered four white kids in dreadlocks and Carhartt overalls hammering, sawing, and measuring away as they transformed a former payday loan outlet into an organic vegetarian oasis. The only other place in the city where I was known as "Jules" was a *carniceria* where each week I purchased a package of entrails for my feline roommate.

Halfway up the stairs, I heard the thump of Punim's paws hitting the floor. As expected, I opened the door to a patrolling puss whipping her tail and meowing demands for the innards of small mammals. Two turkey livers and a chicken heart quickly pacified her lust while I dined on a falafel and hummus sandwich topped with cucumbers, tomatoes, and sprouts, all wrapped in a large collard leaf.

As I ate and Punim meticulously licked the blood from her fur, thoughts of the previous two days gathered. Most of us knew that urban societies had grown numb to annual body counts in the multiple hundreds. We coped with such tragedy by embracing the cold comfort of the assailant's motive—that violence targeted a specific life for an identifiable reason, that it wasn't the random act of a meandering lunatic. In my mind, the blatant disregard of Gelashvili's murder by the cops and media eliminated a chance-encounter scenario. This case was barefaced and screamed for attention, like how a drug mule's car driving exactly the speed limit in the right lane shouted, *Don't pay attention to me!*

12

At five-forty in the morning, a cat's paw swatted my head. Had I shut the door the night before, the door would be bouncing off the jamb. Had I inserted a shim to keep the door still, continuous scratching and yowling would fill my world. Usually, I fed the creature and returned to bed. But this morning I was wide awake. Gelashvili's murder had infiltrated the deeper regions of my consciousness where I imagined impulses to the heart resided. Frownie called this a "personalizin' issue," and no doubt this personalizin' had something to do with Gelashvili's cousin Tamar. Frownie would not have approved.

59

I showered, ate, read the paper, got a cup of chai from Tasty Harmony, and arrived in the Budlong Woods neighborhood at nine *a.m.* I parked on busy Western Avenue around the corner from Gelashvili's apartment and began walking. Western was a wide four-lane street that could have been in any city in the country. Three-story walk-ups lined some blocks while storefronts and offices with an apartment overhead dominated others. Each corner had a gas station–convenience store combo or fast-food joint. I saw no parking devices of any kind. I walked to a side street that took me to Lincoln Avenue, another major artery that offered a landscape identical to Western with the exception of meter boxes along the sidewalks.

You always heard about the omnipresence of parking officers, yet there I stood for over an hour before I noticed a thin, gray-haired man in his fifties slowly walking past the line of parked cars, peering through the windshields to locate the meter receipts on the dashboards. His body movements appeared coordinated in a defined order repeated every twenty seconds or so. He'd stop, look around, lift an electronic ticketing device to within inches of his reading glasses, type in a plate number, then complete the routine with a dab to the nose from a handkerchief he kept balled up in his palm.

I stepped into his path with at least twenty yards between us and waited. When he got close enough for me to read "Jones" on his name plate, he turned on his police radio and performed a microphone check.

"I mean you no harm, officer," I said and smiled broadly. "I come in peace."

Jones did not share the humor. He took off his glasses and said, "You have a question?" His voice sounded hoarse.

"I'm investigating the death of Jack Gelashvili. Did you know him?"

Jones stepped back and blurted some kind of radio code into his mic. Before I had a chance to explain, a police cruiser pulled up. Apparently, I had asked the wrong question. The driver's side door opened and out stepped an African-American officer who did not look amused.

"What now, Rich?" the officer said.

"I'm not sure. This guy's asking about Jack. They found his body about five blocks from here, you know. Kinda weird he should be asking about him."

"I'm a private investigator hired to look into Jack's murder." I took out my identification card and held it up. "I just want to talk for a few minutes."

The cop walked over, and I handed him the card. He glanced at it, gave it back, and motioned for me to follow him a few more steps away. "Rich is a little jumpy," he said quietly. "A little trigger-happy with the radio." He waved Jones over. "Come and talk to the man, for chrissake."

Jones obeyed. "Jules Landau," I said and extended my hand.

He looked at me and then at my hand and then back to the cop.

"Go ahead and shake his hand! What the hell's gotten into you?" Jones took my hand and I sensed he felt better. "That's it! Now, just talk to the man and I'll see you later." The cop mumbled something into his radio and walked back to his car.

An occasional tic under his right eye added to Jones's sickly appearance. "You've been at this job a long time?"

"Twenty-three years," Jones said, taking a wad of tissue from his pocket and wiping his nose. "Damn allergies. In all that time, I never heard of anything like what happened to Jack. Getting spit on was the worst I've had done to me. But nobody ever laid a hand on me or any officer I knew. Weird, though, because when I heard an officer was found dead, I wasn't surprised."

"Once in twenty-three years and you weren't surprised?"

"No, not in a big city. Especially lately. Everyone hates us. They look at me, and I can tell they're thinking of how to kill me. It had to happen eventually."

"How well did you know Jack? Did you consider him a friend?"

Jones wiped his nose again. "Yeah, I guess. We liked Jack but we didn't really know him. He was a good guy, helped you out—covered shifts, that kind of thing. But he never had drinks after work. He seemed lonely."

"But you—personally—were friends? You set him up with Lada, right?"

Jones looked surprised, but not in a happy way. "What do you know about Lada?"

I shrugged. "Only that you introduced them and he fell for her. That's it. Do you remember her last name? Sobor-something?"

"Soboroff," Jones said, still looking spooked. "Who do you think did it? Who killed Jack?"

"Don't know. What do you think?" Jones got fidgety. He looked around several times then shrugged. "C'mon, officer, what're you thinking?"

He stepped a bit closer but looked away as he spoke quietly. "I don't know," he said. "I mean I got no proof, but there's a guy who lives in this neighborhood who's had a running battle with all of us. But I got no proof, so I don't know. But he's like the guy who one day snaps. You know what I mean? And he never learns. No matter how many tickets he gets, he still doesn't feed the meter. But it was when we started towing him I thought he may have reached the breaking point."

I waited for more. "Okay, so what happened? Jack towed the guy?"

"No, no, no. We don't tow; that's another department. But we're the punching bags. It's like if the food sucks, it's the waiter's fault. But I know this guy, Gordie Bastard, got towed last month for the third time. The story is that he showed up when the car was already hooked. He offered to pay, but the boot guys said it was too late. Bastard begged the driver to drop it, but they just laughed. Watching his car towed away must've pushed a crazy button in the guy because he started throwing things, kicking, screaming. He picked up this hunk of loose concrete, slammed it down on the sidewalk, and started screaming how he hated us parking Nazis. When the cops showed up, they put him in cuffs and took him away. But like I said, I ain't got no proof he killed anyone."

"I assume the police questioned this guy?"

"I don't know. But there's something weird. After the guys towed the car, it would reappear parked in the same spot that same day!"

"Somebody would pay the fines and get the car?"

"Uh, yeah, I guess."

"You told this to the cops?"

"We told everything to those two detectives who came by the department. They got pissed off at anything we said and told us not to spread rumors. They started soap-boxing us about a citizen's right to privacy, and we could be sued for slander. Ain't that a twist. Two police snoops lecturing me about a guy's privacy when they can't wait to peek through your window or tap your phone or look at your bank records."

"The guy that got towed. His last name is really *Bastard*?"

"Gordon Baxter. We just call him Gordie Bastard."

"He ever act that way with Jack?"

Jones thought about it. "I don't know."

A kid on a skateboard came rolling down the sidewalk. As he passed, he shouted, "FUCK YOU, METER MAID! GET A REAL JOB!"

Why the hatred in the kid's voice shocked me, I didn't know. Jones appeared unmoved.

"That behavior surprises you?" he asked. "Welcome to my world. Insults from punks who never had a job are routine. And I'll tell you what, that kid's parents are probably just as nasty."

I let Jones get back to his world and walked away with a newfound respect for those who spent their days universally despised.

13

"Jimmy, where do short-timer cops waiting for full pension eligibility piss away their days?" I listened to the ensuing silence while testing the reclining limits of my executive desk chair, feet on my desk, staring at the cracked paint on my office ceiling.

"Oh, right, I forgot. I'm supposed to instantly recognize Landau's voice 'cause we're such good pals."

"You said that last time I called. Christ, Jimmy, after all we've been through, can't you pretend to like me just a little bit? Can't you pretend to respect me just a tiny bit for not becoming a career criminal despite a genetic predisposition to corruption? Would it kill you to think maybe I'm a good guy?"

"Daddy spent too much time in the pen, didn't give you the approval you wanted? So now you want it from me?"

"Yes, Daddy. Getting in touch with your paternal side might be good for your heart."

Kalijero mumbled something in Greek. "What do you hear from Frownie?"

"You asked me that last time, too. His mind is clear, but his body is on its way out. Where can I find Detectives Abbott and Costello?"

"What about your old man? Happy his kid investigates murders?"

"We'll see when I talk to him next. Now, what about—"

"Calvo and Baker are both divorced, I think. So try Reilly's on Milwaukee. That's where the over-fifty badge bunnies still hope to land a cop husband."

"See? That wasn't so hard, was it? Maybe I'll be able to help you out someday."

"You can help me out by leaving me alone."

This time, he didn't hang up on me. I took that as a sign he was only half serious. "Why are you so

66

damn depressed? How about I tell you where I am with the investigation?"

"Stay in this business long enough and you'll understand depression. Go ahead, tell me what you've got."

"I got a lot of weirdness shouting at me to do something . . ." I gave a chronological report starting with Palmer and ending with a chronic scofflaw named Gordon Baxter. "I thought I'd talk with Calvo and Baker and see if they've looked up this Baxter guy."

Kalijero laughed. "Don't expect much from those two. The newspaper editor is a better bet. Either the CEO is the biggest control freak ever to exist or something caused him to impulsively phone this guy. That call is a flashing red neon sign. I suggest you keep your newspaper boy safe."

Kalijero's sudden interest flattered me. Maybe we would be friends one day. "I've got to find a link between an immigrant parking officer and the CEO of a media corporation. Agree?"

Long pause, then, "Yeah, it looks that way. That editor. You expecting him to get *involved* in your investigation?" Kalijero's tone had suddenly sharpened.

"I don't expect anything. It's up to him. He's interested in finding a financial aspect."

"But he knows it's about murder because he was told to play it down."

"What's your point?"

"*Responsibility,* Landau! He's a civilian. You gotta make sure a civilian knows what he's getting into! And the fact I have to tell you this really pisses me off!"

Kalijero's volatile mood pissed me off. It was my turn to hang up on him.

14

Besides the scratchy green shamrock hanging above the door, nothing about Reilly's reminded me of an Irish pub or anything much removed from a tool and die maker's basement bar. The metal stools with their torn plastic cushions, the chipped Formica tables, the folding aluminum chairs suggested décor that had not changed since the last of the department stores and small industries shut down decades earlier. The only food offering came from a vending machine holding three bags of corn chips. I wondered how Reilly's survived among this neighborhood's art galleries and upscale microbrew pubs serving ten-ounce prime beef burgers.

Behind the bar, a scrawny elderly man stood watch over five middle-aged women sitting evenly spaced along the bar, each sipping from a martini glass, and steadfastly ignoring each other. The bartender reminded me of the guy behind the counter in that famous Hopper painting *Nighthawks*. I decided his name was "Philly." A few of the tables had a male occupant bent over a glass mug. The only sign of life came from a table in the far corner where four men of ample girth, each wearing a different colored polyester sport jacket, chuckled and snorted around three pitchers of beer.

I stepped up to the bar and ordered a bottle of Bud. In one fluid motion Philly reached under the counter, popped off the lid, and slammed down the bottle. "Two bucks," he said in the unpolished accent one expected from an old guy named Philly.

Even though I rarely drink alcohol, I sat at the table closest to the four men and sipped from the bottle as if I were just a regular Joe kicking back with a cold one. After struggling a moment with my gag reflex, I caught bits of conversation from the raucous table evoking a reminiscent tone as the men took turns asking "Remember when?" Their overhanging stomachs and patterned sport jackets demonstrated why stereotypes linger through the generations. With references to 'Nam, hippies, and the 1968 Democratic Convention, I safely guessed their age group as late fifties to early sixties.

I waited for a lull and said, "Gentlemen, may I interrupt a moment?"

Two of the men glanced at me. The other two tipped their heads back and drained their glasses. After a refill from the one full pitcher, the group ignored me and returned to stories of their gloried past.

I slid my chair close. They reacted as if strangers often joined them as they got plastered at two o'clock in the afternoon.

"Hey, guys, I'm looking for Detectives Calvo and Baker."

At that, they all glanced up. A Latino-looking cop in a brown polyester sport coat that probably fit

69

him in 1980 said, "So are we," provoking a collective roar of laughter.

"Guys, please. I just have a couple questions about a murder investigation."

Another cop with closely cropped gray hair and wearing an orange "Illini" sport coat stood and said, "I'm Calvo." Then another stood and said, "No, I'm Calvo." Then the same routine took place for Baker and the four stomachs jiggled with joy.

I tried not to be disgusted by watching veteran cops straight out of an old TV sitcom howling like fools in a dive bar. While I waited for calm, the violent aspect of my genetic profile leaned over the table and swept away the glass mugs and half-full pitchers, transporting the mess either across the room or into someone's lap. The Latino cop lunged at me. A sidestep and shove—barely a nudge—sent him to the filthy tile floor. The other three stared at the scene, looking confused. Philly and the girls watched impassively.

"Listen, assholes, you're all fat and shit-faced, which means I'm in charge. I need to ask Calvo and Baker a few questions. If one or both of them are present, squeal for me."

"The one on the floor is Calvo," orange jacket said. Then the same man said, "I'm Baker."

Calvo struggled to his knees and managed to push himself up to a chair. The seam on the back of his jacket had opened up. I almost felt sorry for the slob.

"Hey, tough guy," one of them said, "one day we'll see how tough you really are."

"I'm not tough. I'm sober. How about Calvo and Baker join me at that table over there?"

"How about you go fuck yourself," Calvo said.

"I didn't come here to piss you off. I just need some info." I walked over to the bar and held up a fifty-dollar bill. "Here's fifty bucks for the bartender. It's a prepayment. Fifty bucks worth of booze in exchange for ten minutes with Calvo and Baker." I put the fifty on the counter. Philly glanced at it, then looked back at me.

I walked to a table on the other side of the room. My four friends stayed put. They looked exhausted.

"C'mon, Ray," Baker said. "Let's see what the little shit wants."

My two new buddies wobbled over to the table. It amazed me how booze turned a middle-aged face into a puffy, bloated mug after just a few hours of drinking. They looked like bulldogs with receding hairlines. I tried to picture them twenty years younger and failed. I said to Calvo, "I'm going to pay for a new jacket and the cleaning bill for the slacks."

"Go to hell."

I looked at Baker. He seemed the more sensible of the two. "Gordon Baxter," I said. "A well-known scofflaw. Did you interview him regarding the Gelashvili murder?"

71

Baker's vacant expression suggested they hadn't bothered. Then he said, "Who told you about Baxter?"

"Rich Jones, the parking officer you spoke with."

Calvo jumped in. "It's none of your goddamn business. And we told them meter maids to keep their mouths shut."

"Baxter's under surveillance," Baker said. "We don't want his name circulating. He might disappear before—" The two dicks glanced at each other. "Before we want him to."

I waited a few beats to let the awkwardness fester. "Before you want him to what? Is this about the Gelashvili murder or something else?"

"It doesn't matter," Calvo said. "This is police business. You got no say in it, so fuck off."

I decided to drop Jimmy's name. "Kalijero tells me you both got retirement in your sights. Couple months or so?"

Calvo grinned. "Hey! You must be Landau! Jimmy puts your old man away and you become his little bitch?"

"Just stay away from Baxter," Baker said. "If he takes off, you're going to piss off a lot of people. That's all you need to know."

"Yeah? Do those people I will piss off also spend their days getting wasted in sleazy watering holes while they're supposed to be conducting surveillance?"

Icy stares. Then Calvo said, "I gotta hand it to you, Landau, you crack one case and that's enough to get a reputation as a smart-ass punk. How many murder investigations you think you can survive being a cocky little shit? And don't bet on Kalijero being your pal too much longer. He put his papers in before we did. Any day now he'll be running some greasy spoon in Greek Town."

Not wanting to wear out my welcome, I thanked my new friends for their hospitality and bid them farewell. I walked back to my car with two competing thoughts: linking a dead immigrant to a multimedia corporation just became more complicated, and it hurt to find out secondhand that Jimmy had put in for retirement. I needed a place to sit, eat, and reflect. Tamar had mentioned she worked at the Georgian bakery around Devon and California.

15

I found the Kutaisi Georgian Bakery in a thriving multicultural paradise of skin tones, creeds, and ethnicities. Equally diverse were the delicious smells emanating from the bakery's brick-domed oven as it produced the breads and pastries so well known to District 24 of the Chicago Police Department. Apart from a line of booths along the back wall, rows of square oak-laminate tables filled the eating area. Four police officers occupied one of the booths, clearly enjoying a variety of flaky pastry treats. A guy in a burnt orange leather jacket with a

73

shaved head sat by himself at the end booth. The words "skinhead" and "neo-Nazi" came to mind. Not wanting to be presumptuous, I settled for "gangster." Not far from the cops, a couple of drunks lay passed out over a table. I perused the offerings displayed under the counter, settled on a triangular delicacy, then sat at a table next to the bakery's enormous storefront windows that ran parallel to Devon Avenue. A sweet honey-walnut flavor filled my world as I stared into the street's craziness and tried to make sense of the preceding days.

In my mind, the cliché stood front and center, close enough for me to smell its foul breath: evil corporate devil committed murder to cover his ass. The simplest scenario—Gelashvili gave Konigson one too many parking tickets—was also the stupidest. Or maybe Konigson's chauffeur got too many tickets. Even stupider. The expanse of unattached dots between Gelashvili's world and Konigson's required more connections before I could move beyond the realm of idiotic speculation. Moments like these begged the attention of "Frownie Consciousness," an intruding voice I attributed to the old man when personal doubt hoisted its monstrous face. *Focus on the dots in your immediate vicinity,* the voice said, and instantly I saw Baxter the scofflaw—aka my closest dot.

I sat upright and breathed deeply while twisting my neck and shoulders back and forth. After several rotations, a silky black ponytail caught my attention. She stood in front of the oven, apparently inspecting the dial thermometer. When she turned, I saw enough of her face to confirm Tamar's identity.

I walked to the end of the counter and watched her push a rolling rack stacked with trays of dough back and forth from the prep room to the oven. The back room had one large open entryway through which I could see other workers bent over tables, kneading, glazing, or icing. While I observed the labors of pastry fabrication, an immense figure appeared in the entryway, filling most of the space—if not blotting out the sun. He was bald with a bushy black unibrow over matching black eyes and a bulbous hook of a nose. The face of nightmares, I thought, a kind of beast-like man who materialized in your bedroom doorway and stared at you with an evil eye known to transform children into stone.

When our eyes met, I instinctively turned my back and leaned against the counter, but not before the man's body language had already revealed his intention of approaching me. Moments later I heard, "May I help you with something, sir?" That this kind, gentle articulation could come forth from such an intimidating figure was almost cartoonish in its absurdity. I was about to respond when I caught a glimpse of Tamar emerging from the doorway, which prompted a lateral move out of the man's shadow. I waved. She smiled broadly, walked over while wiping her hands on the bottom half of her apron, and said, "What're you doing here?" Her white V-neck T-shirt revealed a sheen of perspiration running down her lovely neck to the cleavage of her adorable breasts. The warmth of her expression released a swarm of butterflies throughout my abdomen and I forgot all about the demon who had retreated back into the prep room.

"I was hungry," I said. She giggled. "Gordon Baxter. Does that name mean anything to you?"

"No. Should it?"

"Only if Jack had mentioned him. Another officer told me Baxter was a well-known scofflaw whose car had been towed more than once. He was known for his abusive language and threats. And he lives in your neighborhood."

"So he's a suspect?"

"Seems like he should be, but a lot of things aren't what they seem."

Tamar nodded. "That's quite a profound statement."

"By the way, there's a couple of guys passed out at a table near those cops."

Tamar shrugged. "Yeah, we get a lot of those. Drink a lot somewhere, come here and load up on pastries, pass out. As long as they don't cause trouble, the boss doesn't care."

I nodded as if her explanation made sense, then said, "I'll let you get back to work."

Again Tamar held me in her gaze for an extended moment before saying goodbye. The conclusion to my visit would've been perfect had I not sighted the bald demon once again filling up the entryway to the prep room, his scowl scary enough to cause DNA to mutate.

Men took care of Dad. "Associates," I think they were called. They shopped for him, cooked his food, cleaned his apartment, and basically made sure he was comfortable. These benefits were not the result of regularly paid insurance premiums, but of credits acquired over decades of loyalty to various individuals and organizations operating as a de facto syndicate. Keeping his mouth shut for sixteen years in a medium security prison was the equivalent of buying an expensive long-term disability plan.

Dad rarely left his apartment in a six-flat on Pine Grove and Waveland, which is why I didn't bother calling. Through the door's oval glass, I watched him hobble toward me. He employed his cane carefully, keeping his gaze to the floor. Not until he opened the door did Dad lift his head and offer me a fleeting smile. His blue eyes still gave off a spark of youthful vitality that betrayed a body slowly succumbing to prostate cancer. I bent down and kissed him on the cheek. Dad turned then motioned for me to follow.

"Why don't you have one of those guys live here?" I said. "Let them answer the door."

Dad lowered himself to the couch and sat upright with both hands resting on the cane handle. "Because I can still wipe my own ass, that's why. When I can't, then it's time to go. So what's new?"

77

I sat in a chair opposite the couch and got right to the point. "I've taken another murder case."

Dad had no immediate reaction other than to purse and un-purse his lips, something he always did when contemplating. "Well, what are you going to do?" he finally said.

"If I thought you'd never ask me again, maybe I'd keep it to myself. But I'm not going to lie to you."

Dad appeared okay with my answer. "Hey, what I don't know won't hurt me. Just go about your business. No point in worrying."

I waited for more. "That's it? You're going to let me off that easy?"

"You got any friends besides your father and another old man at death's door?"

So much for letting me off easy. "What's the difference?"

"What about that girl? Susie, wasn't it? You sounded kind of happy about her."

"I was happy about her but . . . we wanted different things. It's complicated—and she had to go back to Connecticut, to help take care of her parents."

"Hey, what about Peggy?"

I thought I was hearing things. "What about her? That was high school, for chrissake!"

He looked confused, as if he wasn't sure where he was. Then his face softened. "That's right," he

78

said. "What's the matter with me?" Dad looked at his watch. "Well, I want to watch my show now." He positioned himself at the end of the couch cushion then slowly rose to his feet, gripping the cane handle to steady himself. I watched his painstaking journey down the hall. After he disappeared into his bedroom, I let myself out.

16

I sat in my recliner with a cat on my lap. We stared at each other as I dialed the phone. She blinked. "I love you, too," I said, and as if on cue, she dug her rear claws into my thigh and leaped off. Love is complicated.

A young female voice answered: "Johnny Bail Bonds. How may I direct your call?"

"Jules for Johnny."

Stringed instruments, then, "Mr. Landau! The bloodthirsty Tyrannosaurus investigatorius!"

Johnny "Bail Bonds" Duggan liked playing with words. He found me after liberating a pile of business cards from a fish bowl on a restaurant cashier's counter, thus depriving someone of a free lunch. Johnny credited me with saving his marriage by verifying Sheila really met her friends every week for "girl chat" and that "Shawn" was also a woman's name. Having Johnny insanely grateful had two serious advantages: Sheila worked in the police crime lab and her brother was a cop.

"I need a background check and this time I'm paying for the service."

"You ain't paying for nothing. Not at Johnny Bail Bonds."

"C'mon, John, I can afford to pay, I don't need—"

Stringed instruments with harpsichord. Vivaldi, I thought. He came back on. "Every time you say you're gonna pay, you go on hold a little longer. So what'll it be?"

Johnny was pure blue-collar Chicago Irish. Favors were sacred and never forgotten. Arguing was pointless. "Gordon Baxter, North Side."

"Give me an hour." Johnny hung up.

I leaned the recliner all the way back, which for me was equivalent to swallowing a Valium. Palmer the aristocrat, inveterate newspaper man, slapped by the realpolitik of corporate media. I needed an insight into Baxter, something to suggest a logical connection, something to close the gaps between all those damn dots. I drifted off picturing four men standing in a room. A faceless head on a body wearing a suit represented Konigson. I wanted him to tell me something, even if he didn't have a head. Konigson raised his arm and pointed. I heard a shrill ringing. Konigson pointed again and I opened my eyes. My cell phone spoke.

"It's Johnny. Your boy Baxter has anger issues."

"Tell me."

"Four misdemeanor assaults on parking officers."

80

"What time frame?"

"All within the year. Before that, nothing."

"What's he driving?"

"Two thousand and three blue Buick LeSabre." Johnny read off seven numbers for the plate.

"Give me an address and your job is done."

"Twenty-four fifteen West Farragut, Apartment G6."

I repeated the address and Johnny confirmed Baxter lived in the same building as Gelashvili.

From across the street of Baxter's Farragut Avenue apartment building I failed to see any sign of the police surveillance Baker and Calvo had mentioned. Real surveillance would've been all over my ass by now. I called the bakery and asked Tamar if she knew anyone who lived on the ground floor.

"I see people in the laundry room down there. But unless they were my neighbors from upstairs, I couldn't say for sure what floor they lived on. Why do you ask?"

"I'll tell you more later. Gotta go." It felt good having a solid reason to call her again.

I judged an apartment building's character by how it treated its ground floor. Apart from a slightly musty odor, the freshly painted hallway, the well-vacuumed carpet, and the brightly lit laundry room spoke well of the building's management.

Outside the door to apartment G6, I heard random notes produced one at a time from an electronic keyboard as if a child were poking the keys with one finger. I knocked. The music continued. I knocked again. Still the music played. I was about to put a closed fist to the door when it slowly opened to reveal a tall, thin man in his forties wearing purple jeans and a white T-shirt. He hadn't shaved in days. Wavy black hair reached below his ears. His studio apartment was messy, like a teenager's bedroom. The white walls were bare. Across the room, a digital piano continued playing the music, or whatever it was.

"Yes?"

"Mr. Baxter?"

"Yes, I am Gordon Baxter."

"My name is Jules Landau. I'm a private investigator. I've been hired to investigate the murder of your upstairs neighbor, Mr. Gelashvili. May I ask you a few questions?"

Baxter's only reaction was to lean against the door frame and stare. Finally, he shrugged and said, "Sure. C'mon in."

Baxter sat on the pile of clothes that covered his bed. He offered me the only chair in his studio apartment—the one at the keyboard.

"There's a button at the far left of the console. Push it if the music bothers you. I'm a composer." Baxter spoke like someone bored out of his skull. I let the invisible child play.

"You were aware that Jack Gelashvili, who lived in this building, was murdered about a block away?"

"Of course."

I waited for more. "Did the police question you? About what you may have heard? Whether or not you knew the victim? That kind of thing."

"I saw police talking to some people from the building."

"What did they ask you?"

"Nothing."

"They didn't question you?"

"That's right."

"And did you think it was odd that they didn't question you?"

A few notes and a couple of eye blinks later, "I don't know."

"Forgive me for saying this, but you are acting really spaced out. Like you have no idea what's going on."

"Yes, you're correct," Baxter said then stood, pushed the pile of clothes to a corner of the bed, then sat back down. "When I am medicated, this is how I act."

I would have apologized but I didn't think he'd care one way or the other. "May I ask how you behave when you're not medicated?"

83

Baxter got off the bed and walked to the keyboard, where he stood next to me and pushed a few buttons that introduced an African beat accompaniment to the invisible child's random note playing. Baxter returned to his cleared-off spot on the bed and said, "Uh, yes, I am told my behavior is paranoid and that I am quick to anger."

"Are you schizophrenic?"

"That's what doctors say."

"Have you ever been arrested because of your anger?"

"I believe so."

"Maybe three or four times?"

"That sounds right."

"Why did you go off your medication?"

"I didn't go off my medication."

"But you said you had been arrested three or four times for anger."

"Yes. But I always take my medication. The police monitor my treatment. If I didn't take my medication, I would be in violation."

I rubbed my forehead. "Okay. Do you have a car parked in this neighborhood?"

"Yes."

"And you acquired enough parking tickets to get on the city's tow list?"

"Yes."

"Why didn't you pay them?"

Baxter's eyes narrowed and he started shaking his head. "I—I never got those tickets. They said I did but I didn't."

"Four times the city came to tow your car? Each time your medication failed to prevent your anger? Each time you threatened an officer and were arrested?"

"So I've been told. And I have been shown records of this behavior taking place."

"But you don't actually remember these incidents?"

"Not details. Only a commotion taking place then waking up in bed."

"Did you kill the parking officer Jack Gelashvili, who lived on the third floor of this building?"

"No."

"You are on record for threatening parking officers, yet the police didn't question you. Doesn't that seem strange?"

Baxter's eyeballs bounced around the room. "I didn't kill anybody. Why would they ask me any questions?"

On the one hand, it was heartening to see Baxter functioning independently with the help of medication. On the other hand, his vulnerability to exploitation had no limits. I put a business card on the keyboard and thanked him for his time. He said nothing and watched me leave.

Back home on the couch, I sipped diet ginger ale and thought about calling Tamar. Overall, it had been a good day, but I felt talked out and was content to spend the evening pondering the blatant framing of Gordon Baxter as a potential murderer. It stuck out like the media emperor calling the city editor to kill a story. In Baxter's entire life, I suspected his medication had failed him only four times. The question remained: who would go to such great lengths to set up Baxter as the fall guy for Gelashvili's murder, and why?

17

The next morning I returned to Budlong Woods. I wanted a few more words with parking officer Rich Jones and hoped to find him again in the same neighborhood. Instead I met a Latino boy who looked barely out of high school. First he shrugged and then he pointed east and said in broken English that Jones was working in Edgewater, a neighborhood directly east that bordered the lake.

I took Foster to Kenmore where I turned north and quickly found a parking place. Since it was a nice day I didn't mind strolling this historic community with an architecture as eclectic as its demographics. Tree-lined blocks of one-story brick cottages mixed with high rises, mid-rises, and two-, three-, and four-story stone flats with courtyards.

I spotted Rich a few blocks away on Magnolia, walking toward me along a row of parked cars. His furrowed brow and downward gaze told me he was deep in thought and had no idea someone stood directly in his path. When he was about a car length away I said, "Hey, officer, this isn't a residential parking zone. Get lost."

His head jerked up. "What?" Jones said and wiped his nose. He had kind of a wild look in his eye. "I told you all I know."

"Relax. I just have a few other questions. No big deal. So Baxter's neighborhood is one of the permit zones for residents only, right?" After Jones agreed, I went on, "So he didn't get ticketed there, which means he was probably racking up tickets somewhere other than his own neighborhood."

Jones thought about it. "Yeah."

"Here's what's bugging me: how did you and your fellow officers come across Baxter's car as a scofflaw? I mean, if he was legally parked in his own neighborhood, what drew your attention?"

Jones paused and said, "Abandoned vehicle. All vehicles have to move at least once every three days. But we only enforce on a complaint basis. Someone calls and tells us a car hasn't moved in weeks, we chalk it up and come back in three days and see."

"You plug in the plate, it comes up owing lots of money, then you call the tow truck. You keep an archive of who called in the complaint?"

"Non-emergency calls don't have to give names."

"But somewhere there's a record of the numbers that call in."

Jones looked around. "You know, they watch us. They got cameras everywhere. And they even got guys sitting in cars watching us." Jones moved as if to leave then stopped. "Do me a favor. Don't keep finding me. I never shoulda talked to you." Jones hurried away.

Traditionally a dusty neighborhood of factory warehouses, the South Loop was fast becoming a young professional's idyllic community of modern industrial design. Among the stainless steel, concrete, and glass was an old hotel of the Northern Italian Renaissance style that had managed to maintain its architectural integrity for the benefit of the police department's Crisis Intervention Bureau.

The female receptionist was young with beautiful light brown skin. She didn't smile. She pointed to the guest list where I was required to sign and print my name. I asked if I could speak to a caseworker familiar with Gordon Baxter. Mentioning Baxter by name was a mistake.

"Do you have legal authority connected with this individual?"

"I'm Jules Landau, a private investigator. I just want to verify a few facts."

"But you have no legal status allowing you to see information on this person."

"Do I need legal status to ask someone a few questions?"

"If your questions pertain to this individual, yes."

"What if I just want to know something, like if the guy drove a car?"

She stared at me a moment then picked up the phone and dialed an extension. I heard her ask "Dr. Frank" if he had a minute for "some guy." Then she took the guest list, turned her back on me, and spoke quietly before hanging up, "Dr. Frank will be right out."

I thanked her. She ignored me. The clip-clop of Dr. Frank's shoes trotting down the hallway announced his impending arrival. Six foot, trim, Mediterranean looking with olive skin, brown eyes, and black curly hair, Dr. Frank gave my hand a quick squeeze, said, "I have a couple of minutes," turned on his heel, and began power-walking back to his office. I did my best to keep up. His office door had no name or title. I sat on a plastic folding chair in front of his desk and caught my breath.

"So how can I help you"—he looked at a piece of paper on his desk—"Mr. Landau?"

"I'm investigating the murder of a parking officer who lived in the same building as a schizophrenic individual who has been arrested four times for threatening parking officers."

Dr. Frank opened the top drawer of his desk and produced a toothpick that he put between his lips. "And your diagnosis of schizophrenia is based on?"

"An educated guess verified by the man himself. Apparently he owns a car. I was curious if schizophrenics were allowed to drive."

"Depends. Properly medicated, there shouldn't be a problem. Sometimes a doctor has to sign off declaring the person fit enough to drive. If you don't mind, is the individual of whom you speak a murder suspect?"

"Would it be odd if the individual was *not* a suspect?"

Dr. Frank leaned back in his chair, put his feet up on the desk, and aimed his faraway look just over my head. "In addition to being an MD," he said, "I have a master's in public health with a focus on the mentally ill and the criminal justice system. I'm called a *liaison officer.*" He stopped, although I sensed he had more to say.

I repeated, "Would it seem strange if he was not a suspect?"

"I haven't been consulted."

"Did you expect to be consulted?"

"My department coordinates the information covered under the Confidentiality Act. It would be my responsibility to make sure only legally qualified individuals have access to a client's mental health information. Not consulting us suggests, that, for the police, he is not currently a suspect, and, yes, I understand how one could see that as odd."

"Did you find it curious that Bax"—I caught myself—"that he drove around the city quite a bit?"

"The car is registered to his mother."

"Really? And what does she have to say about it?"

"We haven't established contact with her. She's listed at her son's address, but he doesn't remember when he last saw her."

"Did you check the trunk?" When Dr. Frank didn't laugh, I added, "Sorry. I was in his studio apartment and unless she lives under the bed, she ain't there."

Dr. Frank looked at his watch and then straightened up in his chair. "Anything else?"

"If a man threatens someone while off his meds, would he carry out that threat when he's back on his meds?"

Dr. Frank waited for the gyroscope's rotor and axis to finish adjusting in his head. "Highly unlikely."

"He's got a shitload of tickets scattered over the North Side from Howard Street to State Street," Jones said. He'd called me on my cell. I was standing on the sidewalk in front of Gordon Baxter's building, and surprised to hear Jones's voice. "Thirty-two expired meter citations and four abandoned vehicle complaints," he said. "And get this—the abandoned complaints are evenly spaced between eight meter tickets."

"Are the same officers writing the tickets?"

"I don't know," Jones said. "They're not our tickets."

"What the hell does that mean?"

"I'm a Parking Authority officer, the police department's stepchild. Those tickets were written by Windy City officers."

"What the hell is a Windy City officer?"

"Hang on." I heard him blow his nose. "Windy City Meters LLC. The system was privatized. You been living in a cave the last couple of years?"

"So this company has their own private army of officers enforcing city ordinances?"

"Yeah, something like that."

I started thinking out loud. "Where do they work out of? How can I check their records? Where does all the money go? I don't get it."

Jones cursed. "Shut up! Don't be a dope! I've got a wife and two kids, so I don't gotta *get it.* You wanna get it, you find it on your own." Jones hung up.

Before digesting this new information, I needed to verify what I had suspected all along. Starting from Farragut Avenue, I began walking the neighborhood looking for a blue sedan that also had the first three numbers of Baxter's license plate. As expected, I found the car just a block from Baxter's building. Breaking into vehicles was illegal. I had never done it for real, only on practice cars in the subbasement of Frownie's building. When I discovered the passenger door unlocked, intense relief washed over me. Now it was just trespassing. When I uncovered an oil change invoice in the glove box with a date from the previous January, I felt great satisfaction. When I leaned over to the driver's side and saw a digital odometer, I cursed.

I stuck a screwdriver into Baxter's ignition and prayed for the dash to light up. Nothing. Now I had to remove the panels on the steering column where a cylinder held a bunch of wires. This was the tricky part. Frownie always said if I wasn't sure which wires to connect, try the red ones. I took his advice and watched with delight as the dash powered up and revealed the sacred odometer numbers. Since the oil change nine months ago, Baxter's car had been driven only three miles.

18

I walked past a white van double-parked in front of the Kutaisi Georgian Bakery, backing up traffic. Just as I noticed a large decal on the corner of the windshield with the letters "IIPD," a squat Hispanic man wearing a green work jacket and holding a bag of pastries rushed out, jumped into the van, and drove off. If I knew what IIPD stood for, I would've reported that man.

Tamar and another harried-looking woman busily filled orders and worked the cash register. This time there were two gangsters with burnt orange leather jackets and shaved heads in the end booth while a few dapper men in suits occupied the middle booth. A couple of transients slumped over what I thought was the same table as yesterday. The booth occupants presented a sharp contrast to the horde pushing against the counter crying out for their favorite Georgian pastries. Bitter lamentations over unavailable goodies suggested having a few Cossacks on guard might have been a good idea. It occurred to me that outrage over one's baked goods might represent a Eurasian compliment of sorts. While Tamar looked tired, she maintained a gracious façade. I waited for the mid-morning rush to disperse and watched her step away to take trays off the rack and push them into the huge oven. Thankfully, there was no sign of the large demon lurking about. I walked to the counter and said, "Did I just witness a post-breakfast sugar panic or a pre-lunch munchies blitz?"

Tamar turned and gave me the smile I hoped for. "I haven't figured that out yet. We have a similar mid-afternoon event."

"I wanted you to know I've ruled out your ground-floor neighbor as a suspect," I said and told her the details of what brought me to question Baxter. Tamar knew the man I described.

"He's creepy. I've seen him in the laundry room. Sometimes he leaves his door open while playing weird music. He's never said a word or even made eye contact."

"Someone's been writing tickets to his license plate at addresses over a ten-mile swath of the North Side. But his car has been driven only three

94

miles in nine months. So the tickets never get paid, his car gets towed, and presto! Crazy Baxter loses it and commits murder."

"Then why hasn't he been arrested?"

"Good question. By the way, are those booths reserved for neighborhood VIPs or something?"

Tamar glanced toward the back. "Unofficially," she said as if the policy bothered her. "Cops get the booth at one end, some businessmen have the middle booth, and the boss's Russian friends get the booth at the other end."

"How often do they come?"

"Fairly regularly. I mean, whenever I work nights, the businessmen always show up as we're closing. Sometimes with those two guys with shaved heads. The boss lets them use the space after hours for a more private meeting."

"Is the boss that, uh, big bald man with the frightening expression?"

"Yes,"

"So these are your boss's friends?"

"I guess so. He always refers to them by their first names. The regular customers he calls *sir* or *madam*."

"Who are the two guys with shaved heads?"

"Assholes."

Such an ugly word from Tamar's mouth evoked an involuntary laugh that I suppressed after realizing Tamar was not smiling. "Sorry," she said.

"They look like twin gangster-assholes."

Tamar nodded enthusiastically. "Yes, that fits perfectly. They use a lot of Russian slang around me. I don't know the exact translations, but I know it's crude."

"What would happen if some neighborhood peasant wandered over there and sat?"

Tamar thought about it. "Actually—I don't know. I don't think I've ever seen that situation. It's like everyone just knows to stay away from the booths."

I thought I should get in touch with Kalijero to see if he could glean something from Detectives Abbott and Costello. I asked Tamar if she still had my card.

"I do," she said and walked quickly to the counter where she grabbed a bakery business card from a plastic dispenser. On the back she wrote her cell number and handed it to me. "Some weeks I have very strange hours."

A pile of junk mail lay on the floor just inside my office door. I had yet to receive written correspondence not originating from a four-color digital printing press. But the presence of the catalogs and brochures meant another human being had walked up the shabby flight of stairs to implicitly acknowledge the existence of my office. This I found comforting.

I propped open the door, leaned back in my reclining executive desk chair, extended the foot rest, and called Palmer. I left a message suggesting we get together to discuss recent developments. Apart from Palmer's access to Konigson and ability to operate freely within the *Republic* bureaucracy, his sophistication gave me a valuable ally, if only to engage his intellect as I tried to piece together the puzzle of Gelashvili's murder. On a yellow legal pad, I began creating a "gut feeling" flow chart with thoughts, observations, and questions inside boxes and circles. Baxter was being framed; Detectives Calvo and Baker were aware or were unknowing participants. They most likely received instructions from the higher ranks. Windy City Meters LLC wrote fraudulent tickets. On whose orders? Why would a commander or deputy chief want a parking officer dead?

The outside door creaked open, then shut. The patter on the steps told me someone lightweight or small was ascending the stairs. I thought of a child who had just mastered stair climbing. A minute later, Izzy came into view.

"A coincidence?" I said.

"There is a coffee shop across the street. From there I sit and watch the world. From there I saw you enter the building."

Izzy spoke not of a chic café boasting organic fair trade, locally roasted beans in mochas, lattes, and espressos, but a seedy bacon-and-hash joint existing in a time warp from just before the city's white-flight era. I couldn't help picturing his nice gray suit splattered with grease.

"Well, it's been a couple days," I said. "Time for an update, I guess."

"Does that pain you so? May I remind—"

"We had this conversation last time . . ." I rehashed the events since our last dialogue, starting with meeting Tamar and ending with Baxter's frame-up. As I spoke, Izzy slowly paced the room staring at the floor. His expression, his mannerisms, everything about him seemed contrived.

"Are you suggesting Baxter's medication was tampered with on each occasion his car was to be towed? How could this be engineered so precisely?"

"If one had access to his apartment and if Baxter used some kind of daily pill-dispensing device, it might be quite easy."

Izzy thought about it. "Perhaps," he said. "The tickets issued by this Windy City company. That's significant, I should think. And what of the newspaper editor?"

"I left a message fifteen minutes ago." Izzy took a seat in the club chair in front of my desk and rested his head in his hand. I wondered how someone so young could act so timeworn. "If you don't mind, Izzy, I'm curious about your background."

My words had a restorative effect. "Yes, finally, acting as a detective should. And what took you this long to be so curious?"

I interpreted the question as rhetorical. "It's hard for me to see you as an *Izzy*. Why were you given the name Isadore Himmel?"

"The *given* name is a veil of pretense. I *chose* the name with which you struggle."

His failure to elaborate annoyed me. I should be curious, of course. "Why did you choose this name?"

"It's a devotional name. A testimonial, if you like."

"A testimonial to what?"

"Himmel was made into ashes by Nazis," Izzy said. "I arrived at his name from an obscure book of lists that somehow found its way to the library. The lists were of Hitler's victims from various German towns. I sat in a far corner of the reference floor, my eyes moving past name after name. You could've pushed over a bookcase and I would not have flinched, so transfixed I was. I happen to know some German and when my eyes saw the name Himmel, I stopped. You see, Himmel means 'heaven,' and I found the irony of this image touching—Himmel having gone up the chimney in the middle of a forest."

I waited for the little man to continue, but he offered me nothing more than an antagonizing smirk. Had he not paid me five thousand with the promise of five thousand more, I would have proposed removing his grin at no charge.

"But what *inspired* you to—"

"Forgive me, Landau, you have the right to ask such a question, and for you I will tell quickly my story." Izzy draped one leg over the other. "One day I went to a Catholic wedding where I was to be an usher. It was there, while standing with the priest and several members of the wedding party, that I heard the priest ask the groom if he had gotten a 'Jewish deal' on something he had purchased." Izzy stopped, unhooked his legs, and slouched on the club chair with his head back. "I was familiar with stereotypes and I knew a disparaging remark when I heard one. And it struck me that if a priest could so deftly embrace such an ancient, unflattering image of a people, then anything was possible. If there was a next time, why shouldn't I also be included among the victims?"

Izzy took out a handkerchief and began wiping his eyes. I struggled with a translation of what I just heard. Was this his way of assuaging some kind of guilt over horrible events? Thankfully, my phone rang.

"Jules, it's Wilbert Palmer. I'm a short distance from your office . . ."

I told Izzy that the editor, Palmer, was on the way. The little man was out the door before I could suggest he leave.

19

Maybe it was the lighting, but Palmer looked less burdened than I remembered. And if you stamped his net worth across that shiny billboard of a forehead, I could imagine some women even finding him quite attractive.

I said, "What brings you to this part of town?"

"After visiting with you at Mocha Mouse," Palmer said. "I decided I needed to learn more about the city, explore the nooks and crannies of its many neighborhoods. Working and living downtown offers a restricted view. But I wanted to tell you I received a phone call from a Mr. Ellis Knight. Quite the excitable type. He mentioned you repeatedly. He didn't seem to want information so much as to remind me of some deal he had made with you."

I apologized for Knight's intrusion and gave Palmer an abbreviated version of the events surrounding my first murder case two months ago. He seemed amused.

"I admire his passion," Palmer said of Knight.

For the second time in an hour, I reiterated the facts. "Somebody from Windy City wrote fraudulent tickets to help frame Baxter," I said. "What could this have to do with Konigson telling you to spike the Gelashvili story?"

Palmer blinked a few times and said slowly, "The Republic Media Group used to own Windy City Meters LLC. Konigson sold it to an investment bank a few years ago to lighten the *Republic*'s debt."

"So the company wasn't profitable? Otherwise, why would he sell it?"

"I couldn't say," he said, meaning he didn't know.

I stared at Palmer. "What does this all mean?"

He returned the stare. "I don't know." There. He said it.

Another one of those moments when something so glaring shrieked for attention yet the significance remained just out of reach. Palmer told me the investment bank Decatur-Staley paid the city a billion dollars for the right to collect meter revenue for seventy-five years and then two months later sold their stake for twelve billion to a group of investors somewhere in the Middle East. My brain glazed over as Palmer utilized his vast tax-loophole knowledge to drag me through the weeds of corporate accounting trickery.

I interrupted to steer him back to the headless corpse of Jack Gelashvili. Then my phone rang with Kalijero's number in the display. I answered saying, "How come I gotta find out from a couple of malingering cops that you put in for retirement?"

"Don't tell me I hurt little Jules' feelings!" Kalijero said. "I'll never forgive myself!"

"You are truly one heartless, unfeeling, American."

"They found a body in a Budlong Woods apartment building. I've been asked to check it out. I want you to be the first to know that it's probably my last case. Feel better? Now what was that suspect's name again?"

Gordon Baxter's sheet-covered body lay on the gurney as the paramedics pushed it toward the ambulance. In the lobby, a couple of uniformed officers chatted with residents. To add to the squalor, from an open door down the hall, a baby wailed. I spoke to another officer standing outside the door of apartment G6. He repeated my name to Kalijero, who waved me in and pointed to a spot just outside the bathroom, where I was to remain while he talked with a curly-haired man sporting a pencil mustache and holding a large metal ring loaded with keys. I assumed he was the building super. Yellow tape crisscrossed the bathroom doorway. A crime scene investigator collected fibers with a tweezers. Then he spread powder on the desk, chair, and keyboard before turning on an ultraviolet light. Powder had already been applied throughout the bathroom. On the sink sat a plastic pill dispenser with compartments labeled for each day of the week.

The super walked with an obvious limp. I pushed my back against the wall to give him more room. He was barely a foot away as he passed but said nothing despite looking directly into my eyes. Kalijero motioned me over. "When were you last in this apartment?" he said.

"So Baxter really was under surveillance?"

"You left your card here, idiot."

Oh, yeah. "Yesterday, a couple of hours after I talked to you. First I went to Reilly's and spoke to Calvo and Baker."

"You realize you're now part of my investigation."

I waited for a sign of jest. "Screw you, Jimmy! I told you yesterday I was going to try to find this guy. I can prove he was a legitimate suspect—"

"Calm the hell down, private dick. I'm just saying if there are other forces at work here, you've got to watch where you leave your scent. Think before you go tossing your card around."

"Of course you're right. Now that you mention it, I should've *anticipated* Baxter getting killed."

Kalijero scratched his head. "Right now, it looks like he OD'd. We'll have to wait for the toxicology report."

"Of course, and I'm sure it was *accidental*."

"Detective?" The CSI knelt at the head of the bed, holding a pillow in one hand while pointing with the other to some kind of bracelet wrapped around a note.

Kalijero carefully removed the piece of paper without touching the string beads. He looked the note over and then began reading aloud. "The voices told me to do it. I couldn't help it. I tried resisting, but they pushed and pushed until I could take it no longer. They told me someone had to pay.

104

They targeted me so now I should target them. Why not kill the one who lived in my building? That would be the easiest way. But after I killed him, I knew I had to offer my life to balance out the good with the bad."

Kalijero put the note down and looked at me. I said, "I don't know what's more full of shit, that note or that crying kid's diaper down the hall. That guy had trouble putting three words together, much less holding a pencil for that long."

"Writing is a different brain function," Kalijero said. "What do you know about that bracelet?"

I told Kalijero that Baxter's car had been issued tickets over a ten-mile radius yet the odometer had moved only three miles. The significance evaded him.

"What do you know about the bracelet?" he repeated.

I sat on the bed and stared at the wooden beads. My brain flashed back to my first conversation with Tamar when she told me about a bracelet of prayer beads Jack always wore.

"It's Jack Gelashvili's bracelet, here to leave no doubt that Baxter killed Gelashvili. What a crock."

Kalijero's eyes searched my face. "When you come up with something better, let me know." He started toward the door then stopped short. "And did it ever occur to you that the odometer might be broken?"

20

At the bakery, I found Tamar taking a break at one of the customer tables.

"You just missed the post-lunch, sweet-tooth-madness rush," she said.

I took a seat facing the only occupied booth. "I see the twins, Boris and Vlad, are here," I said, referring to the two gangsters in leather jackets.

Tamar turned. "I guess so," she said.

"You had told me Jack wore a bracelet?"

"A *chotki*. It's like the Eastern Orthodox version of a rosary."

"They're made with wooden beads?"

"More often they're made with rope knots. His had wooden beads. Why are you asking?"

"The creepy laundry room guy that I told you was not a suspect? He was just found dead in his apartment. Under his pillow was a suicide-murder confession note and a bracelet with wooden beads."

"So he *did* kill Jack?"

I told her about Baxter's outbursts at parking officers occurring on the same days his medication mysteriously failed. "He didn't kill anybody."

Tamar rested her forehead on the heels of her hands. "Okay. What's next?"

"Did you know the parking meters were privatized?"

"Oh, sure. We paid close attention to that because we weren't sure how it would affect Jack's job. But after the transition, nothing seemed to change."

"All of Baxter's tickets were written by officers working for Windy City Meters, which had been owned by the Republic Media Group. A few years ago the Republic Media Group sold the company to an investment bank. Remember that reporter who interviewed you? Did you ever wonder why the published story in the *Republic* was really just a glorified obit? The CEO of the Republic Media Group, a guy named Konigson, called the city editor and told him to chop it down to a few sentences. He didn't want to draw attention to your cousin's murder."

I watched Tamar attempt to process my words. "Are you saying this CEO had something to do with Jack's death?" Tamar let her head fall over the chair's backrest. We sat in silence. It was a comfortable silence. "Why do people kill?" Tamar asked the ceiling. "For money or love," she answered and then lifted her head back up. "The only money Jack made was for the city. Many times his salary in parking citations. He gave his life for the city."

I said, "And the ungrateful city never thanked you or offered you a flag." I then asked Tamar to have dinner with me.

"Not tonight," she said, and I felt like a jackass. I still didn't know how to ask a woman out without sounding like an idiot. "I need to finish up in the back and give my neighbor a break from my aunt."

Tamar said goodbye and disappeared into the kitchen, leaving me alone with my insecurities.

Relaxing with a can of sugar-free root beer, I pondered rejection but still anticipated Tamar's voice when the phone rang. Instead, Frownie cloaked me in his rich Chicago inflection. "Julie? Whaddya know, kid?"

That this familiar voice emerged from the cadaverous bag of bones I had seen two days earlier seemed impossible.

"Now that I know you're back on a murder case, I gotta call you. I don't want to be a pain in the ass, but lyin' around this bed all day I got nothin' to do but think."

"Frownie, you know you can call me anytime. But I don't have anything solid. Just a lot of disconnected facts."

"Bullshit! There's always somethin'. You got facts? Then you got somethin'. What about the newspaper editor? Don't tell me he's already dead."

"Nope. Alive and well."

"Tell 'im to get lost. For his own good. Stickin' his nose in others' financial dealin's gets you dead."

I told Frownie about Baxter's frame-up and "suicide" and that Konigson's Republic Media Group had once owned the company that now controlled the parking meters and employed their own ticketing deputies.

"All roads lead to money—you know that! Investigation ONE-OH-ONE. The money that paid the killer, the money to be grabbed by the crime, the people whose money was protected by makin' someone dead. The people who might get more money because the guy was dead. Make up a story and check it out. Investigate—"

Frownie dropped the phone. I heard lots of coughing, hacking, and sputtering. Then, like magic, he returned to old form. "Listen, you got anyone on the inside yet?"

"I think Kalijero's on board. You know, he's developed a real soft spot for you. He wants to know how you're feeling."

"Ain't that typical? When you're still young enough to take a chunk outta someone's ass, guys like that Greek bastard hate you and want you out of the way 'cause they're the police, the real good guys. Then when you're old and crippled, they start with the sentimental bullshit. Tell him I remember how much of an asshole he was and that he can go rot in hell."

"I thought we all got a little more nostalgic as we got older."

Frownie groaned as if in pain. "Ah, hell. I got no use for nostalgia or guys who wallow in it. Waste of time. Just live your damn life and don't cry over the past."

I wondered how long a strong spirit could keep a body alive. There was nothing left to the guy, just parched skin shrink-wrapped over sinewy muscle fibers. Yet at the top of this fossil, brain neurons fired away as if arrogantly demonstrating their disdain for that useless, shriveled body attached to it. Frownie would never die, regardless of what happened to his body.

While Punim dined on hearts, livers, and kidneys, I ran down to Tasty Harmony and bought a grilled zucchini, pesto, and portobello sandwich. I kicked back and ate while thinking that all I really needed in life was a Tasty Harmony close by and a comfortable lounge chair. Good food did wonders for my attitude. My thoughts drifted to my conversation with Frownie and then to the two short-timer detectives who had been "assigned" to the Gelashvili murder. Now that their number one suspect had conveniently confessed in a suicide note, I wondered if their retirement party had been scheduled. I wondered what kind of bonus they got for their brilliant non-surveillance.

I answered the phone, mildly annoyed by the interruption but thrilled to hear Tamar's voice. "Why don't I come over tomorrow night and make dinner?" she said.

In that instant, any residual feelings of stupidity stemming from my date request vanished.

21

I'd always heard bars like Reilly's never really closed, and when I found it open at nine *a.m.*, I thought it was probably true. Inside, a fifty-something woman dressed professionally in a blouse and skirt sat at the bar reading a newspaper under a desk lamp connected to an extension cord. What looked like a glass of tomato juice sat in front of her on a paper napkin. I recognized the geezer sitting at a table staring out the window as the bartender.

"Good morning," the woman said and smiled warmly. "Can I help you with something?"

I introduced myself and told her I was looking for a couple of police detectives I had spoken with two days earlier. "We're collaborating on a case."

She laughed. "I'm Elaine and this is a good place to start, depending on how long they've been cops. You won't find many officers with less than twenty years on the force hanging out here." She had one of those personalities that instantly exuded kindness.

"I'm going to guess you're the daughter of a cop."

"That's a good guess, but I'm actually the daughter of the man who first opened Reilly's."

This intrigued me. "Okay, give me another try. As a child, this place was like a second home and you grew up knowing all the cops that hung out here and they treated you like an adopted daughter."

"That's true! But it wasn't just cops back then. This used to be where all the machinists in the neighborhood came after their shifts ended." She sipped her drink and laughed. "Or before their shifts started."

I said, "Gradually, automation and cheap labor overseas closed the shops and changed the neighborhood."

"Yep. The cops stayed loyal to my dad, but after he died, a lot of the original crowd started retiring and moving away."

"Why do you keep it open?"

"I own the building and don't need to do much. I'm a Realtor by trade." She pointed at the old guy. "Billy over there runs the place. I promised Dad I would take care of him. As you can see, the neighborhood is becoming more well-to-do, so I'll probably shut it down soon and either sell the building or lease it out. Which cops are you looking for?"

"Detectives Calvo and Baker."

Elaine took another sip of tomato juice. "I know them. They're both about to retire. Kind of a dopey duo. A pair of clichés—you know what I mean?"

"I was told they got a couple of months left before calling it quits."

Elaine gulped down the rest of her juice and then carefully pressed the napkin against her lips. "I don't think that long," she said. From underneath the newspaper she pulled out an appointment book and began paging through it. Most of the dates were filled with addresses all over the North Side. One date was circled in red. "Yeah, they want to use this place for a private party next week. Retirement party."

Elaine shut the appointment book and eyed me knowingly. "I can hear the little wheels in your head spinning, private investigator."

"I'd call you a sharp dame, but we both realize how cliché *that* would sound."

Elaine laughed. "Nowadays, most private investigators are retired cops. A bright, nice-looking kid like you with a North Shore accent collaborating with a couple of gold-bricking buffoons like Calvo and Baker? You want something from them. Now you got me curious."

She turned to face me and crossed her legs. Had she been the offspring of educated professionals, she would have been a successful corporate attorney or college professor. But as a bartender's daughter, her intellect would have to first fight through the affections of big-city cops and machine-shop serfs before seeing opportunity in real estate.

"A man they had under surveillance as a prime suspect confessed to the murder in his suicide note. I have a feeling a retirement bonus was paid for not noticing anything suspicious leading up to the suicide."

Elaine frowned. "Well, that's a convenient way to declare a case closed." There was a pause in the conversation before Elaine said, "I may be able to help you. Give me one of your cards." I did as told

113

and watched her put it in a Fendi wallet. "I have a side business," Elaine said. "I use one of my properties to introduce people."

We locked eyes for an instant. I nodded. "Like a dating service," I said.

"Yes, like a dating service. A high-end dating service. One does not have to worry about being rejected. Everyone wins."

"Thank you for the offer, but—"

"No!" Elaine laughed loudly and gave my hand a squeeze "That's not what I meant! I believe there is a detective you are looking for who has recently been utilizing my service. Should I notice an impending appointment, I could give you a call, and, perhaps, you might just find him in an agreeable mood to answer all of your questions."

I thanked Elaine for her generosity and told her I understood the importance of repaying favors.

At The Chicago Diner, I indulged in thoughts irrelevant to the case as I ate a banana coconut muffin and then an apple cider muffin. A few blocks away, Wrigley Field sat empty, as it had every October since 1945. I wondered if the North Side would ever experience a World Series during my lifetime. I was also conscious of hearing the opening motif of Beethoven's Fifth. Then I remembered my new ringtone.

"Yeah, it's Rich Jones, the parking officer. Can we talk?"

114

"Sure, Rich. You don't sound so good. You want me to call a cop?" I was half serious.

"No, no, no, no, I just remembered something, that's all. And I wanted to tell you about it."

After suggesting we meet at the Kutaisi Georgian Bakery, I arrived there a half an hour later to once again see the white van doubleparked, pissing people off. This time I stopped to study the decal, but apart from the letters "IIPD" above a bald eagle holding a snake in its mouth, I learned nothing new. Once inside, I saw Jones in street clothes waving at me from a table near the far corner. His face looked more drawn than I remembered, his eyes more sunken. A large glass of water sat in front of him. Another waited for me. Tamar was nowhere to be seen.

"Want something to eat?" I said.

"Huh? No, not hungry." He wiped his nose with a napkin.

I sat. "Allergies still bothering you?" He nodded. "Today your day off?"

"Huh? Yeah, sort of."

His eyes were bloodshot, pupils dilated. "Rich, relax, man. You look as gray as your hair."

"I didn't tell you everything. About Jack, I mean."

He reminded me of a panicked kid who'd just broke a window. "So tell me. I won't be mad, I promise."

115

Jones took a deep breath. I thought he was about to talk but instead he took another deep breath. On the third try, after exhaling, he laid his torso on the table and sobbed into his folded arms.

"What is it?" I asked. "C'mon, Rich, whatever it is I'm sure we can work it out. I'll help you, man. I know you're a good guy."

It took a few minutes but he managed to sit up and dry his tears on his sleeve. "I think it might be my fault Jack's dead."

I waited a couple beats. "You didn't kill anybody, Rich. Don't give me that crap."

"But I think it's my fault."

"Tell me why you think it's your fault. Take your time. Start from the beginning."

One last deep breath, then, "I'm the longest-serving parking officer. The supervisors kind of look to me, you know? I train new officers. I let them know when someone has a bad attitude or a problem at home. I don't snitch, though. I would just say that I didn't think someone was very happy or didn't take the job seriously, and they would ask me to get that person right or maybe suggest they get a new job or whatever." Jones gulped down half the glass of water.

"So one day the boss called me to his office, which was weird because I'd never even talked to the guy before. And he started saying how he was trying to avoid budget cuts and the department wanted to try to hire foreigners because they work for less. And I asked him how he could get away with that, and he said he already had gotten away with it and pointed out that Jack was working for like half the wage of everyone else and nobody cared. And since he knew my neighborhood had a lot of Mexicans, he asked if they spoke English good enough for this job." Jones chugged the rest of the water.

"Your boss wanted you to recruit foreigners to save money on wages?"

"Yeah. But he was, like, *ordering* me to do it. Then he said it was more than just the budget, that he needed cheap labor to prevent my job from being 'outsourced.' Then he started asking how my kids were doing, you know? So I started getting scared. Because at my age, I don't want to be looking for a job and lose my health insurance. I told him I would do my best, and he patted me on the back and said he trusted me not to go telling everyone because he didn't want the papers and TV to get a story and have all them community organizers screaming about discrimination or this and that."

"Your boss told you to get cheap officers or you and your family might end up on the street."

Jones looked at me, wavered a bit. Then he said, "Yeah, that's what I thought, too. But I started getting mad. My wife kept telling me to play but I got madder and madder. I got a lot of Mexican friends in my neighborhood. They just want a better life. But goddamn it, why do they work cheap? You know?"

"Bring this back to Jack's murder."

"My brain starts taking off with crazy ideas. And I remember seeing on TV stories of terrorist bombs in Russia blowing up all over the place and that they were planted by mafia guys where Jack came from and how powerful and crazy those mafia guys were over there."

I thought of asking about the Russian woman Jones had set up with Jack, but then remembered Frownie's best advice—don't trust anyone. "That was the *Chechen* mafia from *Chechnya,* not Georgia, but go on."

"Oh, okay. But then some guys were talking about Jack being connected to the Russian mob. I asked them about it and they laughed. They said they heard it somewhere else but thought it was a joke. But I get this idea to start playing up the rumors that Jack is part of that mafia group and he's here to get connections so that he can send money and guns back over there. So I thought as nutty as it might've sounded, maybe I could get Jack canned and maybe change the attitude about hiring foreigners. That's what I thought, but I think maybe I just wanted to hurt someone because I was so pissed off. I didn't like that he undercut our wages by working cheap."

"So who killed Jack Gelashvili?"

"One day Jack came to me and wanted to talk. And that's really weird, because he didn't talk to anyone. I mean he didn't just chat about life and all. But he told me the boss took him out to lunch.

Jack's English was not that good. But what I got was that the boss wanted to know about where Jack was from. And I think he tried to explain how things worked in Chicago—in the slimeball politician kind of way. So even though he wasn't sure what the guy was saying, I guess he just went along. And then the boss met with him again, and showed him pictures of dollar signs with arrows going here and there. Jack kept repeating 'money this money that.' I think he was offering Jack some kind of deal."

Jones took out a wad of tissue and began a cavalcade of nose blowing dissonance. I turned away from the noise and was instantly charmed to see several young teens of differing skin shades, clearly enjoying themselves around a table full of baked goodies.

After Jones finished, I turned back to him and said, "You think this rumor made its way to a city big shot who wanted your boss to get Jack as a contact with the Russian mafia?"

"Yeah. Something like that. But then a few weeks before his death, Jack came to me all freaked out and showed me an envelope stuffed with cash. 'What to do! What to do!' he kept saying, and he jammed the envelope into my pocket and backed away shouting, 'You take! You take!' I just stood there watching him. I figured the money got passed down from up top. But what do I do with it? If I take it to the boss, he's gonna know Jack was talking to me. And then what?"

"Where's the money now?"

"I—I hid it."

"You think Jack was killed because of the rumor you started?"

"They found out he wasn't connected. They had shown him stuff about the city he should not have seen."

His scenario seemed plausible although the simplicity of the events troubled me. But under the right circumstances, rumors often took on lives of their own, and this kind of conspiracy fit the tangled world of politics, money, and media empire pricks like Konigson.

"When you told me about Baxter, did you really think he could've been the killer?"

"Yeah, until those two detectives told us to shut up about him. That made me wonder. And something else I should've mentioned. It was the tow truck guys that put Baxter's car back in the same spot. They would just drive around until Baxter was hauled off and then re-park his car."

"You know Baxter is dead, right? Overdosed?" I didn't mention the suicide note. If he knew about it, there was more he wasn't telling me.

Jones looked confused. "Wow. What does that mean?"

"It means nothing. Starting rumors about people isn't cool, but you are not responsible for Jack's death. If anything, you're helping me find his killer. In the meantime, just go about your business. If your boss, uh—what the hell's his name?"

"Robertson."

"What is he, a sergeant?"

"Civilian."

"A civilian working for the CPD?"

"Department of Revenue."

"You guys don't work for the cops?"

"We work *with* the cops but *for* the Department of Revenue."

Strange. I thought about my first conversation with Kalijero regarding Gelashvili. I had said Jack "worked for the police department" and Kalijero had not corrected me. Maybe he didn't know.

22

Jones appeared calmer when he left the bakery, although I feared he could easily swing back into doom and gloom. One of the ladies behind the counter told me Tamar had the day off. I thought of calling to make sure she knew the way to my apartment but realized how stupid that sounded.

I drove east on Devon to Broadway, where I started snaking toward the lake on my way downtown. Just as I merged on to Lake Shore Drive, Kalijero called.

"Toxicology confirmed overdose," Kalijero said.

"Who do the parking officers work for?"

"What? The police—I think. When I started, they worked for the police. Then they put them

121

somewhere else. I don't know. Nobody ever knows who the hell they work for. Did you hear me? Toxicology—"

"Department of Revenue. Overdose of what?"

"What difference does it make? He took too much and died."

"What's more useless than a short-timer cop? Couldn't you have at least verified the drugs were for schizophrenics?"

"He intentionally took too much of some goddamn drug and he's dead!"

"How the hell do you know it was intentional? How do you know he didn't unknowingly take a drug someone put in those capsules?"

Either the signal dropped or Kalijero was developing a behavioral problem with cell phones.

Light traffic allowed an easy drive to Monroe Street. From there I weaved my way to the concrete chasm of LaSalle Street, where I parked at a standard coin-op meter. After loading it up with all the silver in my pocket, I set my sights on city hall, a pretentious neoclassical structure arrogant enough to incorporate an entire city block. I explored the lobby of white marble, gaudy electrical appliances, and numerous bronze tablets honoring long-forgotten political hacks, before finding the Department of Revenue on the first floor. In the waiting area, a morbidly obese man wearing a bright orange vest sat on a folding chair. He cheerfully said "Hi!" and waved as if he were the greeter at Walmart. On his baseball cap, a large button read, "Ask Me About Paying Parking Tickets!"

I asked directions to the administrative offices, and he pointed to a television on the counter of the deserted reception desk showing a woman frozen in time by the pause button. I looked back at the man. He nodded enthusiastically. I thanked him, walked to the reception desk, and after pushing the play button watched the woman on the television explain how to pay bills using the Internet, pay-station machines, or with a customer-service representative located down the hall. I turned and saw only a wall with the mayor's portrait, then noticed an opening set forward about ten feet. The "hall" appeared more like a short passageway to a crowded section of what reminded me of a gigantic Vegas casino. In addition to the multitude standing in a roped-off corridor facing a row of customer-service tellers, pay-station machines along the walls commanded lines ten people deep. Armed security guards roamed about. At that moment, I realized the so-called hallway was really an enormous metal detector.

I remained on the periphery of the patrons and observed the machines sucking in bills of varying denominations through metal slots. Those waiting in line revealed no emotion other than boredom or resignation. Some absentmindedly rolled and unrolled thick wads of cash in their hands while others re-counted what they were about to forfeit.

I repositioned myself against the wall near the end of the teller row. From there I obtained an interesting perspective on checks, credit cards, and driver's licenses being pushed back and forth under thick plastic windows. The continual movement of paper and plastic from one hand to another entranced me. Every transaction represented money flowing from one bank account to another, five days a week, eight hours a day but available twenty-four-seven on the Internet .

Several security guards opened a route to one of the pay stations. An armed Bankroll Warranty driver followed and set up a curtain around the back of the machine. Minutes later, he was escorted out pushing a dolly cart piled with money bags.

About thirty yards behind "teller row," a line of desks spread out evenly across the room, each commanding a queue of Chicagoans waiting to visit with a department agent. I walked closer and observed the troubled faces of shabbily dressed citizens. A man spilled the contents of a coffee can onto an agent's desk and then stood and pulled his trouser pockets inside out. The agent leaned back and crossed her arms while the man pled his case. I caught enough words to surmise the man wanted his car back.

At another desk, a young woman signed documents with the help of the agent's pointing finger. There must have been a dozen or more pages, each requiring several signatures. Unlike the others, her expression and body language did not betray a sense of doom. At one point she looked up and laughed, provoking a similar response from the agent.

When she stood and reached across the desk to shake hands, I hurried back toward the exit and waited for her to approach. "Can you tell me what happens with those people sitting at the desks?" I said.

She gave me a curious look. "That's where you go when they've held your car for two months because you haven't paid what you owe the city."

"I happened to notice you were signing a lot of documents."

"Yeah, that's my payment plan."

"Can anyone choose that?"

"I think it depends. We just bought a new car. We didn't know all our unpaid tickets would transfer to it. As soon as we got our plates, they towed it. We got a huge loan to buy our dream car, and then the city said we owed them eight thousand in tickets and fines."

"So it's like having two car payments."

She giggled. "Except the city offered us a deal. For a slightly lower interest rate, they bought out our loan and added in the eight grand."

I thought she was kidding. "You mean the city is financing your car? Can a city do that?"

Loud laughing. "Well, someone's financing the car. Can a city do that? I don't even care anymore. I just want my 650i convertible back!" More laughing.

"Why is this funny?"

She shrugged. "It's just the way things are. You can fight it or accept it. Start fighting, and it just costs you more money. Luckily we can afford this life. I don't know how the others do it." I thought most of the "others" probably did not "do it."

I walked back to the row of desks and joined one of the lines. I pondered the woman's comment about being able to "afford this life." There was a cheerful capitulation in her voice, as if the merging of private banking and government was simply part of a natural evolutionary process. When my turn finally arrived, I sat across from a pleasant-looking African-American woman with kind eyes who introduced herself as Evelyn. Evelyn asked how I was and what she could help me with.

I tried to talk but started laughing. I apologized. "Does the city really help people reclaim their vehicles by financing them?"

"We offer payment plans to qualifying individuals. Was your car impounded?"

"But how can this be? I mean, what gives the city the right to loan taxpayers' money to make a profit?"

"Oh, there's no profit for the city. It's just a way to help individuals get their cars back." Evelyn rested her elbows on the desk and interlaced her fingers.

"Then what's the interest rate for?"

As if reading from a script she said, "The interest rate helps the city recoup administrative costs associated with processing the vehicles. This also helps eliminate the need to raise taxes to cover those costs. In fact, the city was able to decrease the total sales tax from 10.25 percent to 9.75 percent thanks in part to the payment plan program. Now, sir, do you have an impounded vehicle I can help you with?"

Her kind eyes had acquired a sharpness, as had her voice. "How can I find out how much money the city earned from interest?"

"Requests should be made with the Department of Revenue. Sir, there are people waiting—"

"Who's the boss of the Department of Revenue?"

"That would be Mr. Elon—"

"How can I speak to Mr. Elon?"

She must have activated an alarm with her foot because I never saw her hands leave the desk. How else could I explain a security guard's sudden appearance and polite offer to escort me out of the room?

Because of my family's connection to "Boss" politics and Prohibition corruption, it seemed ironic that city hall's ubiquitous power had a chilling effect on me. I exited the marble lobby onto LaSalle Street and thought of all that money flowing as green as the Chicago River on St. Patrick's Day.

Such a lame metaphor would have provoked an angry lecture from Frownie, who would remind me how nothing had really changed in a hundred or more years and I should know better.

The orange envelope under my wiper blade did not register in my brain until I saw a small, stocky man lumbering ahead about thirty yards from where my meter flashed "expired." He cautiously planted each step as if walking on ice. The back of his jacket read "WCM PEA." I caught up to him and said, "I put at least three dollars in that meter." The elderly Hispanic man finished printing his current ticket and looked at me. I pointed to my car and repeated my grievance.

He slowly maneuvered himself around and started trudging back toward my car. I felt guilty for making the guy retrace his steps and thought it better to stay at his side than race ahead and wait. The challenge of maintaining such a slow, deliberate gait had never occurred to me. It was like trying to keep pace with a three-toed sloth.

When we reached my car, the man pointed to the flashing red display. "*Terminado*," he said.

"I put *mucho dinero*."

"*Treinta minutos solo*."

"Thirty minutes? *Dondé* thirty minutes?"

The man looked closely at my meter, walked to the next meter, then pointed at a white sticker under the display screen that indicated a thirty-minute maximum. Stunned at the unabashed dishonesty of an absent sticker and the meter's acceptance of an unlimited amount of coins, I could do nothing more than smile and nod at the man, who then reciprocated with a friendly nod of his own before lumbering away.

23

My Civic crawled southbound on Clark Street. The damage that lunchtime traffic inflicted upon my clutch irritated me. I winced every time I stepped on the pedal.

Twenty minutes later, I pushed open the front door to my Old Town office building. As I rounded the third flight, I was sorry to see Ellis Knight sitting cross-legged on the landing a few feet in front of my office door. I stepped over him and searched my pocket for the key. Once inside, I sat down and extended the footrest of my executive chair. Knight stood in front of my desk, holding a notepad. How I hated his idiotic grin.

"Are you tailing me, Ellis?"

"Real talk, feel me, bro. Rich Jones told me about your conversation—"

"How the hell do you know Jones?"

"I got sources. Ya dig?"

"I guess you don't care about protecting your sources."

"Not when I'm paying them."

"You *paid* Jones to tell you about our conversation?"

"Ain't no big dilly! But that Jones dude is bent. He'd do anything for a few bills. I'd be careful around his ass if I were you."

"What do you want?"

"The mental dude that topped himself. I want his story."

"When I solve the case, you get the story. That's the deal."

"This could be a good teaser. Ya know? Mental dude punked into murdering neighbor."

"That's fiction, idiot. But that's what you are, a fiction writer."

"Ease up! I mean, we're as good as fam, you know? I gave you the reporter dude Peter Ross, and that's what lit the fire!"

Knight toyed with me. The North Shore brat with a genius IQ and Daddy's money really did have connections. I couldn't afford not to keep him around, and this fact formed a knot in my stomach.

"Here are the facts," I said, giving Knight a simple sketch of the subject's life and death, but omitting names, contradictory details, and suspiciously convenient evidence. "Go write a story."

Knight looked up from his notepad. He had that cocky look, as if I had unwittingly given everything away. Of course, he knew more than he let on. Or that's what he wanted me to think.

"Thanks, bro. I'll go check some vital records and no doubt I'll have loads of info for a totally sick article."

He dashed out like a little boy given a dollar for candy. I looked at the yellow legal pad with yesterday's flow chart and turned over a new page. At the top I drew a box around Gelashvili's name and at the bottom a box around Konigson's name. In the middle they would meet in a box of their own—somehow. Gelashvili had lines connected to the dead schizophrenic, Baxter; the two detectives, Calvo and Baker; parking officer Jones; and now deputy director of the Department of Revenue, Elon. The world wasn't big enough for Elon and Konigson not to share a box or two.

Thoughts of empty boxes competed with when I last spoke to Frownie. How many more opportunities remained? Dinner plans with Tamar. A real date? She always seemed happy to see me. She easily could've blown me off by insisting on a professional relationship. Jones probably was more unstable than I thought. Full of demons. Did he really feel responsible for the murder? I mean, the guy's not an idiot. Desperate for money, though. It always came back to money. What people did for money. Sad, really.

The phone rang. "You like spicy?" Tamar said.

"Holy shit, I forgot to tell you I'm one of those weird vegan types—or mostly vegan types."

"A spicy vegan?"

"Exactly."

"See you about six."

A short, to-the-point conversation that demonstrated forethought. I felt better. But I needed to see Frownie.

He sat upright in bed connected to an IV drip looking virtually the same as the skeletal image seared into my memory three days ago. With his head slumped forward, I thought death might already have stopped by, but his nurse Helen assured me Frownie had not left the building.

I stood at the huge picture window directly across from his bed, observing how the low-hanging clouds turned the lake steely gray. Winter lingered nearby. Doom and Gloom strolled into the room. I told them to fuck off.

"Hey! Who's there? Julie?"

I walked over and sat beside him. "It's rude to sleep when you have guests."

"That newspaper editor—"

"Safe and sound. I'm keeping him in the background. How are you feeling?"

Frownie stared. "Cut the bullshit. You came here to discuss how I piss in a bag?"

"Hey, you called me the grandson you always never wanted. So I'm visiting the grandfather I always never wanted."

He gave me a sideways glance. "When I'm dead, you can waste your time gettin' all emotional—if you want."

His house, his rules.

"A mental case framed with phony parking tickets confesses in his suicide note."

"You talk to the guys who was writin' them tickets?"

"Not yet."

"So whaddya waitin' for?"

"A private company wrote the tickets—it's complicated."

He appeared lost in thought staring out the window. Frownie had enough money to die at home with a spectacular view of the shoreline. The American Dream. Did he appreciate such luxury?

I said, "Did you know city parking officers work for the Department of Revenue?"

The beginning of a smile crept upon Frownie's face, then disappeared. "Revenuers," he said. "Used to be only Feds bustin' bootleggers got called 'revenuers.' Then anyone bringin' in money for the government." Frownie turned to me. "Remember when I told you not to get caught up in Hollywood bullshit? Like there was somethin' special about *the old days*? It was nothin' special. Killin' is killin', stealin' is stealin'. Nothin's changed except the people doin' the stealin' and killin'."

"I visited the Department of Revenue before I came here. It had a real oppressive atmosphere. Like a lord extracting payment from his peasants.

You don't pay, we take your oxen, and you can starve quickly instead of slowly."

I don't think Frownie heard a word. "Don't use me as an example. I saw guys gettin' caught up in the glamour. What glamour? There ain't no goddamn glamour. Why the hell I took you in, I don't know."

"I would've gone into the business anyway. You knew that, so you wanted me to learn the right way."

"But it ain't normal. Not nowadays. Get some money in the bank and find a new job, Julie. Get married, have a kid. Look at me. I got nothin'."

"But you know my family. We're not normal. Dad was a low-level hood, as was Granddad. And Great-Granddad. He made his fortune as King of Maxwell Street! At least I'm on the right side of the law."

"King of Maxwell Street, my ass. He lost it all fightin' a murder rap and ended up with nothin'."

"You're going on and on about having nothing. What about—"

"You packin'?"

"Huh? I gotta carry a gun to see you?"

"You're on a murder case! You take it everywhere—"

"Okay, okay, relax."

"I could tell you to make this your last murder case, but you're gonna do what you want. Maybe I

134

should just shut the hell up already." Frownie looked directly into my eyes and then turned back. "I love you, you little bastard," he said. "And your dad loves you, too." A tear streaked down the old man's cheek.

"C'mon, Frownie," I said but stopped when his eyes closed and his head fell back against the pillow. I thought for a moment—but then saw his chest begin rising and falling regularly.

Frownie had waited until the end of his existence to decide I needed saving from his misspent life. Despite the colorful stories of grifters, hoods, bosses, baby-kissers, and grandstanders, Frownie said he had nothing. I assumed he meant children and grandchildren, but as far as I could tell he had made a conscious decision to avoid that route. And I never once heard him lament the life of a confirmed bachelor. He had outlived most of his friends and many of his relatives, but to say he had nothing didn't make sense. At the very least, he had one hell of a good view of the shoreline.

24

Driving back toward the city, I pondered why I had not already jumped into investigating Windy City Meters LLC. My conversation with Jones was only yesterday, I reasoned—and then Baxter showing up dead had begged my immediate attention. How much crucial information could I check out in a forty-eight-hour period? Frownie would say "at least all of it."

I parked in a three-hour pay zone near my apartment and walked a half block to the pay station. Typically, I didn't mind parking a few blocks away to avoid paying, but I thought it was time to see how the other half lived. I swiped my credit card, hit the three-hour button, printed out a receipt, and walked the half block back to my car where I put the receipt on the dash. Then I re-walked the same half block back to my apartment. What a pain-in-the-ass system.

From the sidewalk, I saw black fur smashed flat against the window where Punim lay passed out in the hammock. She showed no sign of life when I opened the door. I envied the sleep of cats. All sixteen hours a day of it. I bit into a crisp Empire apple, fired up the laptop, and found the friendliest website on earth introducing the great city of Chicago via Windy City Meters LLC. A sun-drenched skyline along a sparkling expanse of Lake Michigan provided the backdrop for a list of diversions that awaited world-class shoppers, art gallery enthusiasts, architectural aficionados, museum lovers, and theater devotees. With the help of Windy City Meters LLC, your parking experience would be but a footnote in your subconscious. And let's not forget that Windy City Meters LLC sees compassionate corporate citizenship as a fundamental feature of their mission. A headline announced a ten grand gift to a children's hospital. How could Chicago have survived this long without Windy City Meters LLC?

I checked the links to *Cost and Hours*, *How to Find Parking, How to Work My Meter, Request a Refund,* but could not find a physical address or a name associated with Windy City Meters LLC. *Contact Us* offered a toll-free number and an email address. I thought of tailing a WCM officer on foot, although the image somehow hit me as embarrassing.

The discomfort followed me back to the sidewalk, where after a short wait, I spotted a skinny boy across the street peering through windshields and wearing a navy blue windbreaker with the letters "WCM PEA."

The officer had dark skin and Caucasian features. Pakistani perhaps. He looked no older than sixteen. A silver headset sat atop his black hair. The cord disappeared under the windbreaker that covered him like a tent. I thought of Izzy appearing five days ago in his father's suit. I gave the kid a fifty-yard head start before crossing the street to begin my walking surveillance. Nice weather and freely moving pedestrian traffic allowed for easy shadowing, but after heading northbound for thirty minutes, I wished I had eaten something more substantial than an apple.

When we reached Irving Park Road, the kid turned west and after a few blocks stopped in front of a two-story red-brick office building. He took off the headset and stuffed it into his pocket. I saw the security system outside the door and dashed toward the boy hoping to see which button he pressed on the panel. Second button from the top, I thought, then waited to catch my breath before pushing the buzzer. A surveillance camera stared at me through the glass from inside the lobby.

A female voice over the intercom. "Can I help you?"

"I have a question about a parking ticket."

Dead air, then, "You need to speak with someone at the Department of Revenue."

"What's this office?"

"We're a private company, sir."

"I saw a parking officer buzz in."

"They're allowed to use the building's facilities. Please direct all parking questions to the Department of Revenue."

"Is this Windy City Meters?"

Another round of dead air, then a male voice. "This is Daniel of BK Corporate Systems. Can I help you?"

"I'm curious about your company, that's all. I'm looking for a software design firm for parking technology. You guys do that?"

"Sir, we're a private company with no obligation to explain ourselves to those unfamiliar with our services. Please move away from the door or I will call security."

I did as told but ambled around the area keeping an eye on the doorway. What could something called BK Corporate Systems have to do with Windy City Meters LLC? The kid emerged twenty minutes later holding what looked like part of a sandwich that he shoved into his mouth. Halfway down the block, he put the headset back on and crossed back over to Halsted Street, this time heading south.

I closed the distance each time he stopped to write a ticket. Three tickets later I had caught up, but he seemed not to notice me as he grooved to his music and checked dashboards. Finally, I waved at him like a fool and we both stopped. He slid the headset around his neck and smiled as if he knew me.

"Yes, sir?"

His grin took a few more years off his age. "Was that a Windy City Meters office where you just had lunch?"

The kid thought about it. "It's just a small kitchen and bathroom we use when working this area. And at the end of the day, we download our computers there and recharge the batteries." He showed me his handheld ticket-writing device.

"But you're a parking officer for Windy City Meters, right?"

Again, the kid had to think about it. "I'm a parking enforcement aide. And my paycheck always has a different company name on it. Windy City is the company we actually work for—I think." He giggled.

"Have you seen a company called BK something on a paycheck?"

The kid stared at me a moment and then dug several crumpled pieces of paper out of his pocket. He examined them closely until he stuck one in my face and said, "Is this what you mean?"

I thought it odd how readily he would hand over his pay stub to a complete stranger. "BK Corporate Systems" was printed with the Irving Park address. The pathetic hourly rate pissed me off. What cheap bastards.

"Do you mind if I walk with you a bit?" The kid smiled again, shrugged, and off we went. "What's the minimum age requirement for this job?"

"You have to be sixteen to work in Illinois."

"A sixteen-year-old can become a sworn officer with a badge?"

"Nope. We're parking enforcement aides. That's what P-E-A on our back means. We're not allowed to be called officers. If someone calls me an officer, I have to tell them I'm a P-E-A." The kid noticed an expired receipt, wrote the ticket, then wrote another for an expired license plate, and another for a missing front plate. "Hat trick!" he said.

"Is Daniel your supervisor?"

"One of them. Each district has an office like this one where we start and end our days. Every month the PEAs are given a schedule telling them

140

where and what time to report. We never really know who our supervisor will be that day."

He seemed to enjoy my company. He told me his name was Ryan, short for his Nepali name, Narayan, and that he was eighteen. I asked how he got the job, and he mentioned a poster on a bulletin board at an ESL class where his mother taught at night. He liked the idea of walking around without a boss looking over his shoulder, although he admitted working outside in the winter "will suck." He hoped to one day study mechanical engineering. His personality had that amiable, polite quality I supposed most parents dreamed of having in their kid. With each block, he impressed me more. When a younger kid passed us on a bike and called him a "pea brain," Ryan just laughed.

Unlike most of the teenagers with whom I'd had previous conversations, Ryan showed a natural curiosity in me and thought I was joking about working as a private investigator. I could tell his thoughts conjured up images from TV dramas, most of which I said were exaggerated, although when investigating a murder or other serious crime, it wasn't difficult to accurately portray the bad guys. "It's really not that imaginative being a crook, killer, drug dealer, or corrupt politician," I told him.

At the next block, Ryan stopped. "I gotta go this way now," he said. I got the feeling he wanted to put on his headset and be left alone. I thanked him for his time, and we parted ways. I hadn't realized we had reached Armitage Avenue. How many miles did they expect that kid to walk in a day?

Instead of going home, I continued on Armitage to Cleveland where I turned south, hoping to see another WCM PEA. A few block later, I saw a city officer standing in front of St. Michael's church, the defining landmark of Old Town. He was a tall string bean of a guy with a military style high-and-tight haircut. I asked what his territory was for the day.

"What difference does it make to you?" he said.

Ryan's pleasant demeanor had spoiled me. I had forgotten stereotypes often had basis in reality.

"I'm trying to find a Windy City officer."

"What for?"

I didn't like his tone and it seemed inappropriate to speak that way in front of a Catholic church that had survived the Chicago Fire of 1871. "That's really none of your damn business."

I enjoyed acting like a prick once in a while, although some parishioners exiting the church gave me a dirty look.

"Why you giving me a hard time? Just 'cause I work for the city you treat me like shit?"

That I could so easily hurt the man's feelings surprised me. Had I overreacted?

"Look, I just asked a simple question, and you threw it back in my face. So I reacted. Could you please just tell me where your district ends and a Windy City district begins? I'm sorry for speaking to you so harshly."

The man frowned, clearly thinking I was full of crap. "The other side of Larrabee Street," he said and walked away, shaking his head like I was the biggest asshole on the planet.

I hung out around the quaint side streets between Willow and North Avenue where rehabbed clapboard houses sat alongside modern glass structures. A breeze off the lake took me by surprise and once again reminded me how vulnerable one could feel in summer clothing on an autumn afternoon. The chill inspired thoughts of Jack Gelashvili. I tried to picture him starting over as an immigrant, his advanced degrees meaningless, his priorities reduced to taking any job available. And his thanks for doing everything required of an immigrant? Having his head beaten to a bloody pulp.

Down the block a figure in a navy blue Windbreaker searched windshields for the required residential permits. He walked quickly to each car and then peered through reading glasses. His elderly appearance surprised me. I followed him farther south across North Avenue and over to Mohawk Street, where he approached a tall, sad-looking powder blue wood-framed house set back about thirty yards between an office building and the elevated tracks. Chipped and peeling paint covered every square inch.

He rang the doorbell, saluted the security camera, and walked in. Minutes later, I pushed the button fully anticipating the same reception I got at the address on Irving Park. To my utter surprise, a loud buzz released the door's latch-bolt and in I walked. Despite the dilapidated exterior, the interior looked worthy of a historic preservation catalogue. Shiny wood floors, Art Nouveau furniture, classic brick fireplace, all hidden behind a ramshackle façade.

Voices drifted from a short hallway that led to the kitchen where the old man sat at a table casually talking with two middle-aged women also wearing blue Windbreakers. They appeared to be talking shop—how many tickets, who bore the worst insults. My choices seemed limited to sneaking around like a burglar or making up a reason for being there. The idea of casually mingling with the folks in the kitchen seemed appealing, but then a voice beckoned me. "Hey, over this way."

I turned and saw a husky man in slacks and a blue dress shirt opened to the third button. "Bathroom's this way—where're your tools?" A deer in the headlights never felt so speechless. Then the man said, "Who the hell are you?"

"Avon calling?"

"How did you get in?"

"I'm sorry. I was just curious about the house—I study architecture. And I'd never seen such a nice example of an early twentieth century bevel-sided house."

"This is private property. You're trespassing."

"Somebody inside the private property buzzed the door open."

The man unhooked his cell phone. "We're expecting a plumber. Now get the fuck out or I'll call a cop. Or maybe I'll throw your ass out."

"Are you running a business out of this house?"

When the man stepped toward me, Frownie's reprimand about forgetting my gun echoed through my brain. I retreated out the door. At the sidewalk, I saw a plumbing van idling under the train tracks. The driver held a map close to his face. I offered assistance, and he said he was looking for a number on Mohawk Street with the name "KB Enterprises." I pointed out the powder blue house with the derelict paint job.

I still had a couple of hours before my date with Tamar, plenty of time for a nap and a shower. The thought of discussing the day's events with Tamar felt good, if not appropriate. The air had turned noticeably cooler. I jammed my hands in my pockets and headed home. Shortly after crossing North Avenue, I caught a police cruiser in my peripheral vision but didn't think much of it until I hit Lincoln Avenue where I turned to angle back to Halsted. The cop did the same.

Messing with cops was a bad idea, but passive aggression in an automobile pissed me off. I cut over to a quiet side street. When the cop turned, he saw an idiot standing in the middle of the street with both middle fingers extended.

145

I blew him some kisses and said, "You lookin' for some action, honey? Ten bucks for a blow job."

"I hear you been ringing doorbells." He was a little guy with a handlebar mustache. I was going to ask if he was sitting on a couple of phonebooks.

"Yeah? That against the law?"

"If you're harassing people, it is."

"And if I ring a doorbell and they let me in, is that harassment, too?"

"The guy asked you to leave and you didn't."

"Really? So I'm not standing here talking to a bored cop?"

"You know what I mean, asshole. Quit harassing people just doing their jobs and quit ringing doorbells. Get it?"

"You're a dumb-ass cliché. Get it?"

I'm sure he didn't get it.

"I'm gonna ask you one more time," he said.

"Right. I see. You're on some kind of extra payroll, and you don't want me ruining it for you. Is that what I'm supposed to get?"

The cop laughed and then waved his arms like he was signaling to someone. "See ya later, pal," he said and drove off.

I doubled back to Lincoln Avenue and replayed my encounter with Officer Shakedown. He had been contacted by one or both "companies." The companies provided services to the people who wrote parking tickets. WCM made their money from meter revenue. Parking fines went into the city coffers. Why would they have a cop on their payroll?

A cry for help stopped me in front of a narrow one-way alley where a woman leaned against the wall, doubled over in pain. She had short blond hair and wore a jean jacket over a long dress. Gapers walked past more curious as to *my* next move than the stricken woman. Maybe they assumed someone would call 911. The public's blatant disregard tempered my impulse to ignore the risk associated with Chicago alleys, and my altruistic naiveté won the day.

"You need an ambulance?" I said.

She straightened up enough to look at me then held out her hand. I let her use me as a crutch while she led me to the other end of the alley which connected to a circular loading area behind several businesses.

"Over here is my car," she said in accented English.

"Are you well enough to drive?" I said. She pointed to a Cadillac with blackened rear windows parked in front of the exit driveway.

"Come." We walked to the driver's side where she let go of my hand. "Thank you, mister," she said then opened the door.

I had expected to assist her into the driver's seat but she moved unaffectedly and closed the door

147

with little effort. The implication of her sudden upgrade materialized just as the door window reflected a figure standing behind me. I flinched in time to deflect a brass-knuckled fist from a husky skinhead in a black jacket and dark orange shirt. My forearm muscle took the brunt of the strike, saving me from a broken radius, but still rocketing painful shock waves through my arm and shoulder.

I stumbled backward holding my arm, looking around for help. The driver's side rear door was now open. The man approached me slowly, nervously looking around to see if anyone was watching. The plan had been to execute a quick knockout, stuff the body into the backseat, and be off. The woman rolled her window down and frantically yelled something in her Slavic language, whatever that was. The man shouted something back, clearly unhappy. He sprinted toward me. I turned, hoping to reach one of the stairways leading to a business's back door, but slipped on loose gravel and fell. Pain shot through every cell.

I maneuvered onto my back and waited until he was almost on top of me before shoving the heel of my foot against his pubic bone. He fell on me with a scream but still managed to deliver a glancing punch to my face before rolling off and assuming the fetal position. The Cadillac pulled up, the woman jumped out. She shouted, started pulling at his jacket. She wanted to leave.

I used the downtime to start crawling toward the alley entrance that connected to Lincoln but made it only a few feet before a cop car pulled in and screeched to a halt.

"What the fuck are you still doing here?" he yelled at the couple and I recognized the voice of Officer Shakedown. "Get the hell out of here!"

While the cop helped the woman drag the man to the backseat, I continued my journey to Lincoln Avenue until I felt a foot press down between my shoulder blades. "Where're you going, shit breath?" the cop said then dropped both knees onto my back and said in my ear, "Just remember. You're getting off easy." I heard him unsnap his gun holster then something hard hit me.

25

A brick wall came into focus, followed by alley stink, and then throbbing pain from my head, right cheekbone, and most of my upper body. Propped against the alley wall, I managed to get to my feet and walk toward the sidewalk. Pedestrians pretended not to notice or simply didn't care.

Unsteady, filthy, sporting a shiner, I forgave the Lincoln Avenue folks who saw a drunk or dopehead. By the time I staggered home, swallowed 4000 mg of acetaminophen, and collapsed onto my couch with ice packs on my face, head, and arm, the day had acquired a dreamlike quality. Typically, I spent ten or twenty minutes rehashing events or newfound facts before drifting off. On this afternoon, only shock and pain accompanied me into a semi-slumber, unperturbed by Punim's occupation of my chest but eventually succumbing to a continuous knocking on the door.

Standing in the doorway, Tamar held two bags of groceries and stared in horror. "Oh, my god!" she said and rushed to the kitchen and dropped the bags on the table. "What happened?"

"I got mugged—sort of." Tamar gaped as if unsure who I was.

"Should you go to the hospital? Did you report this to the police?"

"Actually, a policeman knows what happened. And bruises always look worse than they really are—especially on the face. Let me get cleaned up, and I promise to tell you everything."

Tamar nodded but continued staring. "I'll start dinner."

By the time I stepped out of the shower, a variety of savory smells temporarily eclipsed any nastiness the day had offered. With an awakened appetite and clean clothes, I felt somewhat human again. Observing Tamar from behind, I watched her create a salad loaded with all things green, purple, yellow, and red. Lightly browned vegetables crowded a baking pan, a pile of dumpling-like things sat in a colander, and a basket held a stack of thick, flat white bread. She wore black leggings and a floral patterned blouse with short sleeves flowing freely over her arms. The combination of the blouse's deep V-back and her slender legs and thighs pulled me into her orbit.

"It looks like you've done this before," I said.

Tamar smiled, then cringed. "You look like you're in pain."

"I'll heal. Put me to work."

"I'm done. Sit."

I obeyed and watched Tamar prepare two plates with a little of everything. Bread was sacred to Georgians, she said, as was the walnut spice of the vegetables and dumplings.

"Food is basic nourishment for our bodies, just as blood is the basic component that unites a family forever. There is no stronger bond than blood."

Talk of food and blood in the same sentence caught me off guard. I sensed Tamar was trying to tell me something. But my hungry, battered body knew only that the flavors in her food dulled the pain like delicious morphine.

"Tell me what's going on and start with the internal organs of small animals in the fridge."

"My cat is observing us from an undisclosed location," I said.

"Hey! I saw my boss kick people out of a booth," Tamar said. "A couple came in and sat in a booth. I watched closely. The gray-haired businessman at the next booth walked over to the counter and asked for the boss who then ended up asking the couple to move. Then the boss told me anything the couple ordered was on the house."

"Maybe those guys are discussing secret recipes?" I said. "Anyway, remember Rich Jones, the guy who set up Jack with Lada? He gave me a tearful confession about spreading rumors that Jack was involved with the Russian mob."

"That's insane!" Tamar said. "Why would he say such garbage?"

"Management was twisting Jones's arm to find cheap immigrant labor to work as parking officers. It angered Jones that Jack worked for half the wage of others. The anger got to him. He wanted to hurt Jack."

"Jack never said anything to me about working for less than the others did."

"It gets better. Jones claimed management approached Jack to act as a go-between to get a piece of the action from his alleged mob connections. Then he described how management went as far as showing Jack complicated scenarios of money laundering and allegedly gave Jack an envelope stuffed with cash to demonstrate their sincerity."

"I can't believe what I'm hearing," Tamar said. "You have to be making this up."

"Look, I'm not saying any of this is true. It's just what I've been told in the last twenty-four hours by someone who worked with Jack."

"So when they realized Jack wasn't a crook, they killed him so he couldn't reveal any of the information they had already showed him—and you believe this?"

I thought about it. "Plausible but unlikely."

"And who exactly is behind all this?"

"Well, I'm thinking a guy named Elon, the Department of Revenue boss. And lots of unwitting accomplices working in a fragmented bureaucracy."

Blank stare. "The Chicago Department of Revenue is run by *Elon the Gangster*?" Something about her tone provoked a simultaneous burst of laughter. Then Tamar said, "And the Russians? Are they part of this or not?"

"I have no evidence Elon has access to the Russian mob."

"Phew," Tamar said sarcastically. "I thought for a second we were in trouble."

"There's more," I said. "The tickets written to the guy who lived in your building were from Windy City Meters' parking enforcement aides. That's the private company that leases the meter boxes from the city."

Tamar looked unimpressed. "Let's keep things simple. Jack was killed to protect this complicated arrangement in which a private company rakes in tons of money from parking revenue."

"That's the baseline. I can't tell you if Windy City's breaking any laws—which brings us back to what this all has to do with Jack's murder."

"He wasn't the Russian mobster they hoped for."

"Did they really have to kill a frightened immigrant on the chance he understood what the hell was going on?"

A lot had been said in a small amount of time. We finished eating in silence.

Finally I said, "The months leading up to Jack's death. Did he act different in any way? Anything you could attribute to Jones's story?"

Tamar contemplated a few moments and shook her head. "Jones's story is nonsense. My cousin was depressed about Lada—the girlfriend I told you about—going back to Russia. Although sometimes he would imagine out loud what he could be doing if he had stayed in Moscow instead of taking a teaching job in Tbilisi. I reminded him how much he meant to the family. But he would just stare into the distance and then start mumbling about corrupt politicians and oligarchs ruining the world. Boy, did he hate Putin."

"How's your aunt doing?"

Tamar sort of frown-smiled. "I think Jack's death was the last straw in a hard life. She spends her days talking to St. Andrew." Tamar grinned. "Jack and Andrew are now good friends, you know." We both laughed. "Hey, if it brings her peace, that's fine with me. What about you?"

The question took me by surprise. "What about me?"

154

Tamar looked as if I had just called her mother an infidel. "Family, of course. You must have family in your life to think about, worry about, deal with."

"Oh, that," I said and told an abbreviated version of my forefathers' dubious reputations. "It seemed the families they married into shunned them once they realized who their daughters had chosen for sons-in-law. I have a lot of cousins out there I've never met."

"But don't you have someone you're close to? A sister or brother?"

I told Tamar about Snooky, devoted family friend, genuine big brother, and the tragedy of his becoming my first murder case just a few months ago. Then I told her about my sickly father and described Frownie, what he meant to my family, and that I most likely saw him for the last time a few hours ago.

Tamar looked on the verge of tears. "That's so sad! Why don't you get in touch with your cousins? I'm sure nobody is going to hold a grudge against you for whatever happened in the past. I mean, they're your *blood*."

"I'm fine, Tamar. I have no complaints with my life."

"But what else is there besides family? You can only depend on family to help you get through life's troubles. Only family can make sure your legacy is properly honored."

I let her words sink in. "I don't know. I never thought about it that way. Don't feel sorry for me. I have a lot of freedom."

Tamar gazed into the tabletop.

I said, "How about some sorbet?"

She looked at her watch. "Let's clean up first."

Silence descended upon the kitchen as we wrapped leftovers, washed plates, wiped the counters and table. I could try to guess what pissed her off—something to do with my attitude toward family—but I hated guessing games.

"I give up. What'd I do?"

Tamar acted surprised. "Oh, no, nothing's wrong. I'm just thinking. I guess it's just that I'm not used to your type."

"I gotta ask—"

"Your independence. It intimidates me. Not that there's anything wrong with it, but it's so different from the culture I grew up in. The idea of being alone in the world. It gave me a chill, but you seem so content. So it's my problem."

Punim landed on the table in front of Tamar. She stroked the feline's backside in one motion, starting at her head and ending with her tail.

"I've had other guests attempt what you're doing. They all went home with bloody hands."

Tamar shrugged. "Cats know who they can trust."

I suggested tea, hoping to recapture our earlier rapport, but Tamar had to get up early. "Baker's hours," she reminded me.

Back on the couch, with ice packs, I thought about my so-called independence. I knew my career choice seemed bizarre compared to my peers who filled the professional ranks expected of a North Shore upbringing. But even Tamar, the Georgian immigrant, sensed a peculiarity about me. I was stranger than I realized. I was the foreigner in our relationship.

26

After a fitful night's sleep, the morning introduced me to a universe of aching. I splashed cold water on my face, popped six more acetaminophen, and sat down to reorient my brain.

The usual breakfast of oatmeal with almonds for me and liver and kidneys for Punim. Beethoven's Fifth rocked my head. I stifled the impulse to smash the phone against the wall. Tamar's rebuff last night had hurt more than I realized.

"Seroquel," Kalijero said.

"Screw you."

"The mental case, Baxter. The lab thinks he took at least six thousand milligrams of Seroquel the day he died. Typical dose is around six hundred."

"I get it, Kalijero. You can't accidentally take ten times the normal dosage. Obviously that means he's irrelevant to the Gelashvili murder," I said sarcastically.

A pause, then, "Baxter's shrink never prescribed Seroquel."

Kalijero's acknowledgment of what I already suspected shoved aside, at least temporarily, the sting of Tamar's rejection. "So what's next?"

"Who said anything was next?"

"Then why are you bothering me with what I already told you?"

Kalijero swore in Greek then said, "I gotta go," and hung up. At least he said goodbye this time.

Escaping my bright, airy apartment for the stuffy familiarity of an office seemed appropriate. On the way to Old Town, I left a message with Palmer and then called back Kalijero.

"Sorry, Jimmy," I said. "I didn't mean to bark at you." I told him about my trip to the Department of Revenue and the events leading up to getting cracked in the face.

"You want me to go talk to the principal and tell him kids are picking on Detective Jules?"

"Do you want to help me find Gelashvili's killer or not?"

"Why should I help you?"

"I'll be at my office in fifteen. Meet me there." Dead air. "Please!"

Kalijero grumbled something unintelligible with an affirming inflection, then hung up. No goodbye.

She had just stepped off the last stair to the lobby as I opened the outside door to my office building. Tall, fashion-model thin, high cheekbones emphasizing exotic good looks. I guessed early thirties.

"Can I help you?" I said.

She stared a moment and said with a Slavic accent, "I don't think so."

"Are you looking for someone?"

She searched my face as if wanting to speak and then rushed out of the building, leaving me to wonder what had just happened.

In my office, a legal pad lay on top of my desk with boxes drawn around names in a sea of empty yellow space. I called Palmer again, and he surprised me by answering.

"I got your message, Jules. Very busy. I should be able to get away in two or three hours—after the budget meeting. Will you still be at your office?"

"If I'm not here, call me. I won't be far."

I returned to staring at the yellow legal pad after telling the city editor of the eighth-largest newspaper in the country to call me back. The outside door slammed shut. Bounding footsteps, at least two at a time up to my doorway, where the uniformed mailman stood catching his breath. He was young and plump with a happy disposition that went well with his butterball face and red cheeks. Despite not being very cold, he wore a postman's winter hat with *faux* fur flaps.

"You do exist!" he said joyfully then kind of giggled. He struck me as one of those annoying nice guys who always had a good word for everybody.

"Why don't you just leave the mail downstairs?"

"Can't. There have to be mailboxes. When they get the rest of these rooms rented, then we'll put in a row of locking boxes. Besides, I like running up the stairs. It's helping me lose some of this fat." He giggled again. "So whaddya do here anyway?"

"Investigations."

"Oh, yeah?" The mailman leaned against the door jamb. He looked way too comfortable. "Like a private detective kind of guy?"

"Kind of like that."

"Is that why you got that purple eye?"

"Have a good day, my friend." He caught my hint.

Elon and Konigson separated by four inches of yellow space. Department of Revenue and the Republic Media Group. Big responsibilities, big egos. These kinds of guys liked to talk about themselves, and the Internet provided the largest possible audience. But numerous searches provided only generic background information and personal opinions on various blogs, as if the world assumed men like Elon and Konigson needed no introduction. Elon had come to the mayor's team from "the real estate and banking world." But to show that he was not a one-dimensional billionaire, Elon's biographers always mentioned his Princeton doctorate in Teutonic literature. I clicked on a link to a photo from the late seventies of a bearded forty-something Konigson shaking hands with a twenty-something Elon. Konigson already had "two decades of success in real estate and investment banking" to share with Elon, Decatur-Staley's newest Ivy League wonder boy. *Take our word for it, these guys are good and will look after your best interests. If you have to ask, then you're probably not worthy of knowing.*

The outside door slammed shut again. Heavy, plodding footsteps. Maybe Palmer. Izzy and Knight were both too skinny for such weight. Reaching the top of the landing, then several breaths, Kalijero's stocky frame filled the doorway. His hair now more salt than pepper, he appeared to have aged significantly in the two months since I had last seen him.

"Greetings, Zorba! I'm flattered you came to see me."

Kalijero panted for a minute. "You couldn't have found a building with an elevator, Landau?"

"It's only four flights, Jimmy. You should quit smoking."

Kaljero sat. "I did."

"Your presence here means you're interested in the case?"

Kalijero started stretching his fingers back one at a time. "Ever since you told me Konigson ordered that editor to kill the story. Got me thinking."

Silence.

Kalijero continued his appendage calisthenics, now flexing his hands open and closed.

"Jimmy, what're you doing here?"

Kalijero answered with his own question. "How's Frownie?"

I shook my head. "Any day."

"Way back when I popped your dad, before the charges were officially filed, Frownie came to see me. He begged me to convince the DA to plea to a lesser charge and not apply the ongoing racketeering statute. I refused and he started cussing me out. And then he started crying. I didn't realize how close he was with your family. He kept going back and forth between cussing me out and crying." Kalijero scratched his head.

"I didn't know this," I said.

"I think maybe I should've done what he asked. Your dad would've done enough time and still gotten out to see you become a man."

Something about men in their sixties suddenly becoming sentimental annoyed me.

162

"You were just doing your job, Jimmy. And you don't know, Dad might have hooked me in. Maybe you saved me from a life of crime." Kalijero wasn't buying it. "Why don't I start from the beginning and tell you everything I got on the Gelashvili case?"

Kalijero stood, smiled. "Nah, this one closed too quickly. I'm already reassigned to *another* last case. I'm doing them a favor, they tell me. A body just washed up downriver."

He walked to the doorway and told me to be careful. I listened as he clomped down the stairs and heard the door slam shut. I still didn't know why he had come.

27

The Blue Line let me off near Madison and LaSalle, close to the sacred temple that housed the Department of Revenue. I acknowledged the Walmart greeter and walked through the hallway metal detector. Like the previous day, lines of gloomy-faced citizens waited to exchange cash for having the scofflaw curse lifted from their lives.

Along the margin of the crowd, I shuffled toward the back. Beyond the row of tellers and revenue-agent desks, a woman sat at a reception station answering phones. I presumed Elon and his deputies conducted business from the offices behind her. A steady stream of suits approached the counter before heading into one of the offices. A lull in the action beckoned my entrance.

"I'd like to see Mr. Elon."

The woman's eyeballs plotted GPS coordinates over my face until she blinked a few times and said, "Do you have an appointment?"

I pointed to my purple welt. "I was involved in a car accident with his wife, and he said I should come by and discuss things."

She plotted more coordinates. "I think he would've told us if someone like you would be stopping by."

Someone like you. That hurt. "How can someone like me see someone like him?" I inquired, trying to be polite despite the scary face.

"You make an appointment." She looked at her computer and typed something. "And what is this appointment concerning?"

"I have questions about how the system works. How the money flows."

She dropped her hands to her lap. "What happened to the accident with his wife?" She looked flustered. "We have a public affairs office that can answer all your questions."

"Why can't I talk to Elon about it?"

"It's not Mr. Elon's job to explain how the Department of Revenue operates. That's the job of the public affairs office."

Her posture told me the conversation had ended. The security guard standing stage left reinforced her statement. I retraced my route back to the front of the room just in time to see four

Bankroll Warranty guards march through the metal detector.

From across the street, I watched the armored truck idle in a loading zone. Half an hour later, the Bankroll Warranty men exited the building escorting bags of money piled on a flatbed dolly. I crossed back and leaned against a square concrete pillar about ten yards behind the truck. Nothing really to see, just three beer-bellied guards handing off bags of loot into the truck while one kept watch. A package neatly wrapped in gray paper positioned next to a rear tire seemed out of place and caught my eye. Probably contained paperwork. Another Chicagoan in an ill-fitting suit and smoking a cigarette loitered about ten feet from the passenger door. The cuffs of his pants stopped short of his ankles. A full head of silver hair combed neatly across from a well-defined part gave him a stately handsomeness. But his wrinkled smoker's complexion and deep lines at the sides of his mouth aged him past his forty-something years. He appeared mildly interested in the process but also distracted by the surroundings. I took pictures of him with my phone. When the guards slammed the rear door shut, the man flicked away his cigarette and double-timed it to the package, reaching for it just as the truck pulled out; a perfectly executed maneuver.

I followed the man and his briefcase across the street into a mid-rise called the "Wolfe Professional Building," where he waited for the elevator while humming and drumming his fingers against the package. When the elevator arrived, I slipped in as he pushed the tenth floor button.

Halfway up, he pointed to his eye and said, "You thought he said *stand up,* when he really said *shut up*?" and followed his quip with unrestrained laughter.

I smiled politely and suffered his giggling to the tenth floor, where the door opened to Vector Solutions, Inc. The common area of the office was wide open, just a big room with doors along the back wall. Nowhere to hide, not even a partition. The man breezed past the woman at the reception station while lifting the package up near his head and pointing at it. She glanced at him and then at me as I followed in his wake down an adjacent hallway where two well-filled, size-54-long suits stood outside an office. One stepped aside to allow the man to enter, the other walked directly up to me and stopped.

From behind came a woman's voice. "Sir, it's not like you can just hang around if you don't have an appointment." I turned and saw the receptionist staring at me.

"How about I hang around the waiting area?"

"We don't have a waiting area."

Outside the office, I leaned against the wall next to the men's room. Occasionally, the receptionist frowned at me. From the elevator emerged a chubby future business leader—young, well dressed, bored to death. The knot of his tie needed tightening.

I said, "Wake up, young man. He who labors diligently need never despair."

The kid stopped in his tracks and looked at me.

"I'm just messing with you," I said.

He smiled and gestured with his middle finger.

The receptionist smiled warmly as he approached. She started to say something but stopped when he strolled past. She and I watched him turn down the hallway. The elevator dinged and out walked a security guard. Miss Receptionist had me in her sights.

"Can I help you with something, sir?" he asked me.

"I was just leaving."

At the newsstand opposite the bank of elevators, I ate a giant soft pretzel, unsure what I waited for. Perhaps Package Man had useful information. Young Businessman, too, might have something to share. The smart-ass little bastard reminded me of myself. The name "Vector Solutions, Inc." reeked like bullshit. Solutions for the trajectory of money. The direction cash traveled from one pocket to another.

As the lunch hour approached, elevator activity increased, and the hallway became a frenetic flow of hungry professionals. Standing on the bank of this human river, the chances of seeing either of my new acquaintances seemed unlikely. Two more pretzels and *Catnip* magazine helped me kill another hour while sitting on a marble bench in the lobby near the newsstand. The thought of squandered time weighed on me. Day seven of my investigation and too many unanswered questions. Would finding Jack's killer offer comfort to Tamar?

Maybe Elon's family had an ancient hatred of Georgians and had settled an old score. Maybe Konigson used the emasculated article to blackmail Elon. So much yellow space between squares, so many idiotic scenarios to consider. Then I saw Young Businessman nearby paging through the magazine *Capital Growth*. Opportunity was knocking.

"You always give the finger to strangers?" I said.

He glanced at me and then back to the magazine. "You in the habit of giving strangers unsolicited advice on their mental state?"

"I wanted to cheer you up."

"Who decided I needed cheering up? I'm not surprised by that welt, dude. Hang around men's bathrooms enough and that's bound to happen. In fact, if you're looking to pick up a young piece of ass, I suggest you piss off now because I won't hesitate to smash your other eye."

I stepped back. "All right, already. I was trying to talk to someone and the receptionist had just tossed me out—"

"And you thought I could get you back in?"

"That's not what I meant—"

"What'd you think of the receptionist?"

"Think? As in—"

"You think she's hot?" He tucked the magazine under his arm and waited for my response.

"A little old for me and not my type."

"I banged her. Many times. In the ass. She loves it."

I remembered how she smiled at him. The image sickened me. I said, "That's nice, kid."

"At what age are you allowed to call someone else kid? I'm twenty-three and you don't look a hell of a lot older than me, *pops*."

"Dude, you, like, so busted me! Do you, like, work for those Vector guys?"

"You sound like an idiot. And I'm an unpaid intern. MBA requirement. Like doing things for free will help you make money later on. I suppose it does."

"University of Chicago?"

"Northwestern."

"Top of your class?"

"Not even close."

"What kind of work they have you doing?"

"I'm an errand boy—"

"Sent by grocery clerks to collect the bill. Yeah, I saw the movie." He had the arrogant odor of a future billionaire. "I'm looking for Elon."

169

"Try looking across the street in Revenue."

"Of course! Hey, what does Vector Solutions do?"

"Consult on transportation issues."

"That would include parking?"

"Oh, yeah!" The kid's knowing smile provoked an unexpected laugh.

"Hey, whose office has the two bodyguards?"

"There's another bodyguard inside the office. They belong to Konigson."

This time my surprised expression evoked laughter from Young Businessman, which then inspired a loud display of mirth from both of us.

"You got a laptop in that package?" I asked.

"Maybe."

"I'll give you fifty bucks if you let me use it."

"Are you stupid? You can go to the library and use one for free."

"I'm not at the library and I'd rather pay an unpaid intern."

Young Businessman stared at me a moment and then took out his computer. I placed it on the counter of the newsstand, typed "Illinois Secretary of State," and searched the corporation/LLC database while he watched.

"Decatur-Staley," he said.

"What about it?"

"Vector Solutions is a subsidiary of Decatur-Staley. That's what you're looking for, right?"

I jammed a fifty into the kid's jacket pocket and said, "Do you even know who Konigson is?"

"A billionaire."

"He runs a media empire that includes the *Republic* newspaper."

"He's rich as hell. That's all that matters. And I have no use for newspapers. Their days are numbered anyway. As a business model, I mean. They're finished. A niche market at best."

"How do you stay informed?"

He looked as if I'd spoken Hindi. "Informed about what?"

"About what's going on in the world."

"What do I care? I'll get my MBA, maybe work for someone else a while, and then I'll make my own fortune. What happens in the world is out of my control."

I waited for more. He took out a smart phone and started reading something. I said, "A guy with a package entered that office a few minutes before you arrived. What do you think was in the package?"

"Ask the guy when he gets here."

"You didn't answer my question."

Something he read angered him. He swore and then said, "What do you *think* was in the package?"

171

"Department of Revenue cash."

He nodded while keeping his nose in his phone. "Sounds like a good guess."

"Learning a lot from this internship? Besides sending American jobs to countries that pay a slave wage?"

"Dude, I know you're a Fed. There's no law says you can't carry a pile of cash across the street in a package."

"How do you get an internship like this?"

"You know somebody—*duh*!"

"I bet you rank number one in your class for cockiest little shit."

Young Businessman shoved the phone in his pocket and faced me. His eyes then focused over my shoulder. I turned and saw Package Courier standing with Rich Jones, of all people.

"I'll say hi to my mom for you," Young Businessman said as he walked away. A second later he turned and yelled, "The receptionist. That's my mom. I was just kidding about bangin' her."

What a cretin. I positioned myself near the exit and snapped a picture of Jones and friends. When Jones caught my eye, I waved and yelled his name. His look of terror was something out of a campy horror flick. He pushed his way through the crowded lobby and out the revolving door, disappearing down the street.

28

As I took the staircase up to my office, I saw the black wingtips first, then the tapered cuffs, and finally Palmer seated on a torn vinyl stair cover under the sickly glow of a ceiling fixture full of dead moths.

"My god, what happened to your eye?"

"Had you called, I would've suggested meeting somewhere."

Palmer looked around and said, "This is fine. It's actually quite peaceful sitting up here by myself." I think he meant it.

"Are you still taking the El train around town?" I said while searching for the key.

"Yes! It's opened up a whole new world for me"

"The world of the hoi polloi."

Palmer laughed. "You often see the same faces on the same trains, depending on the time of day. I imagine many relationships are cultivated while riding the subway." I had just put the key in the lock when he added, "Good thing I'm not paranoid, otherwise I might think someone was following me."

I turned around. "You think someone's following you?"

"No, no, no," he said then laughed again and gestured for me to carry on opening the door. Inside my office Palmer took the club chair opposite my

173

desk. "It's been two days, Jules. Judging by your eye, I would guess much needs to be discussed."

"Wil, I'm going to act a little corny and tell you I don't want to discuss my eye. Let's change the subject. It seems that Windy City Meters LLC is run on the franchise business model. As if each district were a separate entity."

"That makes sense from a tax standpoint."

"Konigson has an office across the street from the Department of Revenue called Vector Solutions, Inc." Palmer laughed at the name. I described the delivery of the Bankroll Warranty cash to the office and told him Vector Solutions, Inc., is a subsidiary of the investment house Decatur-Staley. "The same company that bought Windy City Meters from Konigson."

Palmer nodded but appeared unimpressed with my findings. "Yes, last time we spoke you were curious why someone who needed cash flow would sell a profitable company."

I stopped him. "Keep it simple, Wil, or you'll lose me."

"I shall endeavor. Konigson and his unknown backers borrowed an enormous sum to buy Windy City. In these scenarios, one typically assigns the debt to the company just acquired, makes the necessary cuts to capital and labor, and then sells the leaner company for enough to cover the rest of his debt and make a tidy profit."

"But Windy City's debt was too large," I said.

174

"Or its value had been grossly overestimated."

"So Konigson is bleeding red ink out the ass and then Decatur-Staley, that venerable institution where Elon and Konigson forged their friendship, comes to the rescue."

Palmer smiled. "Where they forged their friendship *and* where Elon still sits on the board."

On my flow chart, I drew a line from Konigson to Elon and marveled at how quickly I had covered the four inches of yellow space. I said, "I couldn't find anything on the net about these guys. It was like their lives had been expunged."

"People like Konigson know how to manipulate media. You show enough money, the masters of the Internet will get you erased off the web. There's a good chance someone looking for you won't bother to do the necessary legwork, like in the old days."

Utilizing the *Republic* archives, Palmer had discovered how Elon and Konigson worked closely at Decatur-Staley selling financial products to high-net-worth investors and learned the art of raising capital to acquire companies.

"Ultimately," Palmer said, "they're both great salesmen. They know how to gain an individual's trust. And once you do that, they gladly hand over money—even if they don't understand what you're doing with it."

"Wil, you gave me some great info."

Palmer smiled and jumped back into the story of how Elon and Konigson started many types of businesses and investment schemes until they parted ways and continued creating wealth separately. At some point, Elon became interested in city politics while Konigson built a media empire.

"Most people don't fully understand the influence of men like Konigson," he said. "Supposedly, it was Konigson's money directed at a few senators that finally got a certain piece of FCC deregulation passed. Now one company can own as many radio stations as it wants."

A direct human link from Konigson to a murdered parking officer obscured the significance of FCC deregulation.

"It's a shame," Palmer said. "The more concentrated the media ownership, the less free is our society. But tell me what you have discovered."

"I appreciate your enthusiasm, Wil, but it's probably best that you don't know all the details."

He looked at my eye. "Yes, I see what you mean."

Silence, until I said, "But the information you're providing is invaluable. I mean, to Konigson and Elon, money circulates as their lifeblood. So if they're involved in murder, the motive most likely was money."

"Konigson's money, I'll wager. If we put the financial puzzle together, the motivations will be obvious."

"Elon and Konigson cut a deal."

"Precisely."

"So in exchange for arranging a bailout of his debt-ridden pal Konigson, Elon gets kickbacks, not to mention a chunk of the eleven billion dollar profit D-S made when they sold their interest in Windy City Meters, LLC. But what could the cash in the package represent? Seems like that money is moving in the wrong direction."

Palmer thought about it. "My guess would be money for an operating account."

"A slush fund! To pass cash to lazy cops about to retire. The cash that greases the wheels that make Chicago 'The City That Works.'"

In a city famous for its machine politics, the analogy of money and grease had no equal, but we laughed at the timeworn reference as if hearing it for the first time.

29

On the way home, I called in an order to Tasty Harmony, then relaxed on my recliner while eating a rice-bean-soy burger. Punim sat on my lap, her eyelids heavy from having just devoured two chicken livers.

Elon and Konigson had put together a private-public apparatus where cash flowed simultaneously in all directions. Somewhere in the process the machine spit out a dead parking officer. Rich Jones worked under Elon and with Gelashvili. I assumed his reaction when he saw me in the lobby confirmed his involvement in this mess. But what about his strange confession of having started a deadly rumor?

Beethoven interrupted, followed by Tamar's voice. "I'm not comfortable with how we left things." In the background, the murmur of the bakery.

"Me, either."

"Want to come over later for dessert? About eight?"

"Sounds great."

Seeing Tamar again pleased me but the thought of going to that grim apartment with the candles, old lady, and weird chanting creeped me out a bit. The things we do for love.

Reading closely some of the blogs discussing Konigson and Elon, I was assaulted by the anti-government theme of libertarianism. Also linked to this dogma was a "Madame Zinoyevich," a novelist turned philosopher who preached finding freedom in the pursuit of self-interests. Apparently her best-known work, *The Integrity of Egotism,* was the capitalist bible of her followers. In the late 1950s, Konigson met Zinoyevich, who was so impressed with the young plutocrat that he became part of her inner circle. Konigson credited Madame Zinoyevich's influence with leading him to his early fortune in real estate. Later, he would credit Zinoyevich for his success guiding a young Elon down the same road.

I checked out a few more links discussing Zinoyevich. She saw the "perfect human" as one attaining complete separation from the constraints of society. The world does not exist for this human nor does this human think the world should exist. Therefore, any action is justified since this human cares not the least for anything society cherishes. She actually found her living embodiment of this perfect human in a man who murdered and dismembered a twelve-year-old girl in 1927. I had no doubt Elon, with a guru who idolized psychopathic murderers, and Konigson were involved in Gelashvili's death.

The phone interrupted. "Yeah, Julie, it's me."

Once again, it took a few moments for me to reconcile Frownie's robust voice only yesterday sounding as if it was knocking on death's door.

"Frownie?"

"What's going on, kiddo? You talk to them ticket-writin' stooges? The ones givin' fake tickets to the nut job?"

"I talked to a couple of them. But I don't know who wrote what."

"That newspaper editor—?"

"Safe as kittens."

Frownie didn't respond, and I thought maybe I'd been hallucinating the conversation. Then he said, "I been thinkin' about your family."

"And?"

179

"Well, ya know, they were just doin' the best they could. Your old man especially. He went into the rag business to make an honest livin'. The bookmakin' and the numbers, that wasn't what he wanted."

"He told me all those little towns downstate were already doing it."

"Absolutely they was! Your old man just showed 'em how to do it better!"

"He must've made good money. We lived in the North Shore, remember?"

"He made some dough on the coats, too. But you know they liked him, your old man. The little stores sellin' the ladies' things. He showed 'em how to have fun. He should've stopped with the whores, though. I remember tellin' him nobody cared about a little gamblin' but you start bringin' in them whores to those little towns and people are gonna notice."

"You can have fun, but not too much fun."

Frownie laughed. "That's right! It's like gettin' greedy. He shoulda been satisfied with makin' a few bucks on the gamblin' and let it go at that. He wasn't no pimp, though. Those gals made a lot of cash. Your dad, a few bucks, that's all."

"Why are you bringing this up?"

"They did the best they could. Your dad, his father, and his father. You do what you're good at in these circumstances. Sometimes it ain't somethin' you want to brag about, but it ain't

180

nothin' to be ashamed of, neither. Don't be ashamed of where you come from, Julie."

"I'm not ashamed."

"Your old man is proud of you. I know it don't always look like it, but he is. Even the murder investigatin'. Deep down I think he's proud of your courage. He just worries, that's all."

"He helped me with Snooky's murder."

"Damn right he did! He would do anything for you. He missed out on a lot because of prison. That's where he screwed up, but don't hold on to anger because of that. . . ."

Frownie rambled on about the importance of family and not to follow his example by staying a bachelor. Somehow he transitioned to tell me for the thousandth time the story of his first girlfriend and how he copped her bare breast in the rumble seat of a 1933 Lincoln KB Convertible Coupe, a model now included in his car collection. Next came the story of falling off his bicycle and having an old man ask if he was hurt. The old man was John D. Rockefeller, the story went, and he gave Frownie a dime. Then a reminiscence of all the different mentors he'd had in life and that he could have done anything he wanted but for some goddamn reason he chose investigations.

As he spoke, my mind wandered to Tamar's apartment and the ancient woman staring at Jack's picture while rocking her way to oblivion. When the call dropped, my attention returned. I didn't know how long the line had been dead and I had a sick feeling the old guy may have gone to sleep for the last time. How could I have blown him off like that? What was the matter with me? His call had been a gift, a chance to be with him as he rid himself of that worn-out body. He had gotten great mileage from it, had kept it long past when one usually traded in for a new model. Just like his antique cars, Frownie was a classic. I had to see him.

A half hour later, I arrived to find the front door wide open and the sound of quiet weeping. Helen, Frownie's nurse, sat next to his bed, crying into her hands. Frownie lay dead with the phone on his chest.

"I'm not sure why I'm crying," she said. "It's my job to help people die. The young ones get to me but not usually the old."

Frownie's eyes and mouth were open, giving the appearance of utter disbelief that Death had finally paid a visit. I said, "Once you got to know him, he was hard to let go of. A lot of people will be crying over this old guy."

A policeman knocked on the door. The ambulance arrived a few minutes later. I watched the paramedics zip Frownie into a bag while Helen signed documents with a cop. I called my father. A caretaker answered and told me he was napping. I asked him to pass on the sad news and then called Kalijero.

"Frownie died." No response. Police radio traffic in the background. I said, "I thought you might want to know, that's all."

"Yeah, yeah, thanks. He was a good man. Let me call you back."

A strange feeling of disappointment came over me, as if I had anticipated commiserating with Kalijero. I talked with Helen awhile and then wandered around the condo examining the various collectibles Frownie had acquired over the years. His impeccable antique car collection reflected the pride he felt in the craftsmanship of bygone eras. Inside his home one felt his appreciation in the meticulous care of the maple drop-leaf dining table, the mahogany console, the Art Deco couch and chair, even the square wooden "High Fidelity" box that looked as if it had just been purchased. I fingered through a fantastic vinyl record collection. The sleeves were hardly worn, the corners barely frayed. Glenn Miller and the like, well dusted and the records in their prime. No scratches.

I opened a beautiful walnut mid-century credenza and found a leather-bound photo album. Most of the photos were groups of men in suits with wide lapels and neckties decorated in bizarre geometric patterns. In his younger days, Frownie cast quite a dashing image in the fashions of the era. A few faces looked vaguely familiar as people I had once called "Uncle," although one photo in particular with Frownie's arm around a young man struck me. Stocky, square-headed, jet-black hair. I left a message on Kalijero's phone asking how a picture of a very young Kalijero had found its way into one of Frownie's photo albums.

Tamar stood in the doorway to her apartment, wearing silk drawstring pants and a T-shirt. In her arms she held a bag of garbage. I had been standing in the hallway about ten yards away, killing a little time, but began walking toward her as soon as I heard the door open.

"Hi," I said. "Somebody walking out let me in. Am I early? I guess I should've buzzed anyway."

"Doesn't matter," Tamar said and dropped the bag down the garbage chute, where it clattered down to the cellar. "Come in."

At the door, she surprised the hell out of me by taking my hand. She led me into the candlelit residence shared with her elderly aunt, who remained in the rocking chair in front of Jack's photograph. Tamar directed me to a small sofa on the room's other side. Two plates with pastries awaited us on a coffee table.

"Those are *puff* pastries, aren't they?" I said.

Tamar laughed. "They're called *taplune*," she said and watched me take a bite. Its sweet, nutty taste made me forget the world had any problems or that I practiced veganism. We ate while I chattered on mindlessly about the pastry. Tamar politely listened and reciprocated with useless information about traditional Georgian food. Meanwhile, the old lady started mumbling—soft at first and then loud enough for me to recognize a foreign language.

Tamar sighed. "She's talking to Saint Andrew again."

"What about?"

"She wants him to set her up on a blind date with Peter." Tamar laughed loudly, startling me. "Sorry. Any idea what it's like to take care of a crazy old lady? I gotta laugh. Otherwise I'll end up acting like her. Maybe you should laugh more, Jules." Tamar put the last of the pastry in her mouth and stared at me.

"I laughed when you referred to the Department of Revenue as being run by gangsters."

Tamar smiled and nodded. "That's right," she said. "Elon the Gangster. Do you know what he looks like?"

"I saw a picture of him taken in the late seventies. Skinny, dark-haired, average looking. Why?"

"I'm not sure. Anyway, I'm sorry for leaving so abruptly that night, but something about you upset me. Suddenly, I felt alone, even though I stood right next to you. I had to leave—I really don't understand it."

"This is about me not having a regular family. That upsets you."

"It's about you not *caring* whether or not you have a family, or just a true blood connection."

"Who said I didn't care?"

Tamar put her plate down and scooted a bit closer. "You don't have to say it. It's all over you. I see it in your eyes. You exude *loneliness*."

185

The temptation to angrily defend my psyche from her presumptuous attack almost won the moment. "It's just how things worked out. I'm fine with who I am. Why can't you accept that?"

Tamar thought about it. "It's too foreign a concept for me to accept. It contradicts how Georgians are brought up. Families are crucial for survival—"

"Yeah, yeah, all this blood and honor stuff."

Tamar couldn't stop staring at me. She must care about me, I thought. Why else would she give a damn what I felt? I extended my arm along the back of the couch, a distance that overlapped Tamar's position and a statement impossible to misinterpret. She stayed put, showing not the slightest display of discomfort. I knew I had a chance.

"A guy yelled at me today," Tamar said, looking into my eyes. "He said we had stale pastries and compared us to a terrorist organization."

"Anyone darker than milk is a suspect nowadays."

"You are the darkest person I ever met. So you must be the terrorist."

I moved my hand close enough to play with a lock of her black hair. She did not object and kept her eyes on me. The prattling from the old lady's conversation with St. Andrew became background noise, like a radio tuned to a foreign broadcast, but then the old broad startled me with a hacking cough that became a desperate struggle for air. I looked over at Tamar, who seemed not to notice the ruckus.

"It'll pass," she said and then leaned forward to meet my mouth with hers. Had the old lady let out a shattering death rattle right then, I would have known only the sensation of Tamar's lips against mine. Unfortunately, a moment later I opened my eyes slightly and caught a glimpse of the rocking chair and all the coughing sounds rushed back to my eardrums.

"What?" Tamar said noticing my perplexed look. "She's fine. Don't worry."

She slid onto her back, pulled me on top of her, and wrapped her legs around me. Despite the eroticism, the old lady and her guttural mumbling were an acoustic impotence device. I maneuvered my arms around Tamar's waist and slid off the couch to my knees.

She laughed. "What're you doing?"

What I was doing became obvious when I stood and she fastened her arms around my neck as I carried her to the bedroom.

Tamar's alarm sounded at four *a.m.*—baker's hours. She had gotten up once already to clean up the old lady and put her to bed. She accepted her responsibilities without complaint.

"There are worse shifts," Tamar said. "We have people starting their shifts at five *p.m.* and then working all night." She ran off a list of activities that needed to be accomplished before the bakery doors could open in two hours.

We held hands walking to my car. I dropped her off in front of the Kutaisi Georgian Bakery where, in the darkness of an October morning, Tamar would take over the duties from those who had spent the night mixing, rolling, cutting, frying, baking, frosting, and decorating dough.

After the rapturous spell that follows the consummation of a new relationship wore off, I thought over the previous days' events. Who was this man who delivered cash to Konigson and arranged the nonexistent surveillance of a schizophrenic framed for murdering a parking officer? Rich Jones, too, needed my immediate attention, but considering the way he fled from the lobby, finding him might be difficult.

Then I thought about how Kalijero could have been acquainted with Frownie since childhood. Musings over that accompanied me the rest of my drive home. Any scenario to explain this relationship seemed too absurd to consider. Frownie came from West Side Jewish Orthodox immigrants. Kalijero from Greek Orthodox immigrants. Twenty-seven-year age difference. How the hell did they even know each other?

30

Punim was not accustomed to my staying out all night, and I could tell by the way she strutted about, whipping her tail, that the cigar-sized hairball on my pillow was no accident. Not until sated with hearts, livers, and kidneys did she return to the loving little pussycat I knew. I changed the pillowcase, passed out, awoke around nine when Kalijero called.

"Frownie was a good man. He went in his sleep, I hope."

"Something you want to tell me?"

"What do you mean?"

"What do you think I mean?"

"No idea. That dead parking officer. Did you say he was Russian?"

"Georgian. When did you first meet Frownie?"

"Long time ago. Are they, like, Russian in their religion? Eastern Orthodox?"

"Jimmy, when did you first meet Frownie?"

"I don't fucking remember! Now answer my question. Do they have the same religion over there?"

"They're both Orthodox—you'd think a Greek would know that. What difference does it make?"

"Not sure." The line went dead. Somehow, Kalijero was getting a perverse thrill from hanging up on me, that was the only explanation.

Standing in the shower as hot water poured off the top of my head, it occurred to me Dad and Frownie had a secret regarding Kalijero, something more than the obvious anger over putting Dad in prison. After getting dressed, I returned a missed call from a number I didn't recognize. A woman's voice said, "Hello, Mr. Landau? Elaine Reilly of Reilly's."

"How are you?"

"I'm just swell, thanks. You had mentioned wanting to speak to a soon-to-be-retiring police detective named Calvo?"

"Thank you for remembering."

"Believe it or not, he just asked me to squeeze him in for an appointment today. He'd like to be introduced to one of my apartments."

"I see. And he arranged a private one-on-one showing of this apartment with an associate of yours?"

"Debbie will expect Detective Calvo around eleven o'clock this morning for a one-hour interview."

She gave me the building's West Town address and imitated Mae West with an invitation to see her some time. I think she was half serious.

I took Halsted all the way to Milwaukee, not far from Reilly's, and easily found parking on a side street in front of a row of rehabbed bungalows. The building where Calvo would have his "interview" had spent the previous eighty years as an industrial warehouse before becoming a luxury loft community starting in the low one-millions. The factory gray, high-gloss concrete floor of the visitor lobby created a kind of seedy-chic appeal next to the exposed urban-brick walls. Glass partitions framed the steel security door of an inner lobby that kept stragglers like me away from the elevators. I counted three displayed security cameras, two disguised as Art Deco wall sconces.

For some reason, a smattering of red leather club chairs had been the chosen seating arrangement for the lobby. Comfortable, perhaps, but stylistically incongruent. The seats should've been slashed open to help the lobby's hardscrabble statement. People of all ages came and went, many dressed in classic overcoats and fedoras as if living some kind of captains-of-industry fantasy.

A vintage industrial furniture magazine helped me kill a half hour until Calvo emerged from the elevator, looking sleepy but contented in that disheveled-fat-man way. I waited until he pushed through the outside door then ran to within ten feet of him as he waddled down the sidewalk. I didn't want to judge a regular joe for walking around with his jacket open and shirt untucked, but as a city employee, Calvo could at least try putting himself back together after rolling around with a hooker on the public's dime.

I slapped Calvo's back, startling him. "How ya doin,' Ray?"

"Who the fuck are you?" he asked, squinting at my shiner.

"Think Reilly's but without the black eye. Remember? You called me Jimmy Kalijero's little bitch?"

191

I could hear the rusted, worn-out gears in Calvo's brain grinding away as he tried to recall events from four days ago. Then a circuit jumped and his eyes opened a little wider. "Yeah, I remember. That murdering psycho Baxter killed himself. Case closed. Piss off."

"Actually, my case is wide open and you're in the middle of it." Calvo chuckled and started walking away. "It's all on surveillance, Calvo."

He stopped then turned around. "What're you talking about?"

"In that building. You just spent the last hour with a prostitute."

"Bullshit! And it's none of your business anyway."

My turn to laugh. "Paying for sex on the public payroll is none of my business?"

"How do you know who I was with?"

"Hidden webcams dude! You're an internet star! Your porn name is 'Calvin Cock,' but we could use your real name if you'd rather have the notoriety."

Calvo looked unsteady, queasy. He glanced around but there was nowhere to sit. "You got nothing. Nobody cares about this sort of thing anyway. The whole world's sneaking out for quickies."

"Really? You think the people of this town don't care if their public servants visit whores on the clock?"

"What're you, some kind of reporter now? Is that it? You got a story to sell?"

"Now that you mention it, I do. I also have contacts with the *Republic* and *The Partisan*."

"What do I give a shit what they print?"

"Ever thought your impending retirement may be premature? That's right, Ray. All those years of goldbricking down the drain."

Calvo's jaw clenched. "How much?" He was thinking more bribery could pacify his misbehavior.

"I want to know who paid you to conduct Gordon Baxter's surveillance from Reilly's bar instead of outside his apartment."

From the look on his face, you'd have thought I had demanded a million bucks in cash. "What do you mean?"

"Stop it, silly boy. You were assigned to watch Baxter. He was the prime suspect in the Gelashvili murder. Instead, you sat around the bar with your pals reminiscing about your pathetic careers. Why would you so brazenly disregard your duty on a murder case if someone had not either told you it was okay, or paid you to do so?"

"A lot of guys blew off that assignment. Why don't you hassle them?"

193

"Because I'm hassling you. Never should've called me Kalijero's bitch. That hurt my feelings. So you start talking to me or I'll have Internal Affairs, the auditor general, and every news outlet in the Midwest crawling up your horny ass."

Calvo attempted a derisive laugh. "Nobody cares. You don't know how things work, Landau. You think you got pull? You don't got shit."

"I'll tell you what I know. When they're caught with their pants down, cities love finding a scapegoat. And then they come down hard for show, to let the world know how serious they are about corruption. When they're done frying your whore-loving ass and things calm down, everybody goes their own way, everything gets back to normal, and you're on the street with no pension."

Loud breathing through his nose. Then he mumbled something and forced himself to take deep, slow breaths. "All right. A guy came to me. Never seen him before. This guy told me I'm gonna be assigned to watch a suspect for a murder case. But he said to just sit around, do nothing. I was supposed to hang out nearby in the guy's neighborhood. He gave me an envelope with cash and said there would be another one coming when the case was closed."

"It wasn't just you," I said. "I didn't see anybody even pretending to be casing Baxter's apartment building."

"Yeah. The other guys didn't even bother going over there, so I followed their lead. We was all short-timers."

"All those dopes in the bar about to retire?"

"Yeah."

"You get that second envelope?"

"Yeah. Fatter than the first."

I asked what the guy who delivered the message looked like and he described the package courier at Konigson's office, ill-fitting clothes and all. At this point, I had no reason not to believe Calvo. He had nothing to gain and everything to lose by jerking me around. I got the feeling his heart was about to explode, and I preferred not to be around when it did.

"Congratulations on your retirement," I said. "A grateful city thanks you."

31

Dad wasn't sure he would go to the funeral. This surprised me.

"*Ach!* Frownie don't care about that crap," Dad said. "We go to funerals to make ourselves feel better. The dead don't give a damn." He had a point.

Despite the funeral taking place only two days after Frownie's death, the simple graveside affair was well attended by Frownie's "younger" colleagues of sun-tanned, craggy-faced men in their early eighties, who flew in from Florida to pay their respects. One of them eyed me then approached with a determined look. "He was a *mensch,*" the man said and cupped my ear. "You should be lucky to know one man like him your whole life." Then the man turned and walked a few feet away and as if on cue, stopped and turned back to face me. "He was a *mensch*!" he repeated loudly and then dabbed his eyes with a handkerchief.

Most of the men had wandered away when I noticed Dad standing in the back just inside the cemetery tent. An associate held his arm while he leaned on his cane with the other. Under his open trench coat I saw the same ancient argyle cardigan sweater he wore when he had knocked on my door after having just been released from prison. He shook his arm loose from the associate then walked to me. A torn black ribbon hung from his lapel. We both stared at the nearby grave.

"You decided to come," I said.

"You see the respect Frownie got?" Dad said.

"The number of people?"

"Damn right. All those guys making the trip, a lot of them coming from Boca Raton. And at their age! Former cops, hoods, bookies, gamblers, pimps, Fed hacks, you name it."

"I bet you and Granddad got that kind of respect, too."

Dad laughed. "Me? Not even close. Your great-granddad—you bet he did. Even more. You see,

Frownie knew how to juggle them all, keep 'em all happy. That was his gift."

"I think over time those types wore on his conscience, though."

Dad gave me that familiar scowl, a fixture of my childhood. "You still trying to find a murderer to chase? Just so you can also get killed?"

"I'm now on a murder case. I told you all about it a few days ago."

"Bullshit! When?"

"When I came over. You don't remember me coming over?"

Dad didn't respond. The he said, "I guess you want me to respect murder investigating?"

"Trying to bring justice to the family of an innocent man? Doesn't that deserve respect?"

Dad thought about it. "You want honor. That's what you want. Respect was different in me and Frownie's day. It had to do with being tough! Your great-granddad showed our family could be tough. He saw how they looked at us and he took it right to them. Capone and the rest didn't scare him. And we went to war just like the rest. My cousin Leo navigated a bomber lying on his back after getting hit by flack and won the Distinguished Flying Cross. My cousin Freddy flew fifty missions in a P38. He had twenty missions under his belt when two replacements showed up all cocky. He hears one of them say, 'Ever notice how the closer we get to combat, the fewer *kikes* you see?' Freddy kicked the shit out of both of them while the others watched. He showed everybody who was tough. And he got respect."

This same conversation had taken place many times in one form or another throughout my life. Unfortunately, a definition of respect would never bridge this generation gap.

"So you're mad at me again for working a murder investigation?" Dad waved at the associate, looked me over, but said nothing. I said, "You let me off easy a few days ago. You said you weren't going to worry. You said there's no point in worrying."

Dad looked at me as if I had just called him a piece of shit. Then he seemed to remember something. He turned to the associate and said, "Let's go. My shows are gonna start soon."

32

Izzy's voice mail "greeting" emitted an extra helping of gloom, as if anticipating every call would bring only bad news. In my most cheerful voice, I asked him to call me and then headed to the Old Town neighborhood where I had encountered the oversensitive city parking officer. I wandered twenty minutes before I spotted a female officer. She looked early forties, prematurely gray, with a braid reaching the small of her back. I said hello, and she sort of nodded and said, "Question?"

"Do you know where Jones is working today?"

"Nope. He moves around a lot."

"Can you tell me where the city's parking office is?"

"You can pay your tickets online or at city hall or at one of our payment processors." She handed me a card listing addresses.

"I don't have tickets. I want to visit your office, where you and your fellow officers report before your shift starts."

"We work for the Department of Revenue. Check with them."

"Your office is at the Department of Revenue? In city hall?"

"Check with them."

"So you can't tell me where your office is?"

"We're not required to give out that information."

"But it's all part of the public record. Your salary, your name, your annual reviews, it's all information readily available."

"Then you don't need me to tell you about it."

She had rehearsed this conversation, and had said it all many times before. "I'll bet you've been instructed not to give out information."

"We are not *required* to give out information."

"Then why bother talking to me at all?"

"We're here to help people. Do you have a question about parking?"

"Thanks for your help. I think I'll go over to the Department of Revenue and check with them."

The lady turned around and continued her walk.

It was a nice day and I had a decent parking place near my office, so I walked to Sedgwick and took the Brown Line downtown, back to the tenth floor of the Wolfe Professional Building where I once again stood in front of Young Businessman's mother. Her look told me she had a finger hovering above the "security" button.

"I mean no harm. I just want a word with your son."

"He's not here."

"Is he coming in today?"

"That's none of your business. How do you know my son?"

"We talked in the lobby after you threw me out."

"What's his name?"

"We didn't officially introduce ourselves."

Mommy shook her head in disgust. "I don't know what kind of sicko you are, but if you leave on your own, I won't call security."

Down in the lobby, leaning against a marble pillar, I watched John and Jane Public walk to or from their various conferences, presentations, pitches, speeches, talks, forums, and every other type of gathering associated with that beloved force

200

of nature called capitalism. I couldn't help but notice how the City of Big Shoulders had morphed into the metropolis of expansive stomachs and vast rear ends. Buttons and zippers on Armani shirts and Dior skirts strained against the forces of Italian beef, Polish sausage, and deep dish pizza—a metaphor waiting to be conceived.

"Don't move," said a voice followed a poke in the ribs, followed by laughter. "I'm just messing with you!"

Young Businessman's chubby face then appeared. I pretended not to have been startled. "I tried to find you upstairs. Your mom wouldn't give you up."

"You know what a Judas Chair is?"

His suit conformed to his portly body as if custom made, although the knot of his tie was still loose.

"A what?"

"It's a pyramid-shaped seat. You're lowered onto it. Very painful. That's what it would've taken for my mom to give me up. So what do you want?"

"I'm looking for a guy named Rich Jones." I gave a description and said he worked as a parking officer but that I saw him hanging out with the guy who delivered the package to Konigson's office. "And what the hell is your name?"

He now stared through the lobby as if he hadn't heard me. "Yeah, I know him. He's a pathetic son of a bitch."

"How do you know him?"

"He writes parking tickets. And sometimes he's a driver for Konigson, like a private chauffeur." He gave me a goofy grin.

"I got a feeling there's a lot you're not telling me."

He leaned back a bit and pretended to size me up. "You asked me my name? How about I ask who the hell you are and why I should tell you anything?"

"I'm a private investigator." I gave him my card. "A few weeks ago a parking officer was murdered near his home. I want to find out why."

He stared at the card, said my name, and gave me a smug look. "There are really people who still do this detective stuff? I mean, I know about finding birth parents and cheating husbands, but murder? What kind of money you making?"

"You ask that question as if really expecting an answer. As if you don't expect me to say 'none of your fucking business.'" I took out a roll of cash from my pocket and peeled off two fifties. "I'll tell you what. You give me some useful information, starting with your name, and I'll give you a hundred bucks."

"Jerry," he said and laughed loudly. "That's awesome! You guys really do that? Money talks, right? I mean, it's the norm in city business—"

"That's right, Jerry. It's just business. Everything is just business. Now tell me what you know about Jones."

"Like I said, he's Konigson's chauffeur." Again with the goofy grin. "But only on special occasions when he went out to party with his bitches."

"What do you mean?"

"You know how these fat cats get young babes to fuck them in exchange for buying them whatever they want? That's just the way it is. That's what I'm gonna do someday. Why not?"

"Terrific. So Jones used to drive him on dates but then he stopped?"

"Yeah, I guess he started messing up." Jerry began sniffing the air. "You know what I mean?" He sniffed more. "Get it?"

"Cocaine?"

"Oh, yeah, big time. Jones started moving blow around the city for some gangs but got caught dipping into the inventory. Usually, you're a dead man when that happens. Konigson's got a soft spot. Word is, he bought Jones some time."

"What's he doing at Vector Solutions?"

"I don't really know. He still writes tickets, when they can get him out there. I don't think they know what to do with him."

"What about the guy who carried the package into Konigson's office?"

"He's a Revenue hack. A real crony. Probably mobbed up. I always see Jones with him. Sometimes Jones is in his parking uniform."

"Where's the parking office?"

"In city hall. In the basement somewhere. Too many threats to have the meter maids out in the open when they're just hanging out."

With that tidbit, I peeled off another fifty and handed over three bills. Jerry shoved them into his pocket and said, "It was a pleasure doing business."

Frownie told me the best investigators are the ones who know how to make friends. You never knew who might turn out to be a valuable resource.

33

Before heading into the bowels of city hall, I stared at one of the domed ceilings of colorful frescoes depicting allegorical backdrops of seed sowing and abundant harvests and thought how much more efficient society had become by planting money instead of waiting for rewards to sprout from seeds.

The only signs of visible life in the basement came from the opened doors of various storage rooms where archivists spent their days managing one hundred and fifty years of documents. Compared to the breezy foyers above ground, the silence of the marble and terra-cotta halls reminded me of a mausoleum.

I knocked on one of the open doors and said, "Hello?" From behind a portable shelving unit, up popped a balding, skinny head with half-frame reading glasses on the end of his nose. His face looked washed out under the fluorescent light, as if he hadn't seen daylight in months.

"Yes?" he said, surprised to see me.

"I was told the parking office was down here somewhere. Is that true?"

The man laughed, stood up, dusted off his knees, and smiled as if genuinely happy to talk to me. "Parking, huh?" He laughed again. "Well, I wouldn't be surprised."

"Why do you say that?"

"I don't know. Seems like all kinds of people come through these halls and disappear somewhere. Mayors, aldermen, dignitaries, police chiefs, prisoners in orange jumpsuits. Why not ticket writers?"

I took out my cell phone. "You ever see either of these guys down here?" I showed him the picture of Package Man and Jones.

"Yeah. Usually together."

"Where do they go?"

"No idea. I just see them walk past the door or I pass them in the hall."

I looked down the hallway toward the elevator. "I'm curious. Do you remember if they're always walking in the same direction?"

He pondered my question. "Can't say for sure, but I think they always come from the same direction as you."

"What's in the sub-basement?"

"As far as I know, just doors that open up to the old coal tunnels that run all throughout downtown. You want to leave a message if I see those guys again?"

"No, thanks." I gave the man my card. "If you happen to notice which door they disappear through, give me a call. You'll be rewarded for your services."

The man took the card, then nodded and smiled as if paid a great compliment.

I got the feeling Jones and friend entered the building through the lobby, took the elevator down, opened a locked door to a secret office, and then exited the building at an unofficial location. Outside, I checked the perimeter of the gargantuan building. The solid granite exterior revealed no phony walls leading to secret passageways or planters disguising stairwells to subterranean hideouts.

Back inside, I strolled the lobby with the nagging thought that, somehow, the glittering ostentation represented ground zero for tragedy. While leaning against the marble wainscoting under portraits of three jailed aldermen, I thought of billionaire buddies Konigson and Elon, so seamlessly woven into the fabric of big-city politics that crony capitalism had become a part of their genetic makeup and blurring the line between public and private money occurred without forethought.

I wondered if after decades of success, they couldn't help but buy into their own mythology that their actions had no consequence not easily handled. Someone screwed up. An immigrant parking officer dead. Konigson panicked, aggravated the mistake by calling the city editor of the *Republic,* demanded an otherwise innocuous murder story—in a city brimming with murders—spiked.

"Sir?" Three police officers stared at me keeping a five-foot cushion.

"Careful. With my back against the wall I got nothing to lose—"

"Sir, do you have some business here?"

"I'm waiting for someone."

"Probably better if you wait outside."

"I'd rather wait inside."

"We think it's better if you wait outside." They stepped forward.

"I'm a public citizen waiting in a public building."

"You're a public citizen loitering in a public building."

The officer handed me a card with Chicago Municipal Code 8-4-015. I read aloud, "'Remaining in any one place under circumstances that would warrant a reasonable person to believe that the

207

purpose or effect of that behavior is to enable a criminal street gang to establish control over identifiable areas, to intimidate others from entering those areas, or to conceal illegal activities.'"

"You think I'm enabling a criminal street gang?"

"We think you're loitering."

"You mean loitering as defined in a post-9/11 world."

"Are you going to cooperate?"

"You think I'm intimidating others from entering the building or do you think I'm concealing illegal activities?"

"We don't know what you're doing here, which is why you are going to leave." Another step forward.

"Oh, that's right. The ordinance refers to how a reasonable person would think, not police officers."

"I'm going to ask you one more time—"

"Actually, I could use some fresh air." I stepped away from the wall, and they escorted me through the lobby inside a human triangle. I had never felt so safe.

34

Loitering once again, this time across the street near the Picasso sculpture, I watched for any sign of Jones or some indication of the parking office, but after forty minutes, the only evidence I saw confirmed my previous observation of an overfed populace.

An unmarked gray Econoline van pulled up to the bus stop on Washington Street in front of the subway entrance. The sliding door opened and three city parking officers climbed out. From the way they smiled and joked with each other, I surmised their shift had ended. As they approached the stairwell, I hurried over and followed them down to the platform, where they walked behind the crowd waiting for the Blue Line's appearance, then down a short flight of steps to track level. When one of them reached for a door handle, all but invisible to the uninitiated, I sprinted to catch up but arrived as the door slammed shut. I cursed loudly, grabbed the door handle intending to pull it out of the wall, but almost smashed myself in the face when it flew open with ease. Light from a brightly lit hallway now greeted me. After my pupils adjusted, I stared down the corridor and replayed the previous few minutes to confirm I wasn't hallucinating.

A young Latina officer appeared from behind, smiling broadly. "Excuse me," she said. I held the door open and watched her enter.

I said, "Is the parking office down here?"

"Follow me."

She walked ahead of me at a fast clip, glancing behind occasionally to say, "Still with me?" The hallway turned left at a ninety-degree angle and continued for at least a hundred yards where another door awaited. Along this route, we passed several other doors with the words "Coal Tunnel" painted on them. The final entrance opened into an L-shaped room full of parking officers, some in street clothes looking as if getting ready to go home, others in uniform ready to start their shifts.

"This is the back way in," the woman said. "Over there is the front door."

"Where the hell are we?"

"City hall basement."

"And what's with the van?"

"The vans drop us off at our various districts and then pick us up again."

"Do you have a supervisor down here?"

The girl directed me around the corner to an office defined by two half walls of glass. Sitting at a desk I saw the package courier and the back of a man he spoke to. On the door was the name Dave Robertson. Robertson's face told me he wasn't happy. When his eye caught mine, the other man turned. At first, I didn't recognize Jones's sickly pale face, but he recognized me and bolted out of Robertson's office.

I caught up with him just as he opened the door to the city hall corridor and grabbed the back of his shirt collar. He spun around and shoved me hard in the chest, knocking me to the hallway floor and then sat on top of me.

"What's the matter with you!" he shouted. "You want to get me killed?"

Jones's thumbs dug into my neck, pushing on my windpipe. The pain and vulnerability of this position was a new experience, as was the associated panic. I managed to turn my head enough to relieve some pressure, but he had my arms pinned down with his knees, and I soon felt the full force of his hands around my throat. The butt of my .40-caliber was wedged against his thigh. In a futile attempt to make some noise, I kicked the ground. Then Jones flew backward across the floor, scrambled to his feet, and sprinted down the hall.

I lay panting, looking up at Robertson's extended hand.

"I think I know you," he said as he pulled me up. "You got some bad blood with Jones?"

I coughed a few times. "Water," I croaked, wondering if there were any more packages around full of cash.

Robertson led me back to his office and poured a glass of water. "On the elevator," Robertson said nodding. "I remember the shiner."

We sat in silence as I caught my breath between sips. I took one of his business cards off his desk and left one of my own. I said, "You're not wondering what I'm doing here?"

"Got a parking question?" Robertson burst into hysterical laughter, just as he had on the elevator.

"What's so funny?"

"I don't know." Robertson shrugged. "I should've asked you why Jones was choking you to death."

"He would have killed me?"

"Probably. Guys all messed up on drugs do that kind of stuff."

"Cocaine, I assume?"

"Yep. So how can I help you? Got a parking ticket?" More laughter.

"Why is the parking office hidden away like this?" I asked.

"Who's hiding? You're here. It's a public building. The front door is always open. Anyone can come down here if they want."

"If they figure out where the hell it is. Has Jones killed before?"

"Before when?" Slightly nervous laughter.

"You sure are a happy boy. Department of Revenue lots of laughs?"

"They take care of me. All I gotta do is sit in this office all day, watch over the crew, and let the public bitch at me on the phone. Not much to it, really."

"Why is a guy all messed up on drugs working here?"

"Rich wasn't always like that. We're trying to help him, give him a chance to straighten out.

212

That's hard to do if we just kick his ass into the street."

"From the look of him, he's been introduced to the crack pipe. You think he can survive your straightening-out program?"

Robertson frowned as if I had insulted him. "You got a funny way of thanking me for dragging him off you."

"I was thinking you owed me an apology, for this dangerous animal you created."

"Rich's problems ain't my fault."

"What're you doing for his wife and kids?"

Robertson shook his head. "He don't got no wife and kids. These guys say anything to get pity."

"You think he killed the parking officer in Budlong Woods?"

"Killed Jack Gelashvili? Nah. They got along fine. Everyone got along with Jack."

"Don't you want to know what I was doing at Vector Solutions?"

Robertson shrugged. "What do I care what you're doing? Ain't none of my business."

"What do you think of that private company—Windy City Meters—writing tickets?"

"There's plenty of scofflaws to go around. Windy City does their thing; we do ours."

"You guys don't work together?"

"We got nothing to do with them. They're private; we're public." Robertson stifled a laugh on the word "public."

"I saw that well-executed maneuver by the armored car before you delivered the package to Konigson's office."

"Yeah, I'm good at that."

"What do you know about Konigson?"

"Big bucks. Powerful. Knows a lot of people."

"He's tight with the Revenue boss, Elon. Your boss, right?"

"That's what I hear."

"How much cash was in that package?"

"Who said cash was in the package?"

This time I laughed. "What do you think was in it?"

"I couldn't even guess, Detective Landau." Robertson leaned back in his chair and rested his feet on top of the desk.

"Private investigator. Jones told you I'm investigating Jack's death."

"You got it. I was kind of expecting you."

"Who do you think killed Jack?"

"I got no proof. Only hunches."

"You want to share a hunch?"

"Why should I?"

"Because you're a nice guy."

Robertson laughed. "Says who?"

"Were you shocked by his death?"

"Sure I was. He was a good man. But what do I know? He kept to himself—you know what I mean?"

I knew, but what did Dave Robertson know? "The cops' prime suspect, Gordon Baxter, got a lot of parking tickets. Is that why he hated parking officers?"

"Wouldn't you?"

"Getting towed would piss me off."

"Pay your tickets and you won't get towed. That's all we ever ask."

"You think he got pissed off enough to kill Jack?"

"That's what the cops think."

"Why did your office tow him so often?"

Robertson gave me an odd look. "Because he didn't pay his tickets! I just said that."

"Whose tickets did he not pay?"

Robertson straightened up in his chair. "What do you mean?"

"Baxter's tickets were written by Windy City parking enforcement aides, who work for the private company you guys have nothing to do with.

215

And how do you think he got parking tickets all over the North Side while his odometer stayed put?"

Robertson drummed his fingers on the desk. "Maybe it's broke."

"Nope. Checked out fine." He didn't challenge my lie.

"Here's the thing, investigator. You assume just 'cause I work for Revenue, I know something. You know damn well the city's a big machine. I'm just a little part. I need oil just like all the other parts. So when the boss tells me we're gonna tow this car, we tow the car. I don't ask why the city's towing for a private company, I just do it. If I start asking questions, I don't get no more oil. And when I break down, they'll replace me. Where's a guy like me gonna get a job that pays this well?"

"Here's the thing, Robertson. Two innocent men are dead. One murdered, the other a phony suicide. If you have information you're hiding, then you're an accessory—"

"I got nothing to hide! Why do you think I'm talking to you? You asked me if I think Jones killed Jack and I said no. I never saw the package opened, so how do I know what's in it?"

"How about an envelope? Ever deliver envelopes full of cash?"

Robertson didn't like that question. "What do you mean?"

"I mean, I know a cop who said you gave him an envelope full of cash to forget to keep an eye on a prime murder suspect named Gordon Baxter."

"Bullshit! Any cop-snitch knows the guys upstairs would put the hurt on 'em."

"The thing is, the more parts in a machine, the more likely it is to break down. It's not realistic to expect all the parts to work properly all the time. Sometimes they start squeaking and break. Especially if they're about to retire."

Robertson stood up and walked to one of the glass walls. "What do you want to do, investigator? Take down the city?"

"Give me your opinion. How's that sound? Elon had you deliver Department of Revenue cash to a cop so that Gordon Baxter could be properly framed for murder. The question is: why would the Department of Revenue boss, Elon, want an immigrant parking officer dead?"

Robertson leaned against the glass and stared straight ahead while whistling. Then he said, "It just don't make sense—Elon wanting Jack dead. What does he give a damn about parking officers? As long as they bring in revenue, he's happy. It must've happened on someone else's orders. That's the only thing I can think of."

"And a guy as powerful as Elon takes orders from who?"

"Jones told me he thought Jack had a connection to the Russian mob," Robertson said.

"Jones told me he made that rumor up because it pissed him off that Jack and the other immigrant officers worked cheap. He said if he didn't recruit immigrants, he would get fired. He thinks your bosses believed the rumor and tried to use him to get in good with the Russians. But Jack found out too much and they killed him."

Robertson howled in disbelief. "You gotta be kidding! What a whacko. Sure, maybe we was trying to get immigrants to work cheap, but that had nothing to do with Jones. But I'm not so sure he wasn't telling the truth about Jack and the Russkies. He has some personal experience with them boys."

"Explain, please."

"Jones started working for them—"

"Moving cocaine until he started snorting the goods. But what about Jack?"

"One time I said I didn't think a guy like Jack could be involved with mobsters. So Jones gives me a picture of Jack with some fat baker. Jones says the bakery is mobbed up and the fat guy smuggles in illegal workers. I show the picture to someone else and he tells me not to worry about it—to just forget about it."

"You still got the picture?"

Robertson rummaged through the top drawer of his desk until he found the photo and handed it over. In the photo Tamar's boss stood in a rather defiant posture, hands on hips, scowling at the photographer. I wondered if the camera lens had shattered. Next to him stood the profile of someone who looked like Jack, apparently talking to the baker.

I said, "How do you know this guy is Russian mob?"

"Because my sources say so."

Robertson said I could keep the picture. Maybe the fat baker paid protection money, but human smuggling? Robertson reminded me that his sources knew of what they spoke. I wondered what Tamar could tell me about her boss.

35

On the Brown Line heading back to my office, I tried to imagine the city, the mob, and the Republic Media Group conspiring to murder a parking officer. Too many big fish demanding too much in return for silence. Too many irresistible blackmailing opportunities.

Absorbed in thought as I ascended the third flight to my office, I almost didn't notice Izzy leaning against the wall in his customary pose, arms folded tightly against his chest.

"You are deep in reflection," Izzy said as I opened the door. "I see this as a good sign."

I pretended to ignore him as I entered and sat behind my desk. Izzy remained on the landing. "How long have you been waiting?" I said, not looking up.

"Long enough," Izzy said strolling in, hands engulfed by pockets. He took the guest chair. "Point is, I'm here, after all—and so are you."

"As usual, well said."

"You have much to tell me, I'm sure, and I refer not only to your black eye."

I recapped the days since we last spoke. Izzy appeared to listen intently while leaning forward, elbows on knees, chin resting in hands. When I stopped talking, he remained in that position several moments longer. "Damn it!" I said. "Are you even listening?"

"I have something I want to show you." Izzy took some folded sheets of paper from his back pocket, unfolded them and put them on the desk. "This will be published in tomorrow's *Partisan*."

Reluctantly, I reached for the pages. My stomach clenched as I saw an Ellis Knight byline with the title "When Gordon Baxter Went Off His Meds."

As he did with my first murder case, Knight stretched the definition of journalism to include an omniscient narrator revealing the motivations of all involved, interspersing his fictional thoughts with rhetorical questions.

"Picture Farragut Avenue on the last day of Gordon Baxter's life, where he sits on the bed in his basement studio apartment located in a four-story brick cube as ordinary as Baxter's life is pointless, balancing his daily pill dispenser on his thigh, calmly deciding how many of the taupe-colored pills he will swallow, little round tablets he assumes are the same meds that for most of his life have tamed the electrical forces crashing through his brain like a constant procession of suicide bombers. Picture Gordon Baxter, *sans* meds, a terrorist. . . ."

Knight's rambling narrative of facts affixed to conjecture and assumptions first told the story of an immigrant's life tragically colliding with a schizophrenic who periodically stopped taking his medication. The story appeared sympathetic to the official conclusion until Knight's sudden ghetto slang about-face. ". . . But let's break it down and quit buggin', dig a little deeper, see there's nothing but a busta-crew who don't give a damn. . . ."

While I read, Izzy rose from his chair, stood next to my desk, hands back in pockets, waiting for my reaction.

I said, "You've been feeding Knight information?"

Izzy shrugged. "So what of it?"

"Because you don't show the world what cards you're holding! Because then perpetrators cover their tracks!—wait a second. How the hell do you know Knight?"

"That you did not figure this out right away I find astonishing. At our first meeting I said the article in *The Partisan* had made me aware of your talents. Then a mangled corpse the authorities don't care about shows up in my backyard. Who else

221

would I trust to feel my outrage but the journalist who wrote that article?"

"Knight put you up to this. You're paying me with his—"

"Knight put me up to nothing! We are partners in a common goal. The money is irrelevant and none of your business."

I had trouble seeing two strange personalities like Knight and Izzy cooperating, regardless of the circumstances. "Knight gets his article, I get paid to solve another murder. Tell me again what's in it for you?"

"How many times must I say this? Nothing is *in it* except to know why a man is dead, although now I can confirm that corporations and city machine politics have life-and-death control over us. That a man who knows too much is much feared and often dies prematurely."

Izzy waited for a response. To escape his scrutinizing stare, I closed my eyes and massaged my eyebrows with the tips of my fingers while praying Izzy would leave. When I opened them again, there he stood, gazing at me with an expression of intense curiosity.

"Are we done?" I said.

He remained looking at me several more seconds before taking something from his breast pocket. "Here," he said handing me an envelope.

"What's this?"

"Twenty-five hundred," he said. "A balance of twenty-five hundred remains." Without another word, Izzy walked out.

36

The key had barely touched the lock when the door pushed open to reveal the wreckage of what had been my couch, coffee table, bookcases, and contents of the kitchen cabinets and drawers. My bedroom had suffered the same fate, with the addition of dried blood smeared across the floor.

I called Punim's name repeatedly while piling up the pieces and tried to prepare myself for her body when I turned over the larger chunks of debris. After the dread had welled up through my abdomen and stuck in my throat, I sat on the floor and leaned back against the wall opposite my opened door. It was times like these when one appreciated friends. I thought of calling Tamar, but fear of sounding vulnerable to a woman I had just slept with stopped me.

I shouted for Punim a few more times and then thought of what Tamar had said three nights ago while cooking dinner: how I was alone, without family, without blood relations. Two nights ago she had described feeling so alone just standing next to me and said that I exuded loneliness. I wondered if Frownie sensed a pathetic lonesomeness or even thought of me as forsaken somehow. I wanted to ask him, and it hit me hard that I would never ask him anything again. Tears spilled out of my eyes. Punim, my roommate, my house companion, was missing. Just ten pounds covered in cottony fur, a living, breathing being who acknowledged my existence, if only by her choice to stay with me, had met with violence of an unknown nature. Why? Because my cash was in a safe deposit box instead of a shoebox? Because destroying my apartment wasn't enough? Then the sobbing began, slow at first but gradually engulfing me in loud, heaving convulsions, turning me into someone I had never met. Who was this boy sitting on the floor, alone, feeling as if the world had deserted him?

A black-and-white cat sat calmly watching me from the space between the wall and the edge of the opened front door. Instantly, my grief subsided. I crawled toward her and she allowed me to pick her up and run my hands over her body. I found no signs of trauma nor did she react as if injured, although I did notice the white tips of her paws were stained pink and a crusty substance resembling dried blood stuck to her claws. I put her down and watched as she began meticulously cleaning herself. My furry friend had made sure the perpetrator had not escaped unscathed and, perhaps, had even been scarred for life.

"You don't sound too good," Kalijero said. "Rough night?"

Lying on my back, staring at the ceiling from the futon mattress, I let the phone rest against my ear. I was not accustomed to morning sunlight, but the blinds had been included in the mischief, so there it was. "You could say that."

"You mind if I stop by? I got some things to show you."

224

"I'd absolutely love to see you, Jimmy. Seriously. I really, really, want to see you. Bring bagels."

No response, then, "Are you fucking with me? Landau, want me to come over or not?"

"Yes! But bring some fucking bagels." I hung up and wondered why I had just acted like a prick. Kalijero was a good guy. We were friends—sort of. An hour later, holding a brown bag and leather briefcase, he stared in disbelief from the doorway.

"What the hell happened?"

"I'd offer you a seat, but I don't have one."

We stood at the kitchen island and ate while I filled him in on yesterday's events.

"This looks like someone in a rage," Kalijero said wiping away a schmear of cream cheese. "The parking officer with the drug problem. He's the one I'd keep an eye on."

Kalijero opened his briefcase and took out some papers. "Frownie had a will. He left everything he owned to various labor unions. Except one item. This is yours."

Kalijero handed me a picture of Frownie's most prized possession, a 1933 Cadillac V-16 once owned by the king of Denmark. I stared at the photo unable to comprehend that I would own this vehicle.

"What am I going to do with it? This is a rich man's hobby."

Kalijero started laughing. "Sell it, dumb ass! You don't think he expected you to drive the damn thing?"

I said, "The day Frownie died, I was snooping around his place. I found a photo album. There's a kid, a dead ringer for a young Jimmy Kalijero. Frownie's got his arm around his shoulders."

"So what?" Kalijero stopped chewing. "What do you care? I'm not in his damn will. That tells you something, doesn't it?"

"What's with the secrets?"

"Just because you don't know about something doesn't mean it's a secret." Kalijero closed his eyes a few moments then opened them. "I told you some already. About when Frownie begged me to let your father plea for a shorter prison sentence. I said I didn't realize how close he had been with your family. That's a lie. I knew."

I waited for more. "And?"

"When I was a kid in the fifties, Frownie was like an activist type. He always was trying to help working people, especially immigrants. Everyone loved him. That's how he got to be so good at his job, because he had so many friends. Lots of those people became contacts for his detective work, including your grandfather over on the West Side. Us kids loved listening to Frownie's stories about gangsters and pool halls full of hoodlums. After my dad died in a car wreck, he took a special interest in me. Kept an eye on me, made sure I didn't skip school. He became close to my mom, even though she barely spoke English and Frownie sure as hell didn't speak Greek." Kalijero, laughing, shook his head. "He tried to learn a few simple sentences but always got so tongue-tied and pissed off that he'd start cussing."

"This is all very scandalous. I can see why you didn't want me to know about it."

"I'm not done, smart ass. Word got out about plans to build the interstate through our neighborhood. We all knew this meant the end of Greek Town. A hundred years of history bulldozed under. Frownie organized against it. He used every contact he knew, trying to find out who to beg or bribe or make some kind of deal with. But this was the Feds we're talking about. Even though I was only about seventeen, I knew it was hopeless. And that pissed him off."

"He didn't like your attitude."

"Yeah, especially so readily taking the compensation money. He wanted me to at least fight first. He stopped talking to me for a while. Then he told me how disappointed he was. Gradually he warmed up again. A few years later, I disappointed him again when I went to the police academy. He had his heart set on me going to college. I had already been in uniform a couple of years before we started talking again. We kind of developed a more professional relationship. I gave him tips if I heard something at headquarters; he'd use his contacts for me if I asked. When I made detective, he congratulated me and I think he might have even meant it. When I started working vice,

Frownie was pretty much retired, but he heard about a gambling sting I was conducting. When it all went down and he found out it was your father, he came to me. When I refused to go light with the charges, that was the last straw. Glad you asked?"

"Sure, why not? I'm always glad to learn something new. I got something to show you." I walked to my bedroom and returned with the photo of Tamar's boss and Jack Gelashvili. "You know anything about this guy?"

Kalijero looked at the photo and frowned. "Where'd you get this?"

"Who cares? Just tell me if he's someone I should know."

Kalijero scratched his head. He looked tentative. "He's pissed off a lot of the community because he feeds the bums and lets them sleep it off in the bakery. More and more bums are coming to the neighborhood because of him, they say."

I waited for more. "He feeds the poor? That's all you know?"

"I didn't say that's all I know! But we don't have anything concrete on him. He's one of those characters—it doesn't matter. He's known to us, but that's as much as I can say right now."

"I'm starting to think the Russian mob might have been involved in Gelashvili's murder. So does his former boss at parking. No real evidence yet, just a story."

"Well, if you do get evidence, don't pursue it. You'll end up as dead as Gelashvili. Now I got something to show you."

From his briefcase he took out two enlarged photos of a rectangular copper or bronze object. Embossed on one side was a bearded man with a crown. On the other side, the king's sunken image along with three ornate characters of an exotic alphabet etched into a corner.

I said, "You want to tell me what I'm looking at?"

"Help me figure it out."

"Where did you get it?"

"For now, it's better you don't know."

"Did you check with one of the *eighty* universities in Chicago?"

"I did."

"So what do you want from me?"

"I want you to show it to that girl, Gelashvili's cousin. It's a way of confirming what we suspect."

"Holy shit, Jimmy! Just tell me what you suspect! Is it relevant to Gelashvili being dead? I've got kindling for furniture. I'm not in the mood for games."

"I've been pretty damn straight with you, Jules. In fact, I've gone out of my way to be a good guy when I sure as hell don't have to be. So why don't you pretend I have more experience in these matters than you? Why don't you pretend I've been doing police work for over thirty-five years?"

Kalijero was great at reminding me that he was in charge and would always be in charge if we worked together. It still didn't make sense for him not to tell me what he suspected. But it also didn't matter.

37

On the phone at the bakery, Tamar sounded tired but glad I called. "I didn't hear from you yesterday," she said. "I wasn't sure if something was wrong."

It was true we had not spoken since I dropped her off at the bakery the morning after we had sex— a potential mixed signal if there ever was one. I apologized for not calling and told a brief story of yesterday's adventures at city hall. I did not mention the sacking of my apartment. She suggested I stop by after the late-morning rush.

After I filled several garbage bags with wood scraps and stacked the larger pieces along the wall, I set out to a Salvation Army thrift store down the street where, in fifteen minutes, I had picked out suitable replacements, paid for with cash. Then I left five C-notes with a carpenter-locksmith guy I trusted to repair my door and install a dead-bolt. I enjoyed sharing the wealth.

I loaded the Civic with the refuse and drove to a West Side wood recycler before doubling back to the Kutaisi Georgian Bakery. Despite the absence of the double-parked white van, I recognized the heavyset Hispanic driver sitting at a table near the door, relaxing with coffee and a pastry. Maybe he figured out there's a loading zone in the alley. For the first time, I noticed a patch on the left breast of his jacket identical to the IIPD snake-eating bald eagle decal on the windshield.

Tamar greeted me with a warm hug and led me to a table with two pastries. The booths were empty except for Boris stoically smoking a cigarette, flicking the ashes in a coffee cup. Three hammered guys at the drunk table, one snoring loudly. "Why does your boss put up with that?" I said.

Tamar seemed not to know what I meant. Then she said, "My boss is very compassionate. He understands hard times."

"What about that guy? Is he supposed to be smoking in here?"

Tamar frowned. "No!" she said then stood up, walked to Boris, and said something. Boris initially had no reaction other than to drop the butt into the coffee cup without even acknowledging her presence. After Tamar turned to walk away, Boris said something out loud in what I assumed was Russian. Tamar stopped momentarily, but didn't turn around. Then she continued walking back to our table and sat. She didn't say anything, just stared straight ahead looking troubled.

"Are you okay?" I said. Tamar nodded. "What did he say to you?"

"Doesn't matter," she said quietly.

I tried to lighten things up a little. "I'm gonna get fat if you keep pushing these tarts or turnovers or popovers or whatever they are on me."

"Pakhlava," Tamar said, trying to sound cheerful. "And you could use a little fattening up. What's that?" Tamar pointed at the manila envelope I brought with me.

I handed her the photo of the kingly figure embossed in metal. "Do you know what this is?"

Tamar needed only a glance. "It's an ornament of King David IV. Georgians are known for their metal-working skills."

I handed her the photo of the flip side of the ornament. Her eyes bounced around the image until she focused on the inscription and brought the photo to within inches of her face. She mumbled a word I assumed was in her native Georgian.

"I'm guessing those are letters. Maybe somebody's initials?"

Tamar looked deadly serious. She turned to glance at Boris. "Where did you get this?"

"A cop gave it to me," I said. "He wants some kind of confirmation before he tells me anything more."

Tamar put the photo down. "You're right. Those are initials written in *Mkhedruli,* the Georgian alphabet. The letters are the equivalent to the English B, D, and G. King David's likeness is common on these metal ornamentations. One carves their initials so it won't get mixed up with someone else's ornament. That's what my cousin Bagrat Dogonadze Gelashvili did."

I said, "This is more evidence that the bracelet with Baxter's phony suicide note was planted. This ornament was found somewhere else—or on someone else. It's time to find out."

Tamar slouched in her chair and stared at the table. Her eyes filled, but she wiped them with the back of her hand before a single tear managed to spill out. I moved my chair closer and put my arm around her. She leaned into me and said something in Russian. "That means, *It was over quickly, they say. He didn't suffer. Be thankful.* That's what the gangster-asshole said to me."

Kalijero picked up on the first ring. "Well?"

"It's an ornament of a Georgian king. Where did you get it?"

"Meet me at Area B in an hour," Kalijero said. I agreed and we hung up at the same time.

Tamar stared at the photo of Jack's initials as if in a trance until she looked at me and said, "You didn't tell him it belonged to Jack."

"I got a meeting right now at police headquarters. But first there's something else I want to talk to you about." I took out the photo of the baker and Jack. "This is your boss, right?"

Tamar looked at the photo and back to me. "What's this all about?"

233

"There are people who suspect this man might be connected to the Russian mob. Some even think he runs a human smuggling operation."

Tamar handed the photo back to me. The look in her eye told me she wasn't happy. "And do you think my uncle Gigi is a criminal?"

The word "uncle" hung in the air over Tamar's head. For a moment I pictured death rays shooting out of her eyes. "You heard what that gangster just said! He's implying he knows something, maybe even *participated*."

"That doesn't mean *Gigi* is involved!"

"Then why does he let these scumbags hang out in his bakery?"

Tamar looked horrified, but I couldn't say from what. "Because, because, he has no choice! They're *gangsters,* they don't give you a choice, and Gigi goes along. He has to! You don't think Gigi had anything to do with Jack's murder, you can't!"

The proverbial can of worms covered me. "I don't know what to think. Everyone knows I'm not buying the murder-suicide story. Maybe they're throwing in your uncle to perpetuate the phony mafia theme."

"Let me guess. You want me to spy on the most generous man who ever lived. A man who made sure I had a job and that most of the people who've made this bakery a huge success had jobs."

Her anger was palpable. "I'm not asking you to spy. But if you notice something that might seem weird—"

"Weird? Like what? Crates overflowing with rifles and grenades or bags of white powder lying around the warehouse? Or how about my uncle sitting around with a bunch of guys named Khaber or Sergi or Zakhar performing ancient initiation rites and guzzling vodka while playing Russian roulette?"

"You're overreacting—"

"Am I? If this bakery were run by white Americans, would you be taking this photo seriously? Or does the word 'smuggling' cause your brain to create the image of a scheming Central Asian connected to an international arms or drug dealer?"

"You're calling me a racist? You really think—"

"Just get away from me!" Tamar stood, knocking the chair over. "Get out of our bakery. Just leave. Leave me alone!"

She stormed away and disappeared into the prep room. I left the bakery with a knot in my stomach. I knew what kind of pain it was, but I had to focus on the latest developments. On my way to Area B, I wondered if I was as insensitive as Tamar suggested.

38

The Area B district station was a textbook description of bleak in an otherwise eccentric neighborhood of restored bungalows and rehabbed frame houses. I sat on a wood bench outside the detectives' room and admired framed photos of the smiling mayor and glowering police chief. Against the wall were two vending machines: one for soda, another for yummy sandwiches wrapped in plastic. A bulletin board announced various K-9 and Mounted Units fund-raising events and encouraged participation in the "Area B Memorial Ten-Kilometer Run." There was also a congratulatory letter from the assistant superintendent for Area B's participation in the West Side Greek Parade.

Kalijero stuck his head out the door and motioned for me to enter. The room was filled with 1960s steel desks and a smattering of detectives talking on the phone or dealing with paperwork. I followed Kalijero to his desk, where he directed me to a metal folding chair.

"You want a career investigating murders, right?"

"Talk to me like I'm a grown-up, Jimmy."

"I'm just saying, if this is what you want. You ever see a body after it's been in water awhile?" Kalijero opened the center drawer and slid to me a photo of a woman's bloated, wrinkled corpse.

"Awesome. Thanks for this." I looked at it closely, as if an obvious clue could be found on the face of a gray-skinned cadaver. "You want to tell me who she is?"

"We think she's Russian. Maybe a prostitute."

Kalijero's words caromed sharply off my chest. I could tell he was studying my reaction. "Anything else?" I said.

"That piece of metal with the king? Found in her pocket."

Almost involuntarily, I took a lungful of air and let it out while remembering my first conversation with Tamar, when she told me about Jack's Russian girlfriend, Lada Soboroff.

"She matched the description of a missing persons report. The scorpion tattoo on her left shoulder should clinch it. I'm meeting her sister, Marta Soboroff, at the morgue to identify the body."

I flashed back three days to the lobby of my office and the woman with the exotic good looks speaking in a Slavic accent. King David IV was shouting the obvious conclusion. But what did Jack Gelashvili's falling in love with a prostitute have to do with Jack Gelashvili's murder? I kept Jack's connection to myself but asked if I could join the identification.

"You can watch from a distance. I don't want you talking to the sister until I'm through with her. Got it?"

A twenty-four percent obesity rate, heat waves, gang warfare, New Year's die-offs. Those were just some of the factors contributing to a backlog of

237

bodies that occasionally forced the Office of the Cook County Medical Examiner to double up on trays. Fortunately, late October was still the offseason.

Kalijero's decades of investigating murders gave me instant credibility as I moved through the building with only a "visitor" card clipped to a belt loop. Once inside the medical examiner's office, we walked toward an autopsy table where a sheeted body lay. Kalijero ordered me to stay back about ten feet and keep quiet. A few minutes later, a doctor entered, along with a victim's advocate and the sister I recognized as the woman I'd seen at my office. Our eyes met for a moment when she passed.

The doctor asked the sister if she was ready. The woman clutched her escort's arm with one hand and held a handkerchief to her mouth with the other. I heard the zipping sound and then saw the woman's legs buckle. Anticipating the reaction, the advocate quickly positioned herself to catch the sister under the arms and guide her to the floor where she sobbed for several minutes before being helped back to her feet and led to a grieving area.

Kalijero whispered something to the doctor and then motioned for me to follow him out of the room. Neither of us spoke until we had exited the building.

"Thirty-five years and it still gets to me."

"What can they say about the death?"

"Signs of torture with fire or acid. No water in her lungs. They're thinking her body was dumped in the river three or four weeks ago. The cool weather helped preserve her."

"What can you tell me about the sister?"

"All I know is that her name is Marta Soboroff. That ornament thing with the king? Worth any money? I mean why would she steal a worthless piece of metal from a client? Or is it some custom over there to give whores gifts?"

"When can I talk to the sister?"

"Go home, Landau. I need to spend some time with her first."

Kalijero made a move back to the entrance. I said, "She better not disappear in some kind of witness protection bullshit."

"What's that supposed to mean?"

"A dead Russian prostitute. Imagine all the possible roads where that could lead."

39

Rubber weather-stripping on the bottom of the door pushed an envelope full of coupons across the floor. I breathed in the stuffy air, glanced fondly at the yellow legal pad on my desk, and sat down to see what had become of my murder investigation.

Frownie had always warned me about making things more complicated than they really were. Never lose sight of the simple facts. Nothing about Jack's relationship with a Russian prostitute changed the fact that Konigson, the ruler of a vast media empire, called Palmer, the city editor for the

Republic, and ordered him to spike the story about Jack's murder. The distance between Konigson, Jack, and the prostitute was just more yellow space.

I left a message on Elaine Reilly's voice mail. Ten minutes later, she called back.

"Sorry, hon," Elaine said, "I was on another call. Tell me, did you catch Calvo with his pants down?"

"Yes, and Detective Calvo asked me to thank you for helping ensure his comfortable retirement. And I thank you as well."

"Glad to help. So what's up?"

"Are you aware of any Russian prostitution rings?"

Elaine hesitated. "Hey, you know, I'm gonna be in your neighborhood in an hour or so. Why don't we meet for lunch?" Her voice had always been light and playful, so the sudden awkwardness was impossible to ignore.

Upon entering Murphy's Red Hots on Belmont, a cloud of mustard, onions, sweet pickle relish, and smoky charbroiled beef engulfed me. Instantly, I was like a kid in the 1970s, sitting in the sanctuary of the left field bleachers of Wrigley Field, when tickets were barely a buck and never sold in advance of the day's game. Elaine's waving arm brought me back to the reality of corporate Jumbotron blasphemy.

"This is the best place to have a conversation like this," Elaine said loudly over the crowd noise, a hot dog with the works in front of her. "A little spyware in your cell phone and the Fourteenth Amendment is obliterated." She took a bite of her hot dog, careful to protect her blouse from falling condiments.

"A Russian prostitute was fished out of the river," I said. "Suddenly, she's central to my original murder investigation. Any thoughts?"

Elaine chewed a bit, then said, "My first thought is to recommend you find a new career. But you're not going to hear me, so I'll tell you that, as far as I'm concerned, any illegal activity operated by Russians is something to run from. If this dead girl was part of a Russian prostitution ring, you can be sure it functions without mercy and with lethal efficiency. There's no saying no to these guys. If you do, your replacement will be earning money before your body is found—assuming it's ever found."

"Aren't you afraid they'll try to push you out?"

Elaine shook her head while wiping her mouth. "It's a different market. My girls cater to the guys who can afford to blow a hundred bucks a couple of times a month. The Russkies minister to very wealthy clients. The kind that can drop a grand for a few hours of fun as if they were just buying one of these hot dogs. I'm running a business where the girls are going to make good money and don't have to worry about a psycho pimp. The Russkies run a slave factory."

"I was told this prostitute wore designer clothes and drove a Mercedes."

More chewing while nodding her head. "Sure she did; they all do. None of them own the cars or clothing, but they sure look good in them. And when the girls are all used up, they go back home wearing the same rags they arrived in."

"Someone who knew the dead woman told me she was going back to Russia until some immigration issues could be solved."

Elaine laughed. "There are no immigration issues with the kind of money these outfits have at their disposal. Money makes those kinds of problems disappear real fast."

"If you had to come up with the most probable scenario for this woman's murder, what would it be?"

Elaine considered the question. "She angered a client. But not your average multi-millionaire—someone who had enough power and influence to require the outfit to keep him happy. It's a simple business plan: the customer is always right."

"Just so rich men can have sex with pretty women."

"Sex is just one aspect of the business model. The Russkies have also got their hooks in fraud, money laundering, drug trafficking, murder for hire, extortion—it's all part of a big crime partnership."

Her words had a sobering effect. I longed for the days when it was only corporate and municipal corruption I had to consider.

"If you don't mind," Elaine said, "where in the world are you going with this?"

The concern in her eyes struck me. "The dead prostitute was also the girlfriend of the murder victim I'm investigating."

Elaine closed her eyes and rested her forehead on the heels of both hands. "Jules, these girls don't have boyfriends."

"Well, he wasn't paying for her company. Would they kill her for giving it away?"

"That doesn't make sense if she's a good earner. At most, rough her up a bit."

"Would they kill the boyfriend?"

"Hard to believe that would be necessary. They could just as easily scare the hell out of him."

"The woman disappeared about five weeks ago. Boyfriend murdered two to three weeks later. She didn't drown. Burn marks all over."

"They tortured out anything incriminating she may have said to the boyfriend, dumped her body, then killed the boyfriend."

"That's what I'm thinking."

Neither of us spoke until Elaine said, "Well, can you find a common denominator with the dead girl, the dead boyfriend, and a rich and powerful corporate executive?"

40

Walking back to the office, I thought of Palmer's focus on finding a financial motive for Jack's murder. It now seemed likely the murder had more to do with sex than money—if the two could be separated. Perhaps a man's reputation was on the line. The thought of blackmail caused panic among the powerful. Blackmail: the great equalizer of the classes.

Beethoven's Fifth broke in.

"She wants to talk to you," Kalijero said. "Marta Soboroff. She won't talk to me, but she'll talk to you."

"Really?"

"Really. Why do you think that is, Landau?"

"Have her come to my office—and I don't like your tone, Kalijero."

"You got something to tell me? You got some history with this Russian doll? How does she even know you?"

"Relax, she doesn't know me and I don't know her." Technically, that was true.

"Now listen to me, Landau. I'm working this murder case, so whatever she says you better tell me. Got it? She may need police protection."

"I'll tell you everything that's relevant to the dead woman. Now calm down, for chrissake. Remember you already got one foot in the grave—I mean retirement."

Small creaks from the stairway preceded Marta Soboroff's arrival until she appeared in my doorway looking beautiful in a jean jacket over a charcoal gray wrap dress, black stockings, black ankle boots, and a small black leather bag over her shoulder. Light brown hair framed blue eyes.

"Please come in," I said. She sat in the club chair and draped one leg over the other. I took a box of Kleenex out of my file drawer and placed it in front of her. I assumed her eyes were bloodshot from crying.

"I talk to you about my Lada."

"You were here three days ago."

She plucked out a few tissues and wiped her nose. "Yes, but I ran away. I not run anymore."

"Detective Kalijero said you wouldn't talk to him. Why?"

"I not trust police. Not anywhere."

"Why would you trust me?"

"You are investigating Gelashvili murder, yes?"

I nodded. "Jack was in love with Lada. Was he murdered because of the relationship?"

Soboroff's lower lip began to quiver as she struggled to keep it together. "Let me first tell my story and sister's story. You will listen?"

"Of course."

"I am ten years older than Lada. I was promised job as waitress or barmaid in America. They say they pay my way and I make good money so I can pay them back and start new life. When I arrive, they take passport and force me to be prostitute to pay debts. If I try to escape or find help, they say they harm my family." Marta Soboroff grabbed a few more tissues and dabbed her eyes.

I leaned forward over my desk and said, "You're done with that world. Please tell me it's behind you."

"Yes, I was lucky. We were guarded always except with customer. One day I went to customer who was educated young man. His friends sent him to lose virginity. He recognized my accent. He wanted to know why I did this. I told him my story. He left still virgin. He said he had contacts. Then someone paid my debt for freedom."

"Did you ever see this kid again or find out who paid?"

"Later, I suspected. I got job in laundry. Boring, hard work but happy to have it. People come and go. I don't pay attention. Then guy comes in—big scary bald man. Looks like cartoon person. He starts talking Russian. He's Georgian. He asks if I want to work at bakery. At first, I think not so great because of baker hours. He asks how much I make at laundry and says he give me that times five."

Marta Soboroff appeared suddenly restless and, like all who visited my office, succumbed to the allure of the room's only window. As she took in the view, I admired her beautiful figure.

"Did you ever consider modeling?"

Marta Soboroff turned to me and smiled for the first time. "Yes, I am model," she said and walked back to the chair. "I start working at front counter in bakery. Giorgi Geladze is the man who hire me. The same man who came into the laundry. I think it's just more good luck. Everyone call him Gigi. The work is easy compared to laundry or those working in prep room. The others are from all over Georgia. After few months, he calls me into office. He ask me to help him with charity that find work for new immigrants. I think this is good because others in bakery are also immigrants. Everybody love Gigi."

I said, "All the immigrants were women from Russia. When they arrived, your job was to assure them everything was fine."

Marta Soboroff rested her forehead on her hand and nodded. "Yes, why not? I didn't know yet the real reason. I didn't know Gigi part of those that enslaved me. Then I have more luck. A man come to the bakery. He is photographer. He gives me card. He ask if I want to model clothes. He takes my picture in beautiful dresses. He show pictures to woman at agency. I sign papers and not go back to bakery."

"So now you're a professional model. What magazines are you in?"

"Mostly department store catalogs and runway shows."

I expected more but saw her remote expression and instantly knew to shut up and wait.

"Yes, I am professional model. I make good money. Lada's living in Russia, in small town. No jobs. No future. I send her money to come here. She have no passport, no visa. She wait, wait, wait for documents. Very depressed. I afraid she do something bad to herself. I decide to ask Gigi—"

Her face crumbled into sobs, and I was reminded of my first visit with Tamar when she broke down describing the farewell to her aunt and cousin at the airport. Despite the beautiful, distraught woman in front of me, the memory of Tamar and her outrage during our last meeting hit me hard. And with confirmation that her uncle Gigi was, in fact, trafficking in sexual slavery, the truth twisted my guts.

"Yes, I did," Marta Soboroff continued. "I bring money to Gigi and ask his help to bring Lada here. Gigi was angry I left bakery. But he says he will help me but it costs five times more than what I bring him. A month later I come back with money. Gigi promises Lada come and work at bakery, just like I did. He kisses me on the forehead, says he's forgiven me."

Marta Soboroff stopped talking and stared at me. I said, "Gigi lied. He brought Lada over and kept her as a slave." She nodded and managed to control her emotions.

"How did you finally find out the truth?"

"I keep asking where she is. Gigi swear he doesn't know where she is. He says to bring more money so he can get information. I come again with more money and beg to see Lada. That night man puts razor near my face. Says not to call police or no more modeling. A week later Gigi happy, say they found her. He writes address on paper."

"Where did you find her?"

"I wait at fancy building. I see her walking with guard. She have fur coat, jewels. I run to her. Lada pretend not to know me. I try grabbing her arm and guard push me away. I yell, 'Lada, Lada, Lada. Look to me, Lada!' I not get her face out of mind. I keep seeing my sister walking in the building—"

Marta Soboroff stared silently into the front of my desk. I studied her face, tried to imagine her life reflected in those blue eyes. "Is it possible she didn't want to talk to you? Maybe she was too ashamed?"

A minute passed before Marta Soboroff said, "I never believe that. Money, jewels, Mercedes cars. That not worth it for being prostitute. Not to Lada."

"She's traumatized—shocked, confused. It's not Lada, your sister. They stole the real Lada from you."

Marta Soboroff looked at me. "I went to see Gigi. He says he's sorry but he can't control what happens. He says gangsters decide. I one day sit crying at table. A man ask what was wrong. He speaks Russian. Very kind man. Very smart. I tell him I'm looking for my sister. I tell him I think Gigi know where Lada live. That man was Jack Gelashvili."

"Jack helped you find Lada?"

"He gave to Lada my phone number."

"Jack called Lada? How did Jack get Lada's phone number?"

"I don't know, but I believe him. Then Lada call. She say she is okay and not to worry. She tell me life not so terrible. She have car and clothes and food. In Russia she have nothing. I start crying and she tell me to stop. Lada hang up—" Marta Soboroff dabbed her eyes.

"Did you talk to her again?"

"Yes. We have short conversations. She always say she fine and not to worry. One day she call and say she have boyfriend. A Georgian man. She sound very excited. I tell her if the boss find out they will hurt her. She doesn't listen. She tell me plan to leave with boyfriend. Last time we talk she say rich man help with money so Lada can leave. She talking crazy. She say rich man will help; he care very much for Lada. I never talk again to my sister."

"You told her about the young guy who helped you?"

"Lada know nothing about my time as prostitute."

She seemed to be holding back. I said, "A rich man she worked for fell in love with Lada?"

Marta Soboroff remained frozen in the chair, staring above my head. Then she cleared her throat and said, "At first, I do not believe it can happen." She sat up, opened her black bag. "Then Lada send me these envelopes. It's her proof of rich man helping her."

She dropped a pile of letter-sized envelopes on my desk. No return addresses. All letters printed out on white linen stationery. A quick perusal revealed the repeated desires to "take care" of Lada, "protect my sweetest one," and "free my little bird from her cage." Each letter was signed in blue ink, "Your Prince" or "The King's Son."

"Any idea who this prince or king's son is?" She shook her head. "Who knows you have these letters?"

She reflected a moment. "I don't know."

"Jack's killers searched his apartment for something specific. If it was these letters, your life might be in danger."

If my words threw a scare into Marta Soboroff, she didn't show it. "My apartment was also searched. I always keep the letters with me." She held up her black bag.

"I assume you did not report this to the police."

Marta Soboroff frowned. "Why would I tell gangsters what they know already?"

"I know this sounds crazy, but there are police who are not criminals and would protect you."

She rummaged through her bag and produced what looked like a .45-caliber handgun. "I make my own protections." She put the gun away, stood, and wrote her phone number on one of the envelopes. "I give to you the letters and my number. Find killer, Mr. Landau. Please."

The letters would account for the ransacking of Jack's and my residences, although smashing my furniture to bits was an insult of pure spite. I leaned back in my chair and rested my feet on the desk. A muted excitement buzzed in my stomach. From persuasive but circumstantial evidence, the focus of my investigation had narrowed significantly. I called Elaine to gauge her reaction.

"Oh, hell, yes," Elaine said. "Happens all the time. Millionaire gets to late middle age and suddenly wants to be 'daddy-lover' to the little girl he wants to protect—although he wants to keep screwing her as well. It's a twisted, sick scenario, and at the first sign one of my girls starts getting that treatment, goodbye client. I don't care how much money they have."

On my next phone call, Robertson pretended he didn't remember me. "Listen, Mr. Parking Supervisor, I got another dead body connected to Jack's murder, and I'm starting to think you might be hiding something behind your charming personality."

"Easy, Mr. Detective. What can I do for you?"

252

"I have to locate Jones. You're gonna tell me where he is."

"I don't know—"

"I got a police detective helping me. Ask around about Detective Kalijero. Accessory after the fact, Mr. Supervisor. That's serious time."

"Take it easy! I haven't seen him today. You know as well as I do he takes orders from above."

"You got my number. You find out something, you call me."

41

Eating a sandwich while driving a stick shift in heavy traffic was not a good idea. By the time I parked on LaSalle, hummus, feta, lettuce, cucumber, and salsa covered my lap.

I walked to the lobby of the Wolfe Professional Building and waited around, hoping to find Jones or young businessman Jerry. Kalijero's name appeared on my cell phone.

"What did the Russian say?" he asked.

"Are you okay working together on this?"

"Working together on what? You got a connection between the dead sister and the dead parking officer?"

"Jesus, Kalijero, you should've at least suspected. That metal ornament on the dead girl belonged to Gelashvili."

"Why the hell didn't you say something?"

253

"Gelashvili was Georgian. The ornament was Georgian. What more was there to say?"

Kalijero had no response. I pictured him rubbing his eyes. "What did she tell you?"

I sat on one of the lobby's marble benches and repeated Soboroff's story of Gigi smuggling Russian girls to work as prostitutes, Jack's relationship with Lada, and the love letters from "Prince" and "The King's Son."

"So your suspect is still this media big shot?"

I saw young businessman Jerry and his mother walk out through the revolving door. "And Elon. He's the—"

"I know who he is. Why Elon?"

"They're old pals. A mentor-student-ego affair playing power-finance games for decades, going back to their days at Decatur-Staley. A chunk of Windy City Meters' money is taken out for kickbacks. But first it's laundered through the Department of Revenue, where the cash is mingled with the city's parking ticket money. Then it's delivered across the street to Vector Solutions, one of Konigson's companies and, coincidentally, a subsidiary of Decatur-Staley."

"You'd need auditors and accountants and tax attorneys to prove anything, and there's too many of them greasing the city machine. And the public won't care because they won't understand."

"Damn it, Kalijero, you're missing the obvious again. Jack Gelashvili and Lada Soboroff were in love. Now they're dead. You put Konigson or Elon as the letter writer, you've established murder motives like hiding any connection to white slavery, prostitution, money laundering—not to mention psychotic jealousy. And you know damn well prostitution cash is also cleaned at Revenue."

"Yeah? So how're you gonna prove this?"

Before I could formulate a response, the elevator door opened and out walked three XXL suits surrounding a short, mostly bald man with bushy gray eyebrows and matching beard. The ends of his mustache seamlessly blended with chin hair falling long and straight, giving the impression of a well-groomed schnauzer. I pushed the "end" button on the phone, then followed Konigson as he and his three heavies shuffled through the revolving door.

Once on the sidewalk, I was surprised at the speed the entourage moved considering that Konigson was in his eighties with a significant leg-size differential. Three Konigson steps equaled one bodyguard stride. I caught up then kept pace which drew the attention of the closest escort. "Keep your distance," he said.

"Can I take a few minutes of your time, sir?" I said.

Konigson didn't quite glance at me although the bodyguard shifted laterally, putting me in direct line with pedestrians walking in the opposite direction. At the corner the group turned left which caused me to lose more ground. By the time I caught up, they were approaching a green canopy extending over the sidewalk that served as an entrance of a pub.

"I know about Lada," I yelled. Konigson and two bodyguards continued walking in, the third remained in front of the door.

"Don't harass my client," he said.

"Who's harassing? I just want to ask the man a question."

"You wanna get arrested?"

One of the bodyguards that had entered the pub returned, whispered quickly in the ear of the guy engaging me, then walked back inside. My man looked at me and said, "Let's go."

It was a standard pub-deli with lots of wood trim and rows of two-tops, mostly empty since the downtown lunch rush had long ended. Konigson watched as I was accompanied to his table. My escort joined the others at a table behind the boss. I didn't wait for an invitation to sit.

"What do you want?" Konigson said, sounding more puzzled than suspicious. I took out my IDs and handed them over. He studied each one carefully then handed them back. "I'm under investigation?"

"I'm investigating the murder of Jack Gelashvili."

The waiter brought over a corned beef sandwich and a pint of dark beer. Konigson gulped half the glass then attacked the sandwich, taking several large bites. While he chewed, his shaggy brows scrunched together as if in deep thought. He stayed this way for a full minute before lifting his head to reveal a mass of damp facial hair covered in crumbs.

"What's that got to do with me?"

"Maybe nothing."

Konigson took his napkin and thoroughly wiped his mouth before gulping down what remained of his beer. Then he stuffed the rest of the sandwich into his mouth and returned to his knitted-brow posture. After he swallowed the last of the sandwich and gave his face a final mopping, he said, "Didn't the police solve that case? A mentally unstable man or something?"

"Who told you that?"

"Who's telling you otherwise?"

"My client's money and—" I almost mentioned the spiked story.

Konigson chuckled. "It's good to know one's motivation. *If one does not know to which port one is sailing, no wind is favorable.*"

"I'll bet Seneca is your favorite Roman statesman."

"You went to school?"

"That surprises you?"

"Young people don't know Seneca from Santayana. What's worse is they don't give a damn, because it's not about getting an education, it's about getting smart enough to make money."

"Lada knew Jack Gelashvili. Did she mention him?"

"What makes you think I know anyone named Lada?"

We locked eyes. I said, "Okay, my turn. What do you want?"

"Only to know why you were following me."

"It took shouting Lada's name for you to talk to me."

Konigson leaned back and eyed me thoughtfully. "You young people think I'm just a cold-blooded capitalist pig."

"No, I think you're Mother Teresa. Did you know Jack Gelashvili?"

"I'm wealthy. But that doesn't mean I don't help people."

"Lada Soboroff. A Russian prostitute. Did you help her?"

Konigson appeared to evaluate my question. "I'm a small ugly man with a lot of money. That doesn't mean I have to judge others. I can change people's lives."

He didn't seem to be talking to me. "Congratulations. How about Lada's sister, Marta Soboroff? Did you pay off her debt to some unsavory Russian pimps?"

Konigson looked bewildered. "Is that a crime?" he said. "Helping someone change their life?"

"I thought you prayed to the god of self-interest-comes-first."

"And why can't helping people also be in my self-interest?"

I guess he had a point. "What about your pal at Revenue? Elon. Would he approve of your selflessness?"

"Ask Elon."

"Where can I find him?" Konigson ignored my question. I said, "Rich Jones works for Elon. But he's also a parking officer, and I've been told he used to work for you, too—driving you and your dates around. It was Jones who introduced Lada to Jack Gelashvili. Lots of connections. Anything you'd like to get off your chest?"

Konigson gave a sideways glance to the table of bodyguards. One of them stood then walked to me and said, "Time to go."

I rose from my chair and was about to step away when Konigson said, "I tried to help him, you know. I tried to help Rich Jones. But sometimes trying isn't enough."

42

Across from the lobby newsstand, I leaned against the marble façade. Konigson knew Baxter took the fall for Gelashvili's murder. His dancing around the issue of knowing Lada seemed

259

intentionally ambiguous and was hardly the behavior of a man determined to hide something. His comment about Jones sounded ominous. Through the lobby window, I recognized Robertson double-timing it down the sidewalk before stopping at the entrance and pushing his way through the revolving door. Once inside, he carefully scanned the room. For fun, I grabbed a magazine off the newsstand rack and waited.

"Hey, there, Mr. Landau."

I finished reading the fine print of a mutual fund advertisement and looked up. "Supervisor Robertson."

"Hey, I been askin' around and I think I know where you might find Jones."

"You're shittin' me!"

He lowered his voice. "Look, I don't care what a guy does with his life. Look at me. I know you think I'm a scumbag, but I'm just makin' a living. I take orders from people who are the real scumbags, but they pay me good. I never got a good education or nothin' so maybe you can understand and not blame me—"

"I absolve you, Robertson. So where is Jones?"

Robertson looked around. "Well, you know he's got that problem, right? And that we've been keeping him supplied, just to shut him up?"

I stepped back and gave Robertson the once-over. "This is how you're helping him, instead of—

how did you put it?—'kicking his ass into the street.'"

Robertson looked genuinely hurt. "I just do what I'm told—"

"Yeah, yeah. So where is your little crack slave buying his dope?" Robertson described an alley that ran behind a well-known Italian restaurant on Taylor Street. "How do you know he's still there? Wouldn't he just score his crack and be off getting high somewhere?"

"Well, that's what's weird. Usually, someone comes by with a little something to give to him. We never sent nobody in that alley before. I gotta bad feeling about this."

"Why are you playing the nice guy all of the sudden?"

"Maybe you can help me when this all blows up. You know, tell your cop pals I ain't such a bad guy."

I had not been in this Near West Side neighborhood since my friend's body was found on Maxwell Street a few months earlier. From the sidewalk, I could see the restaurant's staff setting up for dinner while giving the stink eye to a few couples lingering from the lunch crowd. Single-car garages connected to orange brick townhomes lined one end of the alley, while the other end contained the decaying masonry façades of the restaurant and a dry cleaner.

Jones stared at the ground and paced near two Mexican busboys on a cigarette break. His bandaged right hand confirmed who had destroyed my apartment and dripped blood on the floor courtesy of an outraged cat.

I approached to within ten feet and yelled, "What happened? You get attacked by a wild animal?"

Jones looked at me with a face that had not slept in days. "Why are you following me?" He searched the pockets of his shabby overcoat and produced a small knife. He struggled to unfold a three-inch blade and held it awkwardly in his left hand. "Did they send you?"

I stepped back and held up my hands. "Easy. Did who send me?" The busboys inched their way along the wall on Jones's right.

"Esta bien, esta bien," I said to them.

"Who told you I was here?" Jones demanded.

"This isn't really a crack alley, is it?"

"It's none of your damn business what I do."

"You been waiting long?"

Jones looked past me down the alley and then at the busboys. There was nobody else around. "They told me to come here," he said with a touch of panic in his voice.

"Hey, Rich, maybe it's time to tell me the truth about Jack's murder."

"I gotta get a rock."

"It's not happening here, my friend. They want something bad to go down. If they get me out of the way, nobody's snooping around anymore. But if they get you out of the way, they don't have to worry about a squealer."

"I didn't do anything!"

"Jack's murder, Rich. I know you wouldn't kill someone outside their building and then hang around to ransack their apartment. Someone else was with you. Did you do the killing or the ransacking?"

"I didn't kill anyone! I keep telling you that. You're putting words in my mouth."

"Okay. But if you know who did, you're still guilty as hell."

"I can't talk to you, asshole! I'm dead if I talk."

"You're already dead! They got you on the crack pipe, right? That's a fast one-way trip to hell. They used you up and now they're spitting you out."

Jones winced, stamped his foot several times, then shouted, "Fuck! They always *gave* it to me. I need some money!"

I took out some cash. "I can help. But you gotta give me something in return."

Jones stepped toward me, knife still in hand. I took out my .40-caliber and pointed it at his chest.

"You come within three feet of me and you get a bullet through your heart. Self-defense is written all over that knife."

Jones held the knife up to his face for a moment, then dropped it. He took another step forward. "It's the Russians. They do the killing."

"The Russians killed Jack?"

"It had to have been. Why are you doing this to me?"

"What do you know about the prostitutes?"

"I—I didn't work with them. Only sometimes drove them places. That was run higher up. You trying to make me a pimp? I'm not a damn pimp."

"You know any of the girls' names? You knew Lada, right?"

"That's Konigson's whore. She's his, like, private girl."

"How do you know?"

"I drove them around sometimes. But that's it. I didn't pimp girls out. That was the higher-ups."

"Tell me more about Lada."

"I don't know anything. She's a whore. That's all I know."

"That's all you know? You didn't introduce her to Jack at the same time she was Konigson's girlfriend? You didn't think that was a little risky?"

Jones's face became a contorted display of emotions until he settled on anger. "He was lonely!

He was my friend. I didn't know Konigson *owned* her. Who the hell falls in love with a whore?"

"What was Elon hoping you would find when you destroyed my apartment?"

"Konigson's love letters to Lada."

"How did Elon know about them?"

"I told him. Lada had showed them to Jack. She thought they could run away together with Konigson's money. Jack was scared about what would happen if Konigson found out about him and Lada. He came to me for advice. I told him he needed to forget about her, but I knew he wouldn't listen. So I went to Elon. I told him about the letters. I thought Elon would talk sense to Konigson and that would be the end of it."

"Konigson and Jack were both in love with Lada Soboroff. She wanted to run away with Jack. Now they're both dead."

"No! Lada went back to Russia."

"No, Lada was just fished out of the Chicago Sanitary and Shipping Channel."

I took out a photo and tossed it at Jones's feet. He stared at it and then looked back to me. "I need a rock."

He stepped toward me. I held up the cash. Jones fixated on it like a dog staring at a treat. "Who runs the prostitution on the city's side? Konigson?"

"No! Revenue runs everything."

265

"How high does it go?"

"All the way."

"All the way to Elon?"

Jones's eyes never moved from the money. "The money goes to the very top."

"Think, Rich. What have you *seen* with your own eyes? How have you *seen* Elon connected to prostitutes or the money?"

Something I said must've tapped into a deep memory not yet obliterated by cocaine, because his expression morphed into a kind of disgusted look.

"Elon liked to try the new merchandise," Rich said, still riveted on the cash. "The tugboat comes in with all the girls. They line up on the dock and he'd pick one and take her to his SUV. The others they'd put into the van and drive off. That sick fuck would already have a sheet covering the backseat. Then he would bang her in his car while we waited outside. Then I'd drive them to one of his apartments. She'd be his girlfriend until the next shipment came in."

"Tugboat?" I said and began lowering my arm, wondering if his drug-addled brain could be trusted. "Where is this tugboat?"

As Rich reached for the cash he said, "At the port—" Then a shot rang out. I stood motionless, covered in a sticky sheen, watching Jones's legs fold in slow motion, as if he were carefully laying himself down, until the weight of his headless torso tipped him over, leaving a specter of red mist wafting in the air. For an undetermined amount of

266

time the data overwhelmed my bandwidth, suspended my brain while it buffered the shock, until enough bits had been processed and I broke away running with only the thought of getting home to wash the blood, brain, and skull off my body.

Standing in the shower, I had no recollection of driving or parking the car. Only after I dressed and deposited my blood-spattered clothing into the alley Dumpster, did I look at my watch and realize almost two hours had passed since I had witnessed a murder and not reported it to the police.

"I'm going to pretend you didn't call me," Kalijero said over the phone. "Go down to the crime scene and file a report—now! What the hell were you waiting for?"

"A man's skull and brains just erupted all over me. I'm not quite as seasoned as you."

"Did those busboys see this?"

"I don't know. Maybe they went back to work before the shooting. Or maybe exploding heads are no big deal in Juarez."

"Why the hell you would go to that alley—"

"I take chances! Yeah, I know. And that makes me a bad detective."

"It makes you a *stupid* investigator. It didn't occur to you that Robertson was setting *you* up? That maybe that bullet was meant for *your* head?"

Of course it occurred to me, but Robertson's pathetic veneer exploited the ember of goodwill that still glowed in my spirit. My real failure was not realizing Robertson was just a pawn like Jones.

43

I ducked under the yellow tape sealing off the alley and told the patrol officer I had witnessed the murder. He told me to stay put then walked to his sergeant, who was interviewing the two busboys through an interpreter. A crime scene photographer took pictures of the area from all angles. Investigators in white jumpsuits painstakingly examined the alley. The sergeant glanced toward me then said something to the officer who then headed over to where several people stood near the body. From this group a husky plainclothes man about forty with a flattop emerged, holding a notepad. He followed the officer back to me.

"I'm Detective Horowitz. You say you witnessed the shooting?"

"Yes."

"You got some ID?"

I handed over my investigator's license. Horowitz peered at the card then chuckled and shook his head. Contempt glowed from his square face while he scribbled in his notepad.

"What were you doing in the alley?"

"Conducting an interview."

"You told the victim to meet you here?"

"No. I got a tip that he would be here."

"Who gave you the tip?"

"Robertson, at Revenue."

"How did he know Jones would be here?"

"Ask him!"

Horowitz dropped his arms and looked at me. "You got a problem?"

"You haven't asked me how the deceased was involved in my investigation."

"We know the deceased. And I heard about your investigation."

"Really? I guess you boys don't give a damn about Jones or you would've had him under surveillance."

"Did you lure him into the alley, Landau? Were you trying to buy drugs from him?"

"That's bullshit! Kalijero can vouch for me."

"Kalijero?" Horowitz said. "Kalijero was here, too?"

"No—"

"Then what's he vouching for?"

"I meant as a character reference."

Horowitz pretended to think about it. "Oh, you mean he'll tell me you're not lying. But how would he know if he wasn't here?"

Horowitz's smirk begged a *fuck you!* but I stood fast. "The bullet came from behind me. The shooter must've been on one of these roofs."

"Thanks, but we got that part."

269

"So I was right! And I also think the victim's lack of head might mean high velocity rifle? Fragmentation bullet?"

"You're a crackerjack investigator."

"Thanks, but I get the feeling you don't respect my profession."

"I take it back. You're *better* than crackerjack!"

"Cool! Feel free to call anytime." I turned to leave.

"One more thing," Horowitz said. "You know, it's kind of weird you waited over two hours to report the murder."

"Sorry about that. I just assumed *real* detectives like you would've figured it all out by now."

Despite the complications Jones's death posed, not knowing how Jack got Lada's phone number bothered me more. I knew a discussion with Tamar made sense and not only because of our fight that morning. From my apartment, I called and left a message. Then I called Palmer, left a message, and wondered if anyone answered their damn phone anymore.

Pitch-black at six-thirty, a few drops splattered on the window. Late October settled over my forehead, weighed on my eyes. I leaned the recliner back and watched grotesque images float past. Jones pacing around the alley, waiting for crack, then lying headless in the alley; Robertson strapped to a gear meshed with a larger gear in a mysterious machine full of rotating cogs, and Konigson lying shirtless on his side while a litter of miniature suits nursed on hidden teats. From all this, a murder will be solved.

My phone vibrated—I got tired of Beethoven. Palmer sounded almost giddy. "I must show you what I've figured out."

"What do you mean?"

"How they're doing it. How they're moving all that money around."

"We know about the Department of Revenue cleaners."

"That's just one aspect, Jules. It's much more involved."

By "involved" I assumed Palmer meant "complicated," a warning he may have strayed from the path of Gelashvili's murder. An hour later, I opened the door to Palmer, holding a folder and a bottle of wine.

"What's happened?" Palmer said. "You look dismayed."

"Not sleeping well," I said, seeing no reason to mention the vaporization of a man's head.

"It's just a French Colombard," Palmer said, referring to the wine. I pretended to understand the significance of his statement.

Palmer sat on my couch and began fingering through sheets of papers in the folder, carefully examining each one before laying them down in specific locations. I returned from the kitchen with two glass coffee mugs and sat next to him. Flow charts of rectangles and arrows covered half the coffee table.

"There's some serious involvement in those charts," I said. Palmer looked at me with a puzzled expression and then noticed the mugs. "Forgive me," I said. "I don't drink anything that requires a stemmed glass."

He sort of smiled. "So you see, this involves a trust and an IBC. One country hosts the trust while another country hosts the IBC. . . ."

Palmer lost me five minutes into an explanation of international business corporations and foreign grantor trusts, but I was glad to be in his company if only for the pleasure of watching a man thoroughly enjoy himself talking about what most mortals would consider an impenetrable forest of arcane financial tactics.

". . . And believe it or not, a small business is defined as having one hundred or fewer owners!" Palmer burst into hysterical laughter, creating an image I never would have imagined or believed possible from this sober son of Manhattan royalty. Maybe it was the wine combined with some repressed emotion from Jones's murder, but his unexpected merriment took on an absurd quality that provoked my own fits of giggling.

When we both had settled down, I said, "This is all interesting—"

"But what the heck does it have to do with Gelashvili's murder?" he finished for me.

I waited for an answer but realized Palmer did not have one. He leaned back on the couch and cradled the mug on his stomach.

"Yes," he said, "I am obsessed with the financial facets of evil motivations. But this information may be useless to you." He emptied the mug then held it out for a refill.

"How are you getting this *useless* information? We're dealing with private companies, right?"

"Information on private companies is available, although they don't make it easy to find. You have to know where to look—or who to ask. And I'm well-connected, as you might imagine." Palmer sensed my concern. "Don't fret over me, Jules. I take pride in my ability to remain inconspicuous."

His last comment sounded naïve. I wanted to remind him that he was connected to Konigson who was connected to Elon who was connected to gangsters and that investigating the source of money was inherently conspicuous. Instead, I reminded Palmer of our first conversation when he confirmed how odd it seemed that Konigson would call the city editor to kill a story. Then I updated him on my conversation with Marta Soboroff and the love letters to her sister, Lada. "I want to believe that if these letters were worth killing for, there should be an obvious clue about who wrote them."

"If you want to show them to me, perhaps I will see something that only an outsider to the intimate details of the case might see."

Cloaked in Palmer's intellectual timbre, the simplicity of his suggestion had a power of its own. I retrieved the letters and watched Palmer's face as he read to the end of the first letter and then looked at me with a broad grin. Palmer skimmed the next letter and the next, continuing to do so with each subsequent letter while maintaining his grin.

I said, "Yes, they're not very imaginative, just the same letter written in a slightly different way."

"You really don't see it, do you?" He raised his eyebrows suggestively.

"I don't see it. Tell me."

"Clearly, you never studied German, otherwise you would have known the name 'Konigson' is a derivation of the German word 'Königssohn,' which means 'prince' or 'king's son.'"

Palmer's revelation managed to suppress the shock waves of Jones's murder and gave me something to smile about.

"Perhaps it's time I share these letters with the author—just to gauge a reaction."

Palmer lifted his glass and said, "Cheers."

44

"Maybe you were right," she said.

I thought I had been dreaming except I was holding a cell phone to my ear.

274

"What?" I asked. Only when I sat up and saw the red numbers on the clock showing four-forty-five *a.m.* did the voice register. "Tamar?" I heard the sound of aluminum trays rattling on baking racks.

"Uncle Gigi. Maybe you were right."

"Tell me."

"Not now. I have to go."

She could've waited until at least seven to hang up on me. I turned off the phone and drifted back to sleep thinking her call had been a hopeful sign—of something.

A few hours later, from across the street of the Kutaisi Georgian Bakery, I watched an exhausted Tamar fill orders for the last customers of the late-morning rush. She glanced at the large clock above the oven, untied her apron, then disappeared into the prep room. I exited my car and waited for her outside the entrance. A frosty mist blanketed the city. I shivered in my jacket, unprepared for the damp cold. A few minutes later, she emerged from the back and made her way out the door. Scrunched low in her wool coat from the chill, she walked, oblivious that I stood in her path.

"That was you who called me early this morning, right?"

Tamar searched my face. She looked as if she'd been up all night.

"I need coffee," she said, then we walked in silence to a coffee shop in the next block.

After we sat, I said, "Too damn cold for October."

Tamar sipped her mocha latte. "There's a white van often parked in the alley outside the bakery. I've seen it since the first day I started working there. The cargo area has no windows. Sometimes they leave the back door open. Benches run along both sides. I didn't think much of it at first. Sometimes I'd see hairbrushes and makeup kits lying on the floor."

"Is it the same white van that double-parks in front?"

"Yeah. If someone's parked in the alley, he'll do that."

"Any idea what the letters IIPD stand for?"

Tamar looked squint-eyed at me for a moment. "I've seen it somewhere. But I don't know what it means."

"A patch on the van driver's jacket and a decal on the windshield."

"Yeah. That's right. He hangs out in the alley smoking. Anyway, one time I saw a pistol lying on the floor of the cargo area. I started asking questions." Tamar held the cup to her mouth with both hands.

"Who did you ask?"

"First, I asked the other Georgians who worked in the kitchen or did whatever. Some said they didn't know and acted like it was nothing out of the

276

ordinary. Others just shook their heads and said nothing, as if I had asked something taboo. I convinced myself not to worry about it. But every once in a while the van wouldn't be there, but some girls would be hanging around. They usually had some kind of travel bag with them. I started chatting with them. They were young Russian women, maybe eighteen or twenty years old. They seemed to think they were getting jobs in hotels. *Luxury* hotels. They even knew all the names. Hilton, Four Seasons, Park Hyatt, Fairmont."

"So they didn't seem nervous or scared?"

"No, they seemed excited. Like they were on an adventure. The last group, a few months ago, reminded me of happy little kids."

"You asked Gigi about this?"

"He told me he had friends who sponsor people to immigrate here. Once they're here, the sponsors network with people like Gigi to find jobs, just like he helped my family. But they couldn't all work in the bakery, he said."

"Did you ask him *specifically* about jobs in fancy hotels?"

Tamar looked at me, then looked away. "I was going to call all the nice hotels and ask if they had any women employees from Russia. But I didn't."

"Because—?"

"I just told you!" Tamar said, annoyed. "I *convinced* myself not to worry about it." I kept my mouth shut, to let the anger linger. "I'm sorry," she said. "It's just—I had no reason *not* to believe Gigi. I knew him only as a kind man."

"Even though they were all young *Russian* women."

"They were immigrants, just like I was an immigrant and all the people in the bakery were immigrants."

"*Georgian* immigrants."

Tamar put her cup down, turned sideways in her chair. "At the time, I wasn't thinking about politics. Of course, I was naïve. There's no escaping politics. It follows you wherever you go, whether you realize it or not. You're not just an immigrant; you're Georgian. You're not just Georgian; you're Abkhazian or South Ossetian or Ajarian or from some other region nobody has ever heard of where Georgians murder each other."

"What are Gigi's politics?"

"After our conversation yesterday, I cornered some of my co-workers who have known Gigi since childhood. They told me his story—that he believed in a united Georgia under one government. Many of his fellow Abkhazians wanted to be independent. So Georgians started killing each other, with Russia helping the separatists win the civil war. Gigi was kicked out of Abkhazia, his ancestral home. He blames the Russians more than he blames his fellow Georgians."

"Making some cash while taking revenge. How do you think he feels about Russians paying him so they can enslave these women?" She didn't answer, and the conversation needed to be steered back to Jack's death, which meant having to tell Tamar about another murder. "Remember Jack's girlfriend, Lada? I met her sister the other day."

Tamar rotated in her chair to face me. "Jack never mentioned a sister. How did you meet her?"

"She wanted to talk to me about Jack."

"So Lada must know Jack's dead. Is she still in Russia?"

"How did Jack get Lada's phone number?"

Tamar gave me a strange look. "I assume she gave it to him."

"The sister's name is Marta. She came here first, thinking she had a good job in a hotel. Instead, she was forced into prostitution. But she managed to escape, thanks to the generosity of a kind client."

"Wait a second. I remember a Russian woman named *Marta* working at the bakery for a while!"

"That's right. After she got rescued from the prostitution world, Gigi magically discovered her working in a laundry and invited her to work at the bakery. Small world, huh?"

"She was tall and beautiful. Gigi always wanted her up front, working the counter."

"One day Gigi asks her to help with his friend's immigration charity. She was to give assurances to the young Russian women that everything was going to be fine. She still hadn't made the connection between Gigi and her enslavement as a prostitute."

Tamar nodded her head. "I kind of remember that she would leave at odd times to run errands for Gigi."

"So one day, just like in the movies, a fashion photographer walks into the bakery and asks Marta if she wants to be a model."

"And off she goes to make a lot of money. Good for her."

"Except Gigi is angry about her leaving. I'm assuming he thinks she's ungrateful, or that she owes him something. Time passes. Marta makes the mistake of asking Gigi to help bring Lada over from Russia. She thought showing up with a bunch of money would make things right. She was wrong."

Tamar closed her eyes. "Oh, my god. Jack was in love with a woman forced to work as a prostitute?"

"How did you miss it? The fancy cars, the fur coats, the jewelry, Lada half his age."

"I was thinking how happy he was, that she was probably the daughter of a rich oil family, that she wanted an intelligent, handsome older man to take care of her. Why would I have ever thought my cousin would knowingly date a prostitute?"

I supposed her explanation sounded plausible since the girls she had seen were new arrivals in ordinary clothing. Why should I assume Tamar knew how prostitutes dressed once they started making money?

"Maybe Gigi found out it was Jack who helped Marta find Lada. That would've made him pretty angry."

"Are you saying Gigi killed Jack because he gave Lada's number to Marta?"

"There's more I have to tell you."

"Where's Lada now? Ask Marta to get in touch with her."

The look on my face must have given it away. Tamar's expression didn't change when I said, "Lada's dead."

Neither of us spoke for several minutes. Then Tamar said, "Because of Jack, they killed her? They're both dead because of their relationship?"

"It's not that simple. Marta gave me a pile of love letters written to Lada. They're not signed but I'm pretty certain Konigson wrote them. That's pretty damning evidence for someone to get their hands on. You should also remember that the Department of Revenue is *laundering* the prostitution cash."

I could tell Tamar struggled to get her head around all the information. "Elon and Konigson. They would have people killed—as a precaution? Just in case?"

"I think when Elon found out Jack was also in love with Lada, he told Konigson and they panicked. Fearing the possibility of being exposed as part of a prostitution ring. A scandal like that would bring their worlds crashing down."

Tamar buried her face in her hands. "I've been doing some investigating of my own," she said then looked up at me. "Gigi keeps a weekly appointment book on his desk. I've been looking through it during my night shifts, all the way back to January. One day every couple of months he writes, *10 saat'amde, ts'omi ch'amova, 24.*" Tamar leaned back in her chair and stared at me.

"You're going to tell me what that means, right?"

"Ten *p.m.*, dough arrives. Twenty-four."

She didn't need to elaborate. "Code for something else arriving."

"All our record keeping is done on bakery software I talked Gigi into buying. He doesn't want anything to do with the computer so he either gives me a copy of the orders and I enter them, or I do the ordering myself and enter them."

She waited for me to draw her conclusion. "None of these late evening dough orders coincided with anything you entered."

"I've racked my brain trying to figure out a logical explanation." Tamar shook her head. "But it's no use."

"Have we already missed this month's special delivery?"

"Saturday, ten *p.m.*"

"Saturday? As in the day after tomorrow?"

Tamar nodded.

"We've got to figure out this IIPD mystery. An Internet search only comes up with International Institutes of P-something and Development. Professional Development, Property Development, Psychosocial Development."

"Elon," Tamar said. "You know what he currently looks like yet?"

I detected a sprinkling of annoyance in her voice. "Uh, no. Not yet. He's hard to pin down." I could've asked Robertson what Elon looked like, if I had understood the importance.

"What about Konigson?"

"Old, short, bearded, fat. Why? You think you might know these guys from somewhere?" I was half joking.

Tamar looked as though she wanted to say something but stopped herself. "I have the name Konigson to hate, to wish would burn to death. I want to know the face belonging to that name."

The depth of her words impressed me. The buried fury in her voice worried me.

45

Tamar wanted some time alone, but we agreed to talk again later. She smiled warmly as I stood to leave. During the drive home, Kalijero called. "Where are you headed?" His businesslike

283

demeanor sounded weird. "I'll be waiting in front of your apartment," Kalijero said. "Just stay calm, don't overreact."

"What the hell are you talking about?"

"We're just gonna talk, but you gotta be cool."

Fifteen minutes later, I parked my car and crossed the street in front of my building, where Kalijero waited.

"Walk with me," he said and we started down the sidewalk.

"Listen. We've figured out some prostitutes are being smuggled in Saturday night. Do you know what IIPD stands for? Something about immigration maybe?"

"I don't know. But *you* listen. Video surveillance caught Jones's murder."

I stopped in my tracks. "So they know I was just talking to him."

"Somebody called the crime hotline, left detailed instructions, and mentioned your name."

"So they saw me talking to Jones and then his head exploded. That should prove I didn't kill him."

"You waited before reporting the murder. To a cop, that means you're hiding something. Who took your report when you went back to the crime scene?"

"Horowitz."

Kalijero frowned. "Did you piss him off?"

"He pissed me off."

"When're you gonna learn? Guys like you don't get respect from cops. Especially if your name is Landau. You be a smart ass and guys like Horowitz go out of their way to fuck with you. He's probably gonna try for an accessory charge."

"Accessory to what? Murder? That's insane! You're telling me the state's attorney will go for that bullshit?"

Kalijero laughed. "They've got to keep all those lawyers busy. Okay, just be cool. You've got to follow through a little bit, play the game." Two police cruisers pulled up.

"No way! You're arresting me?"

"We've got no choice! But you can't freak out; that'll only hurt you. Play the game, Landau. Let them book you, get a lawyer, make your bail, and straighten this shit out."

One of the cops asked me to put my hands behind my head. Then he patted me down, relieved me of my Glock, and read me my rights. I glanced at Kalijero, he nodded approvingly.

Handcuffed in the police cruiser, wrists bent queerly behind my back, periodic spasms of pain shooting out my shoulders, it occurred to me that bail for a crime of this nature could far exceed my liquid assets. I thought of my father being led away at the conclusion of a sting operation Kalijero had engineered. Perhaps we would one day look back upon this day and laugh at the irony. At that moment, however, I promised both my father and Frownie that if Kalijero didn't help me through this mess, he would be my sworn enemy—whatever that meant.

I was taken to the local precinct where I was allowed to call Palmer and leave a message explaining why I needed a lawyer. An hour later, after fingerprints and mug shots, I was on my way to a holding pen in anticipation of sharing a confined space with men deficient in the basic skills of sanitation and manners. I knew enough to keep my mouth shut, not try to make friends, and to stand as far away from the toilet as possible. From the time they slapped the cuffs on me, I had mentally prepared myself to spend at least one night in the hole since setting an arraignment could take two days. Kalijero showed up after three hours, having secured an interrogation room to question me.

"We got a bond hearing set for tomorrow morning," Kalijero said. He didn't look as pleased with himself as I thought he would. "The DA will try to paint you as a flight risk so they can get a hefty bond."

"More than ten thousand?"

Kalijero frowned. "We're talking about murder. Apparently, the police had been trying to recruit the deceased as a possible informant. Whoever set you up knew what they were doing."

"You know I can prove I was investigating a murder, for fuck's sake!"

"This is why I'm telling you to stay cool. Get a lawyer, plea it down or maybe get it thrown out." Kalijero walked with me back to the holding pen. He looked genuinely sad.

"Jimmy, try to figure out what IIPD might mean. We can bust this wide open!"

"For fuck's sake, Landau! Focus on getting out of here first!" Kalijero held his hands up like he wanted to choke me, then turned and walked away.

Thoughts of spending a night in jail covered a span of emotions ranging from despair to a stupid kind of pride in experiencing a special rite of passage—as if by the next morning I could brag *I had seen the shit and got through it*! But some rituals could be quite unpleasant and would require many years before they could be looked back upon with nostalgic self-admiration. In the end, I knew I could never pull off that kind of bravado and would just be a white boy from the North Shore looking like a fool trying to embrace a cliché.

Palmer's lawyer was Judd Harris, a sharply dressed man of sixty who showed up at eight the next morning, cheerful and confident, but also in a hurry. He asked how I was and pretended to care that I had spent the night sitting on a wood bench occasionally dozing off, only to be awakened by fear of armed robbers, burglars, car thieves, and the moron guard who enjoyed dragging his billy club across the bars every few hours.

"First thing, call me Judd. Second thing, this man who died, he was your star witness and you wouldn't kill your star witness because this is all a big misunderstanding." Judd glanced at his watch and said he would see me at the courthouse. I asked him about the bail amount; he nodded as if I had commented on Chicago's lousy weather and left. A short time later I was herded on to a sheriff's bus that would take me to the immense Cook County jail at 26th and California, but not before making several stops at other police stations to pick up more customers.

Along with eighty others, I was given a number and put in a holding cell to await my turn in bond court. It was then, while standing shoulder to shoulder in a crowd of prisoners, that I considered the cold-bloodedness of a guy like Detective Horowitz, someone who would deposit an innocent person like me into a dehumanizing penal system just because he didn't like me. About two hours later, my name was called.

The DA could not have been more than two weeks out of law school. I had participated in setting up Jones by luring him to the alley—where Jones thought he could buy cocaine—then witnessed his murder and did not immediately report it. A fifty-thousand-dollar bail would be necessary.

"Your Honor," Judd replied and passionately outlined the absurdity of the case, pointing out I was a licensed private investigator talking to a star witness, nothing in the video indicated illegal activity taking place, and my delay in reporting the crime was due to being in a state of shock, having just been showered with the victim's blood and brain matter.

The judge had no comment except to set bail at twenty-five thousand—cash only—and call the next case. The whole process took about fifty seconds.

Outside the courtroom, Judd did not appear too concerned. "Don't worry; it's just a scare tactic. We'll get this thrown out—and Mr. Palmer can get the cash here by tomorrow morning."

"You mean I gotta stay in this shithole until tomorrow?"

Judd looked at his watch. "I have to go," he said. He was in a hurry.

The idea of asking Izzy for a favor was not quite as distasteful as spending another night in the lockup. I saw only his disapproving smirk while leaving a message asking for twenty-five thousand in cash, and as the morning wore on, the smirk became more and more disgusted with me until my jailer informed me I had a visitor and led me to a cafeteria-like room where Ellis Knight waited.

"Hey, fish! You someone's punk? You get the raw dog yet?" His glee bordered on delirium.

"You here to help me or torture me?"

"No worries; everything's *aight*." He took a cashier's check out of his pocket. "See, bro? I got your bank, but I gotta break it all down before I deliver the cheddar."

Already sleep-deprived and hungry, I couldn't handle the added frustration. I lowered my torso onto the cafeteria table, rested my head on my folded arms, and closed my eyes. Such unforeseen behavior had the desired effect.

"Yo, dude. Hear me out."

"What do you want, Ellis?"

"We're making a deal here. Just fill me in on the stiff in the alley, and I'll post your bail."

"Deal," I said and gave Ellis a verbal outline, aware that general references to a life starting in parking enforcement and ending as a stooge running errands for an unnamed cabal of corrupt city officials and powerful corporatists would be all Ellis needed to create a sensational story of tabloid truth.

46

"Home," that sentimental image of a welcoming refuge from an indifferent world, ceased being an abstract concept when I entered my apartment. After devouring a plate of hearts and livers, Punim joined me on the couch, nesting in my lap as I left a message informing Palmer I had been sprung. A few minutes later, he stepped out of a budget meeting to call me back to apologize for his money not being more "liquid."

"And don't worry about this accessory nonsense," he said before hanging up.

I closed my eyes, wondering if I had the ability to stop worrying based on someone else's decision to tell me so. This would be my last conscious thought until three hours later when I opened my eyes thinking if Saturday night passed before I could figure out IIPD, all wouldn't be lost. A confrontation with Elon would be only delayed. Although the good fortune of so easily gaining access to Konigson still skirted the boundary of suspicion, I worried more about finding a way into Elon's world. Then it occurred to me that one world just might lead to the other.

"Hang on, don't push the terrorist-alert button," I said to Konigson's receptionist at Vector Solutions. She gave me an expression I could describe only as homicidal. "Remember tossing me out of here a few days ago?"

"What do you want?"

"I'm Jules Landau. Tell Mr. Konigson I have pressing information about Jones."

"He's out of the office."

"Why do you hate me so much? Can you just tell me when Mr. Konigson will be back in the office?"

Reluctantly, she checked an appointment calendar and said, "In about an hour."

I thanked her and headed across the street.

Maybe it was the dreary weather, but the lobby of city hall seemed more blatantly kitschy than I remembered. The elevator let me off at the basement, and I walked the corridor trying to remember which of the unmarked doors belonged to

291

parking. When I passed the archivist's office and saw the same man on his knees sorting through boxes, I gambled on a door just around the bend and won. Except for Robertson sitting behind his desk in the glass-walled enclosure, the office appeared empty.

"Knock-knock." Robertson looked up. "You are the man!" I said. "Thanks for helping me find Jones."

Robertson smiled tentatively. "Oh, yeah? Things worked out? He give you some good info?" I had a feeling Robertson knew I was being set up, but didn't know Jones was going to get blown away. A blatant lack of respect from his superiors, I thought.

"He did!" I said and walked to the side of his desk but stayed far enough away to provoke Robertson to stand in order to shake my extended hand.

"Maybe things might work out for me if something bad happens? You know? Like you'll help me out a little?" His grasp was firm, like that of a trusting hand thankful for a friend.

"Unfortunately, Jones can't be much help now that he's dead." I yanked Robertson hard into my raised knee, dropping him to the floor. It was the kind of cheap shot a skinny white boy playing detective could not be afraid to use if he ever wanted respect. But just as I felt a tinge of guilt watching his distress, he gasped the word "cocksucker," reached blindly with one hand to open a desk drawer, and began feeling around for a set of brass knuckles just beyond his fingers. I took the groping hand and bent it back in a maneuver that put Robertson flat on his stomach.

"Who told you Jones would be in that alley? Was the bullet meant for Jones or me?"

Robertson cried out in pain. "You're breaking my wrist!"

"Four dead people, one broken wrist. Is that a fair trade?"

"I just got a note telling me what to do."

I let up a bit. "You told Elon I was looking for Jones, didn't you?"

"No! Elon's not involved with guys like me. A kid comes down and gives me a note."

"And the note said to tell me Jones was in that alley?"

"Yeah, yeah, it was a setup. But I didn't know they was gonna kill him. C'mon, let me up."

"Who the hell is your boss?"

"I don't know. Everybody. It's a bureaucracy, all done with email or notes. I do what I'm told. There must be a couple dozen hacks between me and guys like Elon."

"That way he keeps a lot of white space between the headless corpse and himself."

"For fuck's sake, let me up!"

I pushed Robertson's hand against my holstered gun. "Feel that? That's my backup gun. A lousy .38 revolver. Because I'm out on bail, the cops kept my beloved Glock. My license to carry a gun is suspended. Can you imagine investigating murder in Chicago but not being able to legally carry a gun? That really pisses me off and I'm blaming you!"

I unbent his hand and backed away. Robertson got to his knees, rubbed his wrist a while, then climbed into his chair. He looked pathetic.

Robertson said, "Even I know what a big-city machine is about. The money flows up to the top through dopes like me."

I said, "How long are you going to stay aboard this sinking ship? You're now an accessory to a murder."

"I swear I didn't know—"

"It doesn't matter what you knew! If I go to trial, you think I'm going to take the rap for you? I've already given your name to the cops. It's over; you're done."

"So what am I supposed to do?"

I put another card on his desk. "Keep this one in your wallet. You're a double agent now. I need evidence linking Elon with Gelashvili's and Jones's murders. I don't care how many people are between you and that note. When it all unravels, I'll see what I can do for you."

I turned to leave, then stopped. "Hey. Do they still use tugboats around here?"

294

Robertson struggled a few moments with the non sequitur. "Well, in the river you see 'em pushing barges. And I seen them in the harbors sometimes."

"That's right," I said. "Thanks."

47

"You can go on back," the grouchy receptionist said as soon as I walked in, surprising the hell out of me.

Konigson stood on the threshold to his office talking to someone behind the partially opened door. He signaled me to join him. Inside the office, a man sat at one end of the sofa with an open briefcase on his lap. Konigson pointed me to the other end of the sofa. From there, I watched the master deftly employ scornful laughter and blunt retorts to the man's sales pitch. Clearly, Konigson was showing off.

"You get my money, I get fifty-five percent of the company," Konigson finally said with a dismissive wave. "Take it or leave it and get the fuck out of my sight." The man walked out mumbling something about, "Vulture capitalists," before closing the door.

As he walked around his desk to sit, I said, "That's no way to talk to the king's son." Konigson faltered just enough for me to notice, then continued to his chair.

"Bernie Landau," Konigson said. "I remember a Bernie Landau who sold women's coats."

"How did you know my father?"

"When I started making some real money, I wanted to diversify. I was invited to invest in a fund that I could assist in managing. Your father was in on some meetings. He was good at recruiting small-town investors."

"Yeah, he did well—until."

"Until some cunt fucked him over. Now what do you want?"

"How does one so thoroughly diversified know which investments are paying off?"

"Who cares? And what does this have to do with Jones?"

"I'll get to that. I'm trying to learn something."

"How do you *think* you know? You keep track. See what's paying off and what isn't. Most people don't have time for this. That's why they hire a professional to do it."

"Most people just assume their money is being used in an ethical manner."

"Ethical?" Konigson spat out. "Nobody gives a shit about ethics. Ethics has nothing to do with Joe Blow getting rich."

"I would guess a man of your background would know where every dollar is invested."

Konigson was becoming impatient. "Okay, you got me. I profit from the defense industry, the gaming industry, the energy industry, and many other evils. Now what about Jones?"

"How about prostitution?"

"What are you talking about?"

"Pimping out beautiful Russian girls to wealthy clients. I'm going to take a wild guess and say barely legal women provide a pretty good return on investment."

"I don't know anything about prostitution."

"A package of cash walked into your office five days ago."

"Other revenues."

"Like what? Parking-ticket earnings?"

"Enough. Say what you want about Jones and get out."

"Jones is dead."

A pause, then, "Tough luck. He wasn't a bad guy."

"He knew you were in love with Lada."

Konigson stood then walked out from behind his desk. His face began turning red as he formulated a response. "I protected her! I took care of her! Nobody could hurt her because of me! Do you have any idea how much money I spent making sure nobody else touched her?"

"Are you sure *nobody* else touched her?"

Konigson's mustache lent a ferociousness to his stare, but his response was measured. "Nobody else paid for her company."

"You knew Jones introduced Lada to Jack Gelashvili. The dead parking officer."

"So what? You think I killed Gelashvili because of that?"

"Gelashvili was in love with her."

"Oh, you're so clever, aren't you? Nail a murder on the rich man because he was jealous. What horseshit. When she gets back from Russia, she'll tell you the truth."

"Prepare yourself, Konigson. Her swollen corpse was just pulled out of the river."

Konigson stared at me a moment then stumbled, as if from a blow. Bracing himself against the desk, he maneuvered back to the chair. I watched closely, observed involuntary physical reactions bounce around his body. It looked as though breakfast might reappear. Instead, he fell forward onto his desk and began sobbing into his arms. "My little Lada," Konigson whimpered. "Why? That bastard. That fucking bastard."

I waited for Konigson to regain some control. "Who killed her?" I said.

Konigson looked up then wiped his eyes. "It's the Russians who do the killing. It has to be."

"Why did they kill Gelashvili?" Konigson sat frozen. "Just come out with it already!"

"I told Lada I wanted to buy her freedom and take care of her. But she had to end it with Gelashvili. Like a fool, I thought Elon would then

298

leave Jack and Lada alone if they had nothing to do with each other."

"*Elon* would leave them alone?"

"It was my fault. I told her too much."

"Elon is the *bastard*? Just say it already."

Konigson nodded while slumping low into his chair. "Elon makes the decisions."

"Who does he give the orders to?"

"I don't know. But Lada told me about two guys that scare all the girls. She called them mafia soldiers. They're Russian. So I assumed Elon has a connection to Russian mobsters."

"Let's get back to the *other revenues* of your portfolio. Prostitution earnings—"

"Christ almighty, Landau. I don't know where all the money comes from. What I *know* doesn't even matter. It's what I can be *connected* to that matters."

"How about Elon? You think he knows where all the money comes from?"

"Russians give Elon money to launder. You think he gives a damn where it comes from? What does anyone care?"

"Didn't your relationship with Lada potentially connect you?"

Konigson looked away. His chin started quivering then he blinked away a few tears. "Elon told me not to worry. But I had to *give her up,* he said. Nobody would get hurt."

"Then you offer to buy Lada's freedom. Elon doesn't like it. He's worried about what she knew. He's worried about what Gelashvili knew. He's worried about what Jones knew. He's worried about a newspaper story inspiring someone to poke around Gelashvili's life. So he tells you to make sure there's no article." We sat in silence awhile until I said, "I referred to you as the king's son."

Konigson shrugged. "You know some German."

"Elon is trying to get the letters."

Konigson leaned forward on his elbows and covered his face with both hands. He stayed silent for about thirty seconds. Then he said, "How did you find out about the letters?"

"Lada gave them to her sister, Marta, to prove a rich man was going to help her. Marta came to see me. She told me about Lada's journey to America. She gave me the letters hoping they will help me find Lada's killer. Each letter is signed, Your Prince or The King's Son."

"What are you going to do with them?"

"How could you be stupid enough to write letters?"

Konigson pounded his fist on the table. "Because I'm a weak, pathetic old man! Is that what you want me to say?" Konigson returned his face to his hands for a couple of moments then slammed his fist on the table again. "Goddamn Elon! Lada and Jack are dead, what does he want the letters for?"

"He's scared," I told him. "Elon's in bed with Russian mobsters, for fuck's sake! He can't risk the flow of money being disrupted by some prostitute or her boyfriend. The letters provide a motive for *you* to be Gelashvili's killer. He'd use those letters against *you*, if it came to that. My apartment and Gelashvili's apartment were ransacked looking for them."

"Killing and pimping."

"You don't seem too shocked."

Kongison looked at me, snarled, "I would never kill anyone!" then looked away.

"Jones told me everything runs through Revenue. Whether it's cash from parking tickets or prostitution, it all spends the same. And like you said, the Russians do the killing—and the pimping. They've just become part of the red tape. Elon's got a huge bureaucracy between him and the nasty work. He's like an overseer making sure the money flows in one direction and the girls in another."

"I'm a businessman," Konigson said quietly. "I'm no goddamn Boy Scout, but I never crossed into murder and pimping."

"For some capitalists, it's just the cost of doing business. In the last year alone, a vitamin tycoon, a real estate mogul, and an Internet billionaire all hired hit men to kill their wives because it was *cheaper* than divorce."

"I've known Lou Elon for forty years. And all that time I was in denial. I pretended his narcissistic, egomaniacal behavior was just his style for business and nothing more."

"Put yourself in Elon's head. He's thinking about what an infatuated old man might say to a beautiful young woman. He's thinking about what the same beautiful woman might say to her lover who happens to be a parking officer—one of several dots connecting back to Elon. Think of all he has to lose."

"So now you want to bring him in, huh? The great Detective Landau vows to see Lou Elon frog-marched off to jail."

"I think Lada and Jack deserve justice. Don't you?"

"How?"

"Not sure yet. But before I leave, tell me what Elon looks like." Tamar needs to know, I said to myself, and it suddenly occurred to me why.

Sitting in my car, I dialed Tamar's number. When she answered I said, "Gigi is on a first-name basis with the big shots who meet at the bakery after hours, right?"

"Yes."

"Is one of those big shots named Lou?"

The initial silence confirmed what now appeared ridiculously obvious. Then Tamar said, "Fifty-something, gray hair, tall, slim."

"Yes," I said. "That's Lou Elon."

48

Kalijero answered his phone with, "What's up, jailbird? I heard you got sprung."

Why was Kalijero happiest when something bad happened to me? I told him I had more information but wanted a meeting with his boss, Deputy Chief Hauser.

"You gotta give me something now for Hauser to bite, and I don't mean some crazy-ass finance conspiracy."

"I've had a couple of nice discussions with Konigson."

Kalijero waited a beat. "No kidding. And?"

"I want a meeting with you and Hauser."

"Did he confess? You want me to go arrest Elon?"

"I want you to go fuck yourself."

Kalijero laughed. "Settle down there, tough guy. I'll see what I can arrange. Happy now?"

I pushed "end" and, after a quick shower, kicked back on the couch. Of course they still use tugboats, you idiot, I said to myself. Chicago's the commercial "crossroads of America." Highways, railroads, and yes, waterborne cargo, all

303

interconnected. But where would Elon's human goods embark on dry land? The river is at least a hundred miles long and has three branches. Any hope of Hauser allocating police resources my way depended on keeping things simple. Forget about cash streaming into the pockets of business and political elites after cycling through a municipal washing machine. This was how "The City That Works" worked. Instead, sell corpses, crack, Russians, and whores.

Kalijero called back an hour later. Too soon for good news, I thought. "Get over here," he said. I asked if we had a meeting. "Just get your ass over here."

Kalijero sat on the bench outside the detectives' room. "Hauser's in his normal shitty mood," Kalijero said. "I told him I needed to talk. He said, 'Later, now get the hell out.'"

"You didn't mention me?"

"We'll have to ambush him. I'm sticking my neck out for you, Landau. Make sure you weren't bullshitting me about talking to Konigson."

I reassured Kalijero and waited for him to clue me in on the plan. Apparently the plan was for Kalijero to say, "C'mon," and for me to follow him through the detectives' room, where he conducted a no-knock raid on Hauser's office.

Hauser looked up from his desk with a savage expression. "What the fuck are you doing, Kalijero! What's he doing here?"

304

"Now, Karl, just relax. We've known each other a long time—"

"I said we'd talk later! And I don't care if you're about to retire, you don't just barge in like you own the place."

"Landau might be onto some—"

"He's looking at a murder rap, for chrissake! What're you doing with him?"

I said, "Four stiffs, a prostitution ring, cocaine, city officials, and a powerful business icon—all connected."

"Konigson," Kalijero said. "He's got Konigson's ear."

Hauser looked back and forth between Kalijero and me. "Of course. You're pals with a billionaire. And you're here to tell me the billionaire is what? A crook? Why would a billionaire trust a little shit like you?"

"It's complicated."

Hauser rubbed his temples. "So I've got nothing better to do than listen to a murder suspect out on bail who doesn't know why the billionaire trusts him."

"You know damn well Landau's got nothing to do with murder and that Horowitz is just fucking with him!" Kalijero nudged me. "Talk!"

"It was a setup. I was told I'd find Jones in that alley by the Parking Authority supervisor who works for Elon at Revenue."

Working backward from Jones's murder, I retraced my steps to Lada's body and followed the dots all the way back to Jack Gelashvili's corpse outside his apartment on Farragut Avenue. Hauser avoided eye contact but didn't interrupt. I took this as a good sign.

Silence greeted the end of my speech until Kalijero said, "If Konigson—"

"You bust in here," Hauser interrupted, "to tell me the deputy director of Revenue is running a whorehouse out of city hall and that four people are dead to keep it a secret."

"Well, it's—"

"A conspiracy with dozens of city employees who don't notice a damn thing. And all this came about because your media billionaire pal personally called an editor of one of his newspapers."

I said, "Prostitutes are coming in Saturday—"

"What's gotten into you, Kalijero?" Hauser said. "You're buying all this? This is what you wanted to meet me about—to help Landau bring down the big bad politician and be the people's hero?"

I said, "I want to know who killed Jack Gelashvili. If I've got to go through Elon's white slave trade to prove he's a murderer, fine."

Hauser grabbed a folder off his desk and held it up. "See this? A report by another dumb-shit commission telling us how we stink at being cops. Everybody telling us how to do our job. So in response, I'm supposed to prove city hall ain't nothin' but a big cathouse? Goodbye, Landau. Kalijero, you stay."

Back on the hallway bench, I caught snippets of the ensuing argument. Kalijero reminded his boss that solving Lada Soboroff's murder was his assignment. Hauser declared nobody cared about a dead whore.

Kalijero emerged from the detectives' room looking like a beaten man. "Let's go," he said and I followed him outside. "The pressure's killing Hauser," Kalijero said as we walked down the sidewalk. "He's a shithead, but all the deputy chiefs got *chiefs* breathing down their necks and the chiefs got *superintendents* doing the same, and it's coming down all the way from the city council and the mayor. The streets aren't safe; the schools aren't safe. What are you doing about it?"

"So what's he got against me? I'm trying to help."

"Gelashvili's case is closed. You want it reopened. That's moving in the wrong direction."

"So focus on Lada and connect it to the prostitution and money laundering."

Kalijero groaned. "Use your brain! Whores and money launderers aren't killing kids walking to school."

"How the hell were you allowed to bust my dad? He was a petty crook."

307

"An informer wanted cash so he came to me with everything we needed. That was an easy sell. You don't got anything like that with Revenue. And what you're claiming is pretty tough to swallow."

"Jesus Christ, Jimmy! I saw the money moving, the motivation is obvious—"

"Landau, go tell the world the city operates a giant money laundering machine through Revenue and the boss has people killed. See what happens. I don't care what evidence you have, you'll be torn to pieces, called a tinfoil-hat-wearing lunatic. You'd be finished!"

I paused to let Kalijero simmer a bit. Something else was bugging him. "Does Chicago have a main dockyard where commerce is off-loaded?" I said.

Kalijero gave me his *are you a dumb shit?* look. "Haven't you lived here your whole life?"

"I grew up in the *suburbs,* remember?"

"It's called the Port of Chicago."

Jones's face flashed before me with the words "at the port" coming off his lips just before his head exploded. I grabbed Kalijero's arm. "That's it!" I said. "I can't believe it took me this long. The tugboat where Elon brings in his merchandise is at the Port of Chicago! Pier twenty-four!"

"What're you talking about?"

"Just before he was killed, Jones told me the smuggled illegal aliens—all beautiful young

308

women—are lined up and then Elon picks one out and takes her to his car while the others are driven off in a van. Jones would wait for Elon to get his rocks off and then drive them to one of his apartments. She would be Elon's new sex slave until the next shipment of girls arrived. That's ten *p.m.,* tomorrow night, pier twenty-four!"

Kalijero's stare bored a hole into my skull. I dared think he saw some light. "Where are the girls in the van taken?"

"I don't know the whole process, but they're sometimes brought to the bakery. Tamar's seen them. The prostitution biz is run by that *character* you said is known by the cops. He uses the bakery to hold after-hours meetings. A couple of Russkie mob soldiers are always present, too."

Kalijero paced within a small invisible cage, very jittery as he mulled things over. His hands moved back and forth from his face to his hair, scratching, rubbing, squeezing, pinching, until he suddenly stopped and looked at me.

"Okay," he said. "We sit on this for now, start staking things out for the next—"

"Tomorrow night!" I said. "We can end the whole thing tomorrow night—"

"Goddamn it, Landau! This isn't a bunch of sailboats at Montrose Harbor! It's a giant commercial port with barges and cargo ships! You've got to get people down there watching, taking pictures, seeing patterns." Kalijero stopped, breathed in deeply then exhaled. "We want to do

309

this right," he continued calmly. "It's worth waiting to make sure we get it right."

"What's so complicated? They bring the women in on a tugboat—"

"It's a *huge* port," Kalijero said, struggling to keep his voice even. "You need time to get the lay of the land, see where people are hanging out, when they leave, when they return—"

"Pier twenty-four! Gigi *gave* us the information in his appointment book! Ten o'clock delivery at pier twenty-four. It's a fucking gift, Jimmy! What are you afraid of?"

Kalijero shook his head. "You think you can just go down there and be a hero, huh?"

"Give me the *tiniest* bit of credit. If they catch me, I'm dead. Done. Fish food. I *know* that. That's why you have to help me. Just think if you're there and you see Elon inspecting women he just helped illegally smuggle into the country so they could be forced into prostitution. Imagine testifying that the deputy director of the city's Department of Revenue looked them over like dogs at the kennel club, then took one away for a quick fuck? C'mon, how awesome would it be to wrap up your career with that?"

Kalijero started pacing again. I wanted to believe if I could get through to him just the slightest bit, he might picture himself easing into retirement, immortalized by one final epic bust.

"I'll go down tomorrow," I said. "I'll find pier twenty-four. I'll email you a few pictures of the setup. I promise to follow your lead. If you say forget it, I go home and we live to fight another day."

Kalijero stopped pacing but didn't look at me. After staring into the distance awhile, he quietly said, "Fine. Now do me a favor and leave me alone."

Something ate at Kalijero's insides, but I didn't dare ask what. His beleaguered expression reminded me of the contradiction that made up this hardened, sixty-something police veteran; like it or not, the man responsible for putting my father in prison had sentimental roots intertwined with my family. Knowing I was determined to confront Elon and those he worked with must have brought up complicated feelings.

"Before I leave you alone," I said, "where the hell is the Port of Chicago?"

49

I went for a walk along the shoreline, an activity on a gloomy autumn day guaranteed to encourage depressive, self-defeating thoughts. Robertson's pathetic image kept flashing in my brain, his face distorted by pain after I had driven my knee into his gut and twisted his wrist into an agonizing posture. What had I become?

It was dark when I got home. A restless night awaited me. I lay in bed staring at the ceiling, wondering why Izzy viewed the world allegorically and had chosen me to portray his protagonist in a morality play. He knew the reasons. I knew he paid me.

The phone rang just after midnight, arousing me from a semi-conscious slumber barely qualifying as sleep.

"Landau?" Kalijero said.

"Jimmy?"

"Responsibility for civilians, Landau. Remember?"

I struggled to clear a lingering cobweb from my brain. "What do you want, Jimmy?"

"Before you showed up at Area B today, I found out your editor buddy washed up along Navy Pier. The back of his head caved in."

A meteor swung around Earth a few times in its elliptical orbit before crashing into me and dispersing my particles around Palmer's round face. An intense ache filled my belly, a pain that throbbed from allowing a kind, helpless man to end up floating lifeless in a cold lake. Frownie's disapproving mug came into view. *What about the newspaper editor?* he said. *Don't tell me he's already dead.* Frownie faded away shaking his head, thoroughly disgusted. *It's for your own good you should feel such pain.*

I heard myself say, "You're sure it's Palmer?"

"His wallet had a driver's license and *Republic* ID. Wilbert J. Palmer. We're still looking for his next of kin."

"It's my fault."

"Shut up! He was a grown-up, Landau, and he knew you were investigating a murder. You can't tell me this guy was just some babe in the woods."

But he had been protected, I wanted to say, groomed to see only what the privileged owners of media saw. To Palmer, neutralizing threats to financial exposure were just clichés of Gotham.

"Did you hear what I said about staying clearheaded?"

I heard him, but his words had no effect. I hadn't yet hardened enough to do what Kalijero advised. Maybe I never would. Then what was I doing in the murder business? I let the phone drop to the floor and lay awake thinking about my last conversation with Palmer, when he told me not to fret, when he told me that he took pride in his ability to remain inconspicuous.

Saturday morning arrived barely distinguishable from the previous night's quasi-sleep chaos. Palmer's death wrenched my guts. Lying low to deal with my turmoil was out of the question. I told myself that I needed to proceed as planned, if only because that's what Palmer would've wanted. Having no appetite for breakfast, I sat on the couch stupefied—as if drugged— watching Punim gorge herself on a pre-mixed combination of muscles, organs, brains, and bones.

Kalijero could've waited until Sunday to tell me about Palmer. Maybe he hoped the news would discourage me from going to the port.

Soon after finishing breakfast, Punim's inner wildcat showed up. Her pupils the size of nickels, her ears unnaturally askance, she batted a yellow crunched up Post-it note around the living room, occasionally stopping for a quick, intense groom and then an equally brief glance at me, before carrying on. I usually took great delight in watching her so thoroughly amused, but this morning her antics appeared ordinary, barely registering as novelty behavior for which cats expected exaltation. So absorbed was I in Palmer's death and my mission at the Port of Chicago, I didn't notice the show had ended until I caught sight of her sitting at the end of the couch, staring at me. When I reached to give her a scratch behind the ears, she bolted then disappeared down the hall. In a matter of minutes, she would be dead asleep. Somewhere, a metaphor lurked in Punim's lifestyle, meant for my spiritual growth.

I called Tamar and asked her to meet me somewhere. Since her shift started in a couple of hours, she suggested the bakery. "You don't sound so good," she said.

"I'll see you shortly," I said.

Late-morning pastry mania engulfed the counter. Tamar had not yet arrived. I took a table in the back, away from the clamor. Six teenagers occupied one of the booths, none of them speaking, all transfixed by some kind of computer screen, be it phone or laptop. Their varying shades of brown and tan temporarily lessened my pain over Palmer. I hoped nobody would hassle them for sitting in a booth.

A guy wheeled in a stack of *The Partisan* and began loading them on the magazine rack near the front door. So much news, corruption, entertainment, so many crooks and characters, a paper like *The Partisan* needed to be semi-weekly if only to fill in the holes left by a daily corporate shill like the *Republic*. I walked over and grabbed a copy. One of the kids did the same, returning with a paper for each friend. Below the fold: "THE CRACKHEAD AND THE SCHIZO" with a subhead, "Meter Maid and Scofflaw—Both Expired."

Ellis Knight asked what a guy named Gelashvili and a guy named Jones had in common with a guy named Baxter. Two of the three needed drugs to survive, two of the three lived in the same building on Farragut Avenue, two of the three were parking officers, two of the three knew the third— and three of the three were dead.

"Anonymous Sources" in bold letters prefaced the next paragraph followed by "Wassup B? My aces say things ain't *aight*, three sidewalk outlines without a fight, but nothin' an AK couldn't set right. Them wangstas think they all that, but they ain't nothin' but a hood rat . . . booya!"

Without an interpreter, I could only read the article assuming that my vague understanding of ghetto slang was accurate. The project quickly became tiresome. To the kids in the booth as well as those younger faces sitting at surrounding tables, Knight's style was familiar and customary. Many read quotes aloud from the article, eliciting sympathetic laughter and cynical comments relating to social injustices.

Boris and Vlad appeared, each carrying a pastry and a cup of coffee. They took their customary booth at the end of the row. Tamar walked in soon after. On the way over to me, she looked at the vagrant passed out at his usual table. Something about her demeanor told me she was all business this morning.

"Are you okay?" she asked as she took a seat.

I told her about being arrested, my conversation with Konigson, and my staunch belief Elon was behind her cousin's murder. "Other than that, I'm fine."

"You sound terrible."

"Okay, you got me." I explained who Palmer was and told her about his murder.

"That's terrible. Horrible. But you can't blame yourself—"

"Yeah, yeah, he had to have known how cruel the world was, et cetera and so on. But listen, I figured out what Gigi's twenty-four is. It's at the Port of Chicago; that's where the girls are brought in. The number twenty-four in Gigi's appointment book must mean *pier* twenty-four. A reliable source told me Elon uses the occasion to pick out his new girlfriend. This means we can actually catch Elon and Gigi in the act of smuggling women into the country to be prostitutes."

"That's tonight, remember. The next delivery."

"I'm going down there today to find pier twenty-four. Then I'll call Kalijero and give him the lay of the land. If Kalijero thinks he's got a good chance of catching Elon involved in human trafficking or prostitution, he'll respond—or I hope he will."

"Gigi, Elon, and probably those two clowns will be there," Tamar said, nodding toward Boris and Vlad. "God!" she said. "I'd do anything for this to be my last shift with Gigi." I sensed a chilling undercurrent in her voice.

"Try to stay cool," I said. "You can't let Gigi know you're onto something. Trust me, we'll get his ass in prison but you gotta be patient."

Tamar was anything but cool as she sat with those dark eyes intently fixed on Boris and Vlad as they casually sipped coffee and nibbled pastries. She radiated anger like heat shimmering off blacktop. Despite the seriousness of our endeavor, I found myself fascinated by this fiery side of her and, unexpectedly, more than a little turned on.

"Look at those two morons," Tamar said. "They just sit here all day, waiting to cause pain in someone's life as soon as they get instructions from Big Bunny, or whoever they take orders from."

I thought I was hearing things. "Did you say Big Bun—?"

Tamar jumped out of her chair, climbed on top of the gangsters' table, then began pounding her fists on Boris's head. Running over just as Vlad grabbed the back of Tamar's neck, I drove my shoulder into his ribs, knocking him sideways over the seat. From behind, I bear-hugged Tamar, trying to pull her off the guy, but this made things worse since Tamar now had two fistfuls of hair, eliciting horrifying screams. I put my hands around her wrists and shouted in her ear, "Let go! Just let him go!"

Movement from my periphery convinced me I should let go first, then swivel around to plant a foot into Vlad's stomach. This time, Vlad made it all the way to the floor, where he would remain. Gigi was now on the scene taking his turn at trying to get Tamar to relinquish her grip. I put a hand on each side of her face and spoke calmly into her ear. She had stopped shouting but tears streamed down her cheeks.

"Please," I said. "Just let go." I kissed her then repeated, "Please, Tamar, let go," and kissed her again. Gradually, she loosened her grip enough for Boris to pull away. Gigi and I grabbed her, practically carrying her out the front door, as an astonished crowd of pastry patrons watched.

"My god!" Gigi said, sounding more concerned than angry. "What's happened to you? What's going on?"

318

Keep it simple, I wanted to say, fearing Tamar might let her anger give away our newfound knowledge.

"I'm tired of those two stupid idiots sitting there all day making nasty comments, insulting our heritage," Tamar said, making up the story on the spot. "The one I attacked called me a little Georgian whore. Tell them this isn't Russia and they need to respect me."

Gigi stared wide eyed at Tamar as if a spiraling horn had just popped out of her forehead. "Why didn't you say something before?" Gigi said. "*Of course* they should respect you. You're one of us, my child!"

Gigi re-entered the bakery then stormed up to the gangsters' table. Through the glass, we watched him stand defiantly with hands on hips, as he dispensed a tongue-lashing to the bewildered tough guys.

"See if you can skip this shift and go home," I said.

"No. I'd rather work. If there's a delivery tonight, I'll watch closely what goes on here."

"Just be careful not to give yourself away. I'm sure Gigi's compassion has its limits."

"Gigi and I are blood. He wouldn't hurt me no matter what—if that's what you mean."

"A white slaver with a heart of gold."

"Stalin was nominated for the Nobel Peace Prize." Her ironic comeback only added to the intensity of my attraction.

"I better get ready for my shift," Tamar said. "The Port of Chicago. Be careful. I mean it! I'm going to call you around five or six. You better answer and tell me what's up." Tamar took hold of my jacket collar, pulled me toward her into a kiss, then walked back into the bakery.

50

Southbound on the Chicago Skyway, I exited at 95th Street, then parked on Avenue M, a quiet block of small ranch-style cottages and frame houses. From there, I walked to an industrial canal known as the Calumet River; it wound its way through a post-apocalyptic landscape of abandoned steel mills, oil refineries, and dark mounds of their toxic by-products.

From the way Kalijero had described the port, I expected a logjam of vessels moving through a gauntlet of longshoremen operating enormous cranes, forklifts, and grain sifters. But apart from a single freighter being nudged along by a tug, the only other reminders of nautical activity were a mostly submerged sailboat and a rusted ship lying on its side near an abandoned silo.

I was hoping to simply ask someone where pier twenty-four was located, but not much in the way of sentient life could be observed on this sad October landscape. Walking east a block, Lake Michigan's sparkly beauty held my gaze long enough for me to notice two men fishing from a jetty. A little local flavor seemed in order.

It only took a few minutes to reach the lakeshore. The fishermen looked to be in their seventies. They used live bait from a white bucket and had their poles lying on the concrete while they relaxed, resting their arms on generous bellies rounding nicely from their arrangement in folding chairs. The men were engaged in animated conversation but quickly stopped talking when I came within about ten feet of them.

"Hello," I said then sat down dangling my feet over the edge, quite aware of my presumptuous behavior. "Largemouth bass?"

"That's the idea," one of them said with the slightest Hispanic accent.

"Probably too sunny, though," the other said in blue-collar South Side. He wore a baseball cap that said "U.S. Merchant Marine." "Them bass don't like sunny. They hang out in da' shady parts."

I nodded as if I knew well this very dilemma. "Yeah, but what's the difference?" I said. "It's still a beautiful day, right?" Both men smiled politely and grunted. "You guys lived around here a long time?"

Neither made a sound, just nodded with a kind of pained expression while continuing to stare out over the lake. As I formulated my next question, the Hispanic man said, "Almost sixty years now."

"I was born here," the seaman said.

"A lot's changed in that time I bet," I said. They grunted in the affirmative. "This port must've been a lot busier, right?"

Both men laughed. "Used to see barges all day long," the Hispanic man said.

"Lot of them freighters, too," the seaman said.

"I've seen a few tugboats," I said.

"It ain't safe to navigate the channel without tugs."

"Do you know where pier twenty-four is by any chance?"

I wasn't sure the seaman heard me, but then he shook his head. "Yeah. It ain't really a pier, though. Just a dock in the turning basin near the 95th Street bridge, next to that boat storage joint." He shrugged then spit into the lake. "I don't know anymore what the hell they're doin'."

The Hispanic man sighed loudly. The ambience had shifted. I sensed the freshness of my presence had worn off. I bid the gentlemen farewell and wished them luck on catching bass. They both nodded and waved the way people do when they're glad you're leaving.

I followed 95th Street back to the canal then cut through the lot of the boat storage place and immediately saw the masts of three tugboats moored to a small dock in a wider part of the river. A sign on a modular office trailer about thirty yards in front of the dock said "Pier 24." It seemed too easy. Everything Elon needed to quickly conduct business was right there. The white van could drive right up to the edge of the water, pick up its cargo, then disappear onto busy 95th Street.

51

I called Kalijero from my car on Avenue M. He answered saying, "Illinois International Port District."

"What are you talking about?"

"IIPD. Illinois International Port District."

Mystery solved. "Thanks. Did you get the pictures I sent?"

"What pictures?"

"On your phone! I found pier twenty-four. Perfect for off-loading the women. Easy in, easy out. Just north of the 95th Street bridge, next to a boating storage place. The highway runs right behind it."

"Hang on." I waited for Kalijero to check his phone. "Yeah, I got 'em."

I sensed residual ambivalence and it was getting on my nerves. The ensuing silence only added to my irritation.

"What!?" I said, probably louder than I should have.

"I'm looking at the pictures, Landau!" A minute later, Kalijero said, "How much time have you really spent checking that whole place out?"

"When's the last time you were down here?"

"I don't know. Why?"

"Let's just say things have changed. There are only a few businesses and the occasional barge. Meet me there tonight, say nine o'clock. You'll see for yourself. I'll be near the office trailer."

I had been gambling that Kalijero would get excited when he saw the perfect setup, but I had to accept that even if he did come down and take a look, he could still call the whole thing off for any goddamn reason he wanted. I let out a string of obscenities under my breath, directly into the phone.

"Fine," Kalijero said. "Nine o'clock. I know that boat storage place you're talking about. Maybe I can get an unmarked car to hang around, but don't count on it. Just assume we'll be on our own until I know I have something that's absolutely clear with no question that the law is being broken."

Assume we'll be on our own. I stuffed the urge to laugh. If there was one single thing I knew for sure, it was that I was on my own.

Being home at three o'clock gave me plenty of time to relax, but also plenty of time to think about Palmer, which is what I started doing as soon as my ass hit the recliner. Exhaustion also demanded my attention. My eyelids became manhole covers. Maybe just a short nap, I thought as I watched Palmer sip wine and describe Elon's arrogance, how the ease in which we figured out Elon's flesh-peddling venue was the height of pomposity.

I awoke when Punim touched down on my lap. My neck ached from ninety minutes of unnatural angles. After preparing Punim's bowl of viscera, I ordered the usual from downstairs. A minute later, Tamar called.

"Where are you?" she said.

"I got home about three. I found a spot where I'm convinced the girls come in on a tugboat. I'm meeting Kalijero at nine."

"What if nothing illegal happens tonight?"

"Then we wait for the next delivery. I'm not a cop, Tamar. I can't arrest people."

"Where is this spot? In the middle of a hornets' nest?"

"No, it's pier twenty-four, like it says in Gigi's datebook."

"Then there shouldn't be a problem."

"Who knows what Kalijero is going to do?" I waited for some kind of acknowledgment that Tamar understood the situation. "You still there?" I said.

"I'm here. Just be careful. Call me when it's over."

Most of the streetlamps on Avenue M were broken and the ones that worked already had cars parked under them. But I wasn't worried. Driving a nondescript 1983 Honda Civic had its advantages. Apart from a yellow taxi that passed me as I got out of my car, the street was quiet.

Any remaining warmth from a sunny day had been sucked into the clear night sky. I wore a wool sweater under my jacket and a navy blue watch cap that seemed somehow appropriate. The lighting along the river's asphalt corridor consisted only of whatever incidental glow from a neighboring business provided, which left large areas of blackness. The trailer's windows were dark and both floodlights on the roof were off, leaving the dock only dimly lit from the security lights in the boat storage lot. From the back of the trailer, darkness extended a good forty yards, almost to the highway. Hanging out in the shadows behind the trailer felt like standing in the wings of a theater, waiting for the lights to come up on stage.

Nine o'clock, and no Kalijero. I moved farther back, staying in the darkness all the way to a small patch of dirt. From this vantage point, I glimpsed other figures, dodging in and out of the shadows. These impoverished local residents didn't move quickly, as if afraid of being seen, but more like wandering souls not sure what to do with themselves. Had I been a poet, the flash of lighters and the glow of long drags on cigarettes would've been East Side's fireflies.

Nine-thirty. Still no Kalijero. I swore, then called him a Greek bastard. Then I called him a lazy fucking piece-of-shit cop. As I thought of more flattering adjectives, a lumbering figure trotted across a break in the traffic on 95th Street. Kalijero was now the greatest of men. As he made it to the asphalt and slowed to a walk, a low rumbling from

326

the north caught my ear. I anticipated the sight of a moving light, but heard only the rumbling as it became louder. A business on the opposite bank gave off just enough light to shimmer off the water. The tug glided lazily through the illumination like a phantom.

I hurried to the back of the trailer and waited for Kalijero, who was now about twenty yards away. I gave off a loud "*Pssssst*."

"Relax," Kalijero said. "I see you."

"Hear that rumble?" I said. "The boat's coming in. It came down the channel with no lights on."

Kalijero walked to the edge of the trailer to have a look. I got on my knees behind Kalijero to peek around the same corner. As we watched, the tug appeared from the darkness, floating up to the dock between two moorings. About ten young women huddled close together on the main deck. They looked around eighteen or nineteen, tops. Their frumpy clothes indicated that selling their bodies had not been anyone's intended career goal. With the engine still idling, from the wheelhouse a well-built man appeared, dressed in black and wearing what looked like a child's ship-captain's hat. He rushed down the ladder, tossed rope from the bow to the dock, ran to the stern to do the same, then jumped onto the dock and tied the ropes around the two moorings. With the boat secure, the captain returned to the wheelhouse to shut off the engine. After returning to the dock, he leaned against a wood piling and lit a well-deserved cigarette. A few puffs later, he took out his phone and began texting. One of the women stepped toward the dock and said something in Russian. The captain barked back in Russian. She shrunk back to the others.

Kalijero looked down at me and said, "Where's Elon and the baker?"

"I think the tug's early. It's not ten yet."

Kalijero took out his radio and said, "Goods arrival."

"Backup?"

"I decided to call in some favors."

I stood up and looked toward 95th, where I spotted a Crown Vic across the street. At the same time, a van pulled onto the shoulder of our side of the road, switched off its lights, then angled to the asphalt. I nudged Kalijero. "That's the van that takes the girls away."

We watched the van creep toward the dock. The same heavyset Hispanic man I had seen at the bakery got out. He walked to the captain, who made it clear he was not in the mood for small talk. Still desiring human interaction, the driver strolled over to the girls and stood facing them. I imagined he had a stupid grin on his face. Then he said something in Spanish and began gyrating his pelvis while positioning his hands as if standing between a woman's parted thighs. The girls turned away and moved as close to the other end of the deck as possible. The wind blew our way, and I heard the captain say as he threw down his cigarette, "Be a good boy. Sit in van."

The driver did not appreciate the comment. As the two men sized each other up, headlights flashed from the north end of the asphalt. The driver ran to this vehicle and started the engine. The captain waited. Slowly, a black SUV made its way forward until it parked in the darkness just beyond the dock area. Gigi stepped out from the driver's seat wearing the white apron he wore in the bakery. Boris and Vlad emerged from the backseat. From the passenger side, a well-groomed businessman with a wool overcoat draped across his shoulders stepped out.

Kalijero whispered something into the radio. The Crown Vic across the street came to life then sped away. Other noises from behind us momentarily caught my attention. Boris and Vlad stayed near the car while the captain, Gigi, and Elon congregated on the dock. After exchanging pleasantries, the captain beckoned the women to join them. They did so cautiously, obeying the captain's order to form a line.

"Now, listen," Kalijero said. "Stay here, pay attention, and keep down. There are three officers behind us waiting for my signal, and more support on 95th with vehicles. They know this is where you will be."

Elon started his grotesque inspection by passing slowly down the front of the line, giving each young woman the once-over, like an officer on a parade ground.

I whispered, "This is human *trafficking,* which is worse than human *smuggling* because—"

"Shut the fuck up!" Kalijero said.

Coming to the end, Elon wheeled around to stand behind the last woman in line. Despite the faint light, it wasn't difficult to get a sense of what he was up to. First, his hands appeared on her thighs before sliding slowly up, stopping a few moments on her groin then moving to her belly and then to her breasts, where they remained for his groping pleasure. By now, some of the women were openly crying. Others stood frozen in shock. Even with shadows distorting the already dull light on their faces, one couldn't miss their expressions of horror.

Elon repeated the routine with each one of them, acting as if he had all night to make a decision. Gigi became downright fidgety. Finally, he summoned the captain and whispered into his ear.

"Stand by," Kalijero said on his radio.

Boris and Vlad stepped onto the dock. Their smug looks told me they also anticipated sampling the goods. The captain took the hand of one of the girls and led her to Elon's side. Elon took his coat and draped it over the girl's shoulders. Meanwhile, the captain led the rest of the girls to the van and waited with the driver next to the open cargo door. Elon put an arm around his new girlfriend. With a gangster flanked on each side of the couple, he began walking her toward the SUV. Gigi followed close behind.

Just as Kalijero brought the radio to his mouth, the sound of feet advancing quickly from behind blew past us and the back of a small figure entered the stage. In an instant, my brain processed a subtle mannerism in the figure's movement that registered as familiar. A lock of hair flopping into the dusky light was enough to bring the posture together in the shape of Tamar. I jumped up.

The choreography had played perfectly into Tamar's strategy and execution. By the time I reached the dock, she stood facing Elon, Gigi, Boris, and Vlad, covering them with a .22-caliber Ruger target pistol—a lightweight peashooter, really but, at close range with a ten-round magazine, deadly just the same. Tamar said something in Russian to Elon's chosen, who then ran toward 95th Street, where the other women were now being herded away by a fast-moving female Chicago PD officer. The boat captain and the van driver were already sitting inside a patrol car in the boat storage lot. Kalijero had done a stellar job planning.

"Listen up, people!" his voice boomed. "I am a Chicago police officer. Other officers are present. Our weapons are drawn. We have all of you covered. So unless you want to take a swim in the channel, nobody is going anywhere."

"My god, Tamar! My god!" Gigi said, the tips of his fingers pushed against both temples. "Have you gone crazy?"

Despite Tamar's leverage, Boris and Vlad concerned me most. Apart from knowing they both carried guns, they looked bored, exactly as you'd expect psychopathic killers to look. I took out my Glock, pointed it at them and said, "Get your hands up. If I only *think* you're going for a gun, I'm shooting first." They humored me with a half-assed attempt to hold up their arms.

Tamar held the pistol with both hands while shifting her aim back and forth along the length of the line. "Put it down, Tamar," I said. "The police are here. Let them do their job."

Elon's expression now resembled how the girls had looked as he groped them.

"Landau!" Kalijero shouted. "Tell your girlfriend to trade places with me."

"I got at least two bullets for each of you," Tamar said. "Recognize this gun, Gigi? I found it in the van. Let me guess, you used it to terrorize Russian girls, the ones you were helping to find jobs as whores?"

"You don't know what you're saying!" Gigi said.

"It's not what you think, kid," Elon said.

Tamar ignored Elon. "Gigi!" she said. "Did you have these bald-headed dirtbags kill Jack?"

"I—I didn't kill anyone," the baker said.

"That's not what I asked!" Tamar screamed, startling me. "Did you have your gangster pals do the dirty work? *Russkaya mafiya,* Gigi. Or are you calling it *Bratva* or *krasnaya mafiya*? Take your pick."

Boris and Vlad started shouting at Tamar, spitting out words with laughter and exaggerated facial expressions, like little kids emphasizing disgusting details for shock value. Gigi turned to them. "No! No! Please," he said, sounding pathetically feeble. "Don't listen, Tamar."

"Tamar!" I said. "We've caught them in the act. *Human trafficking,* Tamar. The police saw everything. Let them take it from here."

"You wanna know what the gangsters just said to me?" Tamar said, tears falling off her face. "They were describing how easily Jack's head broke open. How it fell apart like an egg."

The urge to empty my revolver into these men was strong enough to provoke my index finger to test the trigger's resistance. I knew if I fired once, I wouldn't be able to stop. "I know it's hard," I said, my words sounding ridiculously inadequate. "But don't throw your life away. Killing is killing, even if you kill scumbags."

"Listen to him," Elon said. "You're surrounded. You can't get away with this."

"I don't expect to get away," Tamar said without looking at Elon.

Elon did not like that answer. "For fuck's sake, kid! You got your whole life. You're gonna throw it away for some trash-talking thugs?"

Tamar looked at Elon for the first time and laughed. "Uncle Gigi should've explained to you how deep the tradition of blood revenge runs in our culture. You should know these things before going into business with someone like him. Tell him, Uncle Gigi, tell him why I have the right to kill both of you in the name of honor."

"Tamar!" Gigi said. "I'm begging you, child! Think of your parents. Would they want this for you? You're here in America to leave that world behind."

Tamar laughed again. "Have you left it behind, Uncle Gigi? Enslaving girls to make money? Oh, but they're just *Russian* girls. Who cares about *Russian* girls?"

"I'll help you," Elon said, a quiver in his voice. "I'll get you a good lawyer. You're grief-stricken over your cousin, that's all. Landau! It was all Konigson. Lada was *his* whore. He was obsessed with her. I tried to talk him out of it—"

"Really?" I said. "Your mentor? All those years you've known each other and now you're just gonna throw him under the bus? I suppose Jack Gelashvili's death was Konigson's fault, too, which was why you told Konigson to make sure the story was spiked. You were saving Konigson from himself, after all."

Tamar pointed the gun at Elon. "Admit it. You and Gigi had my cousin Jack Gelashvili murdered by these two Russian scumbags."

"We're not going to stand here all night," Kalijero said loudly, as he appeared from the shadow of the trailer, pointing his gun in our general direction. He stopped about ten yards from

334

the dock. "Listen to your boyfriend, Tamar. All you have to do is step back. Let me take your place. You can watch us arrest everyone."

"You're absolutely right, kid!" Elon said to Tamar. "Gigi had Gelashvili killed. He runs the whole prostitution—"

"Tamar, sweetheart! You know me! I would never harm your relatives, another Georgian—"

"Do I really know you?" Tamar said, her voice cracking.

"He's lying," Elon said. "He's with the Russians. He's had many people killed. I can prove—"

"Muteli!" Gigi shouted. *"Ushno ylis mwovelo."* Elon's betrayal turned Gigi's stoically menacing face into a snarling, Eurasian hellhound seething with homicidal vengeance. The violence of his demeanor affected all except Boris and Vlad, who passively watched the world go by. Tamar stared at her uncle as one looked in disbelief at a horrific car wreck.

Kalijero stepped toward Tamar. A sick feeling washed over me. Another officer approached from behind the hostages, another approached from behind us, stopping at the SUV. "Step back and put the gun down," Kalijero said.

"Gigi!" Tamar shouted. "Walk over to the nice cop and get arrested. I've decided to let you live—in prison."

I kept my gun trained on Boris and Vlad as Gigi walked to Kalijero who cuffed him and pointed to the officer who stood next to the SUV. Tamar focused on Elon.

"Okay, Landau," Kalijero said walking toward us. "I think it's time you backed off."

"You've got to disarm and cuff these two gangster clowns first," I said.

"Yeah," Tamar said. "Take 'em away. Give me and Elon a little privacy."

Kalijero signaled at the cop behind the hostages, then moved over to me, the two of us now covering Boris and Vlad with our guns.

"Let Tamar move away from these guys," I said.

"Shut up!" Kalijero said. "I've got them covered. You're a civilian. Back off and holster your gun."

Reluctantly, I did as told but didn't back off enough for Kalijero's liking. "I said beat it!" he growled.

"You're not going to really shoot me, are you, kid?" Elon said.

"So now you're scared—just like all those women who got off that boat and didn't know what was going to happen to them?" Tamar said. "As soon as your dirtbag friends leave, you'll know what's going to happen."

I wanted everyone to shut up. Regardless of Kalijero's experience, all brains were vulnerable to momentary lapses of attention, and that's all it took for disaster. The cop approaching from behind ordered Boris and Vlad to interlace their fingers on the back of their heads. They quickly obeyed, which made me more suspicious. I backed off another step, just wanting to get out of Kalijero's peripheral vision, hoping he would forget about me. He stood about four feet in front of Boris and Vlad, his gun fully extended in arms straight and locked, while the other cop gripped Boris's fingers with one hand and began patting his upper body down with the other.

While waiting his turn to be handcuffed, Vlad once again started yelling in Russian at Tamar in a derisive tone, undoubtedly describing her cousin in the most offensive way possible.

"Shut up!" Kalijero shouted but Vlad kept it up. Tamar showed no emotion, just remained focused on Elon.

This seemed to anger Vlad more. He began yelling louder, practically screaming like a lunatic. The other cop was just about to twist an arm behind Boris's back when Vlad leaned forward and spit on Tamar.

Kalijero's initial response was to raise his leg, suggesting he was about to kick Vlad in the stomach, but Tamar responded first by rotating her gun to shoot Vlad once in the thigh, before aiming it back at Elon, now curled up on the ground, covering his head with his arms.

337

The next twenty seconds unfolded as if we were on stage with a director shouting instructions. Despite Vlad dropping to the ground screaming, clutching his bleeding leg, he still persevered to produce a gun from under his jacket, even though Kalijero stood over him, screaming at him to show his hands. I unholstered my .38 as Boris thrust his elbow backward against the other cop's head, stunning him long enough to move a hand under his own jacket, which meant Kalijero was now dead to rights. I fired into Boris's chest then watched him drop beside Vlad, now also bleeding from the chest, although I had not been conscious of Kalijero firing his weapon.

The image of Tamar kneeling over Elon, holding a gun against his head, sent me airborne with two tragic images racing through my mind, the first being Tamar gunned down by Kalijero or another cop. Considering the gory anarchy that had just taken place, one could argue they were within their right to do so. The second thought was Tamar's gun discharging into the back of Elon's head as I landed on top of her, before I had the chance to wrap myself around her like a straitjacket, making sure the gun remained pointed down.

With Tamar securely in my clutches, I closed my eyes and held her tightly, happy to just lay on the ground, waiting for the delirium around us to play out.

52

One week later, Ellis Knight got his story and more. "BOOYA!" One hundred and forty-four-point type, above the fold.

"East met West the other evening on the banks of the Calumet River, where, for one night only, delicious *khachapuri, ajarian, churchkhela, gozinaki,* and *pakhlava* were served *à la mode* Chicago-corruption style with a traditional side of Georgian blood revenge, and a generous sprinkling of white slavery. The attorney general served up dessert in the form of an indictment of Deputy Director of Revenue Lou Elon for numerous felonies." The article recounted putting the smack down, busting caps, and working girls, as Knight and *The Partisan* scooped the world with a story of murder, prostitution, and the Department of Revenue Money Laundering Service.

Subsequent editions gave accounts of Giorgi "Gigi" Geladze's cooperation with the Illinois and U.S. attorneys general in exposing the Russian mob's involvement in human trafficking, prostitution, and the murders of Jack Gelashvili, Lada Soboroff, Rich Jones, and Wilbert Palmer. Because Gigi claimed to have no knowledge or information regarding the death of Gordon Baxter, the manner of death was re-classified to "pending investigation." Several weeks later, with no evidence of a third party's involvement, and after interviewing family members and his doctor, the fatal outcome was deemed accidental. In exchange for his cooperation, Gigi would get to spend the rest of his life in the Witness Protection Program. As suspected, Gigi's testimony included detailed descriptions of how the murders were carried out by the two Russian gangsters, Andrei Fyodorov and Evgeny Kozlov, who had been sent to Chicago "on loan" from an unnamed branch of Russian organized crime.

The prosecution was unsuccessful in proving Lou Elon had anything more than an *implicit* knowledge of the killings, which spared him from a first degree murder charge. Notwithstanding the prosecution's failure, seven months later Elon received a fifty-year sentence for his role in human trafficking, prostitution, and money laundering. The Russian gangsters survived their wounds only to bask in their devotion to blood oaths and codes of silence, refusing to cooperate or show any remorse. It took ten months before they were sentenced to life imprisonment at the supermax prison in Florence, Colorado.

Konigson's cooperation with prosecutors served him well. Despite admitting he solicited the services of a prostitute, no charges were filed.

News organizations from around the country picked up the story, focusing particularly on Tamar, her life briefly becoming a *cause célèbre* that brought attention to the plight of Eurasian immigrants and their vulnerability to organized crime. For my fictional role in the murder of Rich Jones, I was allowed to plea to a Class C misdemeanor and pay a one-hundred-dollar fine, the result of my failure to report the murder within an acceptable time frame.

With the future of the Kutaisi Georgian Bakery in doubt, due to many years of unpaid taxes and the district attorney seizing all assets, Tamar desperately tried to raise enough money to satisfy all the statutory and municipal vultures flying lethargic loops around the North Side neighborhood. The Georgian community pitched in what they could, but with all the various penalties and fines, the debt seemed insurmountable.

I felt a touch ashamed that it took me several weeks before I thought of Frownie's 1933 Cadillac V-16. Having no idea how antique cars were valued, a cursory search on the Internet revealed that, in excellent condition, this model could command in the neighborhood of four hundred thousand dollars. I immediately spoke with Tamar about the importance of diversifying investments, and my intention of offering the vehicle as collateral until it legally came into my possession and could be put up for sale. "I'm just looking for a safe investment," I said to Tamar.

The Kutaisi Georgian Bakery reopened with great multicultural fanfare as all ethnicities of the neighborhood showed their support and appreciation for a fellow immigrant's outrage over organized crime. Izzy, Kalijero, and Knight were also in attendance. Kalijero stayed only long enough to claim he never would've shot Tamar and he always intended on showing up at the port with backup. He also thanked me for possibly saving his life.

Izzy gave me an envelope with my final payment and congratulated me on *brilliant* work. The first time we met, he had said that my *genius* for exploiting the momentum of my first murder case would drive me to solve Gelashvili's murder. I still had no idea what he meant and no desire to ask him. As I stuffed the envelope into the breast pocket of my jacket, Izzy watched me with a judgmental smirk. Inviting him had been a mistake, I decided.

"What is it, Izzy?" I said. "What am I doing wrong?"

"I'm just wondering if you're as happy about solving this murder as you are about receiving the money."

I tried to think of a quick, insulting retort, but just said, "I'm going to walk away now," then headed to the buffet table for a cup of syrupy carbonated Georgian punch.

Dad opened the door, said, "C'mon in," as if expecting me, then started hobbling away. I hadn't called first.

"You're not alone, are you?" I yelled. "Where's the associate?"

Dad stopped in front of his bedroom door, performed a multi-step about-face, said, "He just disappeared," then rotated himself back to face his bedroom.

After he shuffled inside I walked over and watched him struggle to place himself into an overstuffed chair next to his bed. On television was an old episode of *The Rockford Files.* I put a hand under his elbow to help him sit. "Don't do that!" he hissed and I jumped back.

I sat on the edge of the bed, next to his chair. He stared at the TV looking disengaged from the program, like someone staring out a window. "I have a girlfriend," I said. "Her name is Tamar."

Dad turned his head slightly toward me and said, "Oh, yeah? Very nice," then turned back. I heard the front door open along with the sound of crinkling paper bags. I walked into the hallway to see the associate carrying groceries.

"Hey, how ya doing?" he said. "I'm Arthur."

I followed Arthur into the kitchen. "Dad said you just disappeared."

Arthur rolled his eyes. "I told him I was getting groceries and that I'd be back in an hour."

"Seems like he's getting worse."

Arthur agreed and told me Dad had an appointment with a neurologist the following week. I returned to Dad's room and watched him stare at the TV. "Arthur's back," I said. "He just went out for groceries." Dad didn't respond. I said, "I miss Frownie. The world isn't the same without Frownie."

Dad turned to me, smiling. "They don't make 'em like Frownie anymore," he said. "Boy oh boy, you should've seen him in the forties, wearing a fedora and a herringbone tweed overcoat. He was made for this role, you see, because he gave off an air of confidence. Frownie was a natural at sensing which people became friends you trusted and which became friends you knew *not* to trust. They were both important, you see. . . ."

Next, I asked Dad about the old days, back when Great-Granddad ruled the Bloody Twentieth Ward, and listened to romantic stories of Prohibition era Chicago, stories I had already heard in one form or another, extolling Great-Granddad's skill at playing the game of corruption and how it paid off handsomely—until the cost of defending against a murder indictment ruined the good times.

"Yeah, too bad," Dad said wistfully. "It was all a frame-up, you know. It was Capone's bodyguard, Machine Gun Jack McGurn, that killed the guy. But Granddad stayed loyal to his guys, you see. He had to defend them, too."

Dad didn't want to talk anymore and returned to staring at the television. I observed him for a while, wondered what memories those blue eyes were watching. When I said goodbye he gave me a haphazard wave. Just as I reached the doorway he said, "Say hi to that girl of yours."

###

Like his character Jules Landau, Marc Krulewitch, the author of *Maxwell Street Blues, Windy City Blues, Gold Coast Blues,* and *Doubt in the 2nd Degree,* is descended from an infamous Chicagoan. He grew up in Highland Park, Illinois, and now lives with his wife in Colorado.

Thank you for reading my book. If you enjoyed it, won't you please take a moment to leave me a review at your favorite retailer?